Praise for the works of Dana L. Davis

Roman and Jewel

"An entirely showstopping story of star-crossed love on the modern stage."

—Emily Wibberley and Austin Siegemund-Broka,
authors of *If I'm Being Honest*

The Voice in My Head

"A moving tale of faith and sisterly love. Booktalk this with friends and family!"

—Tiffany D. Jackson, *New York Times* bestselling author of *Grown*

"Fun, catharsis, a bit of endearing strangeness amidst heartfelt familial drama. It's everything you want out of a road trip novel."

—Adi Alsaid, author of *Let's Get Lost* and *We Didn't Ask for This*

"An endearing and compelling coming-of-age story. Dana L. Davis captures the messy, complicated love of family in a road trip novel that redefines what it means to truly live."

—Nancy Richardson Fischer, author of *When Elephants Fly*

Tiffany Sly Lives Here Now

"The novel tackles a wide range of important issues—racism, mental health, religion, class, family—through the lens of a spirited and tough protagonist you'll fall in love with."

—*Bustle*

"This debut grabbed me from the very beginning, and kept the hits coming till the very end."

—*B&N Teen Blog*

"This #OwnVoices YA novel delivers moving, realistic, and fully developed characters that you'll feel deeply connected to from the very first page. Don't miss Dana L. Davis' lovable debut."

—*HelloGiggles*

"Utterly engrossing... A terrific teen read for our tumultuous times."
—*Washington Independent Review of Books*

"Honest, funny, captivating."

—*Kirkus Reviews*

Books by Dana L. Davis
available from Inkyard Press

Tiffany Sly Lives Here Now
The Voice in My Head
Roman and Jewel

DANA L. DAVIS

ROMAN + JEWEL

Recycling programs
for this product may
not exist in your area.

ISBN-13: 978-1-335-07062-3

Roman and Jewel

This edition published by arrangement with Harlequin Books S.A.

For questions and comments about the quality of this book, please contact us at
CustomerService@Harlequin.com.

Inkyard Press
22 Adelaide St. West, 40th Floor
Toronto, Ontario M5H 4E3, Canada
www.InkyardPress.com

Printed in U.S.A.

For Laura G.
Because you said, "I think you should write it!"
And so I did.

And to all the lovers of Shakespeare...

"'Tis But Thy Name That Is My Enemy"

"What's in a name? Is something profound and meaningful supposed to live deep within the string of letters? Is a name supposed to say something?"

I stare into the camera of my phone and take a dramatic pause.

"Take my mom for example," I continue. "Her name is Monday. You know, the saddest day of the week? And have you ever met a black man named Dusty? No? Well then, you haven't met my dad. I mean, what if my dad was a *surgeon*? He's not. He teaches fourth grade. But can you imagine? You meet your brain surgeon and his name is Dr. Dusty?" I shift in my seat. "Dust aside, my older brother's name might take the cake. It's Judas. Like the stupid snitch who ratted Jesus out? For thirty silver shekels or shillings or whatever money was called back in the days of yore when people were actually named *Judas*.

"They saved the best for last. Monday. Dust. Jesus killer—meet Jerzie Jhames. Born where? New freakin' Jersey, y'all. I'm not kidding, that's my real name. And I'm not kidding, we live in New Brunswick, New Jersey. I swear I'm like the defunct superhero Stan Lee contemplated before deciding it was a really bad idea. Is it a bird? Is it a 747 jumbo jetliner? Nope. It's Jerzie Jhames in her silk cape and go-go boots. Watch her *werk*."

I lean forward to read a comment from one of my most loyal followers.

Eye_Eat_MonkeyBrainz: What about Cinny?
That's a name that makes a really bold statement.
That's the best name ever.

"Cinny?" The mention of the superstar makes my stomach churn like I just ate something super spoiled. "That name's okay. I guess. Not sure if she lives among the other one-name greats like Cher. Rihanna. Beyoncé. Ciara. Drake. The name Cinny is unique, but I'm not sure it's simple enough to relate to."

"Oh, it's simple, all right."

I turn to face my aunt, who is twisting her braids into a bun on top of her head as the subway rattles across the tracks.

"Simple. Trite. Silly. Dumb."

I turn back to my phone. "That's my aunt, y'all. *She* lucked out in the name department. Karla. A sensible name. Karla's reliable. Upright. Stable. Lovely. My aunt is *such* a Karla."

I lean forward, reading another comment from one of the eight people watching this livestream.

Ram_Butt_Booty16: Why'd yer Mom and Dad name you Jerzie Jhames? You sound like a porn star.

I nod. "Good point. It *could* easily be a porn star's name. But then again so could Ram Butt Booty."

Aunt Karla snatches the phone out of my hand.

"Hey! I'm livestreaming!"

She fiddles with the phone. "Not anymore." And hands it back to me.

"Aunt *Karla*!" I whine.

"Jerzie, you had eight people watching that. It's not a big loss. And why are you doing a livestream on a public train?"

I glance down the aisle. There's only six other people riding in this car, and five of them are on the opposite end, not even in hearing range, engrossed in phones or books, minding their own business in typical New York fashion. The sixth person, a lady near the closest set of doors, is in deep, whispered conversation with herself; I'm pretty sure she's not paying any attention to us either.

"Aunt Karla. Most Instagram accounts are *so* fake. I want my account to be genuine, so I speak truth and talk about real issues."

"Complaining about your name? That's a real issue?" She frowns. "Why not show them your life—what's more real than that? You're a busy kiddo. Voice lessons, dance lessons, piano lessons, too. I follow you on Instagram. You haven't even mentioned you're gonna be on Broadway. Talk about *that*. Show them what it takes to make it to Broadway. Show 'em you can sing."

"So you want me to be like those Instagram accounts with

narcissists singing into the camera? Desperate for followers? Bragging about all their accomplishments?" I shake my head. "There's a million accounts like that. I may only have 114 followers, but they're loyal. And they appreciate my unique style." I log back on and scroll through the comments that were left before Aunt Karla canceled the stream. Perhaps *scroll* is an exaggeration. There is only one additional comment, after all...

GiggleMeister727: Take off your shirt!!

Uggh. These boys are so annoying!

The subway screeches to a slow stop. I hear a muffled station announcement through the speakers. Can't make out what's being said, but I'm pretty sure Forty-Second Street is next. That's where we get off. Then it's only a short walk to the rehearsal space, where we'll be almost every day for the next few weeks.

"So, you excited to meet Cinny?" Aunt Karla asks as quite a few people file into the subway car and plop down onto empty seats.

I shrug.

"Aww, Jerzie. Don't be like that. She's your idol."

"Was."

"Stop it. You got all her posters in your room. Downloaded all the girl's music. You're a superfan."

"My musical tastes have evolved. R & B pop fusion, or whatever it is Cinny sings—it's not really my style anymore." The train jerks into motion again. "By the way, you think Mom and Dad will get mad at me if I change my name when I turn eighteen?"

"Why you wanna do that?"

"Actors do it all the time. Did you know Olivia Wilde's real name is Olivia Cockburn?"

"Cockburn? That's tragic." Aunt Karla grimaces. "So whatcha gonna change yours to?"

"I dunno. Like a one-name name. Like Saran. That's pretty, huh?"

"Honey…" Aunt Karla's big brown eyes stretch wide. "That's plastic wrap."

"Okay, fine. Not Saran. But you get my point."

"I get it. You want a name weirder than the one you already got."

"Not weirder. More amazing than *ever.*"

"Jerzie, please. Beyoncé at four years old? During preschool roll call? Trust me, she was cursing her parents, too. These wacky names like *Cinny.* What is that? Short for Cinnamon?" Aunt Karla pauses to roll her eyes. "These names become amazing because they're attached to amazing people."

I accidentally make eye contact with the lady near the door talking to herself.

"Is that girl lookin' at me?" she whispers to empty space. "Why she lookin' at me?"

Damn. I quickly avert my eyes.

"So don't change your name," Aunt Karla goes on. "Change your trajectory. Make Jerzie Jhames the next dumb name attached to greatness."

"So you admit my name is dumb!"

She tugs on my mop of curls. "Do all teenagers have selective hearing, or just you?"

"Doesn't matter anyway." I press the side button to lock the screen on my phone as the train starts to slow again. "Because under the current circumstances, I *can't* change my trajectory."

"Why you think that? You're about to be on Broadway."

I give Aunt Karla a look that I hope says, *You know exactly why I think that.*

She tosses back a look of her own. I'd guess she's saying, *Jerzie? Stop acting like a sixteen-year-old.* I'd toss back yet another look, but Aunt Karla's now gathering her purse and tote bag.

"We get off here." She stands.

I grab my backpack and sling it over my shoulder as the train screeches to a stop. Once the double doors slide open, we both hurry and step onto the platform. The terminal has an interesting odor, a mixture of sweat, must, dust—*not* my dad—and excitement. An energy you can literally inhale. It's electric.

The platform is crowded, but I'm always amazed at how expertly Aunt Karla weaves through rush-hour crowds. She's barely over five feet—I'm a good five inches taller than her—but she's lived in New York since she was eighteen and is not the one to try. She sort of exudes that New Yorker don't-even-think-about-effing-with-me vibe, and I swear swarms of people disperse when she approaches. Like the way the Munchkins scattered when Evilene walked through the sweat-shop on *The Wiz.* She's basically got it like that. But as my gaze drifts away from Aunt Karla's Wicked Witch of the West march down the platform, I screech to a halt like somebody pulled the emergency brake on me.

It's one of those digital posters. For *Roman and Jewel.* I place a hand over my chest in hopes it'll dull the ache. It's like my heart is in a free fall after being hurled off the roof of a building. I've lost track of where my aunt is, but I can't worry much about that, because I'm not sure I can move anyway. I'm glued to the platform.

It's real. Suddenly so *real*. And even though the poster isn't much to look at—two shadowy figures and the words *Roman and Jewel: A Hip-Hopera Starring CINNY. Previews begin August 18th!*—it still hits me like a sucker punch from an MMA fighter.

I feel a hand rest gently on my shoulder and look over to see Aunt Karla standing beside me.

"See?" I point to the poster. "It *is* all in a name."

She squeezes my shoulder. "On the hero's journey, you're obviously gonna run into other heroes along the way. All at different stages of a marathon. So this is the first mile of yours. Twenty-five more to go. You're gonna get your time to shine."

"I wanted it to be now," I admit softly.

Aunt Karla wraps an arm around my waist, and I lean my head on top of hers. I'm glad she's here, because my knees feel weak and the weight of my heart is working hard to drag me down. "*Now* is here. You're on Broadway, baby. 1681 Broadway, to be specific."

1681. The address to Broadway Theatre. Where *Roman and Jewel* will be performed live onstage. Hopefully for years to come. I force a smile. "I'm on Broadway?"

"*Girl*. You really are."

I'm finally able to will my legs back into motion. Aunt Karla guides me up the stairs and away from the underbelly of Times Square. The city seems to magically swell, welcoming us as we slowly ascend.

"For Never Was a Story of More Woe"

"Why do you think they're taking so long with her?" I whisper. "They didn't take that long with me."

"Stop worrying," Mom whispers back, scrolling through the news on her phone as if this isn't the most exciting thing to happen to us in like...ever.

"Stop worrying? How do I do that again?" With visibly shaking hands, I grab my stainless steel S'well bottle decorated with pink and red hearts from the floor beside me, twist off the cap, and down a few gulps of water, choking on an ice cube in the process.

Mom's eyebrows rise. "Do I need to do the Heimlich?"

I toss the tiny ice cube back into the bottle. "No, I'm good." I pound on my chest and lift the bottle to take another sip.

"Jerzie Jhames." Mom snatches it from my hands. "Your bladder is gonna explode. *Stop.*"

The door to the rehearsal room is pushed open. A girl about my age slinks into the dimly lit hallway. She flips her perfectly straightened hair over her shoulder and blinks dramatically as her mom, who was sitting across from us, stands and rushes toward her.

"Well?" her mom whispers, pulling her purse over her shoulder. "What did they say?"

The girl tugs at the sleeves of her white leotard. A leotard that makes her pretty brown skin seem to glow like liquid gold.

"First off." She licks her lips, painted deep purple, and I notice she has a similar shade painted above her eyelids and dusted across her cheeks. "They like, literally started clapping when I finished that last song."

The mom squeals and hugs her daughter tightly.

Clapping? They didn't clap for me.

"And then what did they say?" the mom asks anxiously.

The girl shrugs. "They said we're free to go. For *now*." Her eyes meet mine. Shit. I look down at my hands as if they're somehow interesting. "But they stressed that I *will* be hearing from them later today."

Seriously?! I pull at my fingers. All they said to me was *thanks and have a seat in the hallway.*

"Thank You, God." The mom folds her hands in prayer and stares up at the ceiling as if God is on their side alone.

"Hey." I call out as the two move gleefully toward the elevator. They stop and look back in our direction. Actually, *look* isn't the right word. They more eyeball us the way you would a family of rats in a dark corner of the subway station. "I could, uh, hear you in there." And I could.

"Okay?" is the girl's only reply.

"Just wanted you to know you sounded good." And she did. "Really good." I notice she's wearing LaDuca dance heels. And a *feather boa*. Where in New York City does one purchase a lime-green feather boa? Should I have dressed up? I'm only wearing yoga pants, a T-shirt, and a pair of old sneakers. I have LaDuca dance heels, too. Should I have worn mine?

"Aww." She seems to soften. "You're like, the *sweetest*."

I wait for her to extend the same compliment. After all, she was sitting in the hallway during *my* audition and had to have heard every note I sang. But instead she sighs dramatically.

"Well. Off to my *next* audition." She flips her hair again. "I'm so tired."

Another audition?

"What, uh, other show are you auditioning for?" I ask, hoping green-with-envy isn't something you can emote.

"Not a show," her mom cuts in, wrapping an arm around her daughter. "A feature film."

"Yeah." The girl smiles. "It shoots in Athens. I like, *love* Greece. Anyway." Another flip of the hair. Jesus, she could use a hair tie. "You two have a blessed day."

"Yes." The mom nods. "Stay very blessed."

"But don't count your blessings before they hatch." I laugh. They only stare quizzically at me. "It was a joke." I shrug. "So smile while you still have teeth?"

They don't smile. Instead, they exchange expressions that both seem to say, *What a weirdo*, quickly turn, move down the hallway, and disappear around the bend.

"I thought it was funny." I turn to Mom. "I'm funny, right?"

"'I like, love Greece'?" Mom rolls her eyes. "Who says that?"

"People who love Greece?"

"Jerzie?"

I look up.

Nigel, one of the production assistants who's been help-ing to facilitate auditions, is standing in the doorway to the rehearsal room.

"They'd like to see you again."

Of course this is the moment that I realize my bladder *is* about to explode. I stand so quickly that the metal chair wob-bles beneath me. "Would it be okay if I ran to the bathroom?"

Nigel slides off his cap and runs a hand through his mat-ted mess of dishwater-blond hair. "Uh. Yeah, I guess. Hurry up though."

"I will!"

I'm almost at a dead run as I make my way over the lino-leum flooring of Beaumont's rehearsal studios. The bath-rooms are at the opposite end of the hallway, so I'm a bit out of breath as I push open the heavy door that leads into the ladies' restroom and move into one of the bathroom stalls.

It's my *seventh* audition for *Roman and Jewel*. Is this what all Broadway stars have to go through?

I still have the Playbill for the very first Broadway show I ever saw. It's stored safely in a Ziploc bag in the top drawer of the tall dresser in my bedroom, where I keep all my stage memorabilia. *Phantom of the Opera* was celebrating its twen-tieth anniversary at the Majestic Theatre, and Mom and Dad had scored third row center seats. They both graduated from the University of Rochester in New York and have always been big theater nerds. Which explains why, at six, I was listening to things like Lin-Manuel Miranda's *In the Heights* instead of "the wheels on the bus go round and round." That song makes me so dizzy.

Anyway, on the drive up to see the classic Andrew Lloyd Webber musical, as we got closer and closer to the city, giant billboards started lining the freeway.

Wicked.

The Lion King.

Hairspray.

The Little Mermaid.

Each billboard seemed to be welcoming us, like giants with rectangular-shaped hands pointing toward the promised land. *Right this way to glory*, they all seemed to say. My face was pretty much smooshed against the glass as I gazed up at the signs, imagining what it would be like to be connected to something so otherworldly. And then, when we came out of the Holland Tunnel and rolled into New York City, I seriously started *crying*. I didn't even care that my brother, Judas, who's two years older than me, was laughing and calling me queen of the drama dorks. Seeing those skyscrapers reaching over the horizon for the first time, driving down tree-lined streets with beautiful brownstones, the hordes of pedestrians rushing under covered walkways... Don't ask me how I knew (I mean, I was only *six*), but I *knew* I belonged.

I was home.

After emptying my bladder of the near pitcher of water I ingested, I rush out of the stall to wash my hands and give my natural hair, which is pulled on top of my head in a high ponytail, a quick fluff. I twisted it last night, so it's all coily and full the way I like it. I splash a bit of water on my face and watch the droplets slide down my cheeks and drip back down into the sink. Should I be wearing makeup? That other girl was wearing a full *ton* of it. My skin is dark brown, like Lupita Nyong'o's, which Mom says is gorgeous and I want to agree cuz like, Lupita is ridiculously pretty. But sometimes I have my doubts about what *I* look like and how people perceive me.

Blotting my face dry with a paper towel, I can't help but wonder what sort of privileges could be awaiting me backstage at a Broadway theater. I hear the stars of the shows have their own personal dressers. I've done theater my whole life; at school, local city theater, I even did a show at Aunt Karla's church. She goes to one of those megachurches in Brooklyn, so it was *kind* of a big deal. Still, no matter the show, I've never had anybody help me get dressed and undressed. That's rock star status.

I yank open the heavy bathroom door, toss the paper towel into the trash, and rush back down the hallway. Nigel is leaning against the wall, staring at his phone.

"Hey." I'm all outta breath. "I'm ready. Sorry about that."

Nigel nods. "Come on in." He motions to my mom. "You, too, Mrs. Jhames."

"Me?" Mom stands. "You sure?"

"I don't give the orders, I just repeat them." He pulls open the door.

Mom stuffs her cell into her purse, and we follow Nigel inside the rehearsal space.

At the far end of the room, three people sit behind a long,

rectangular folding table. The casting director, Sandi Finn; the director, Alan Kaplan, and… When did *he* get here?

"Have a seat, Jerzie," Sandi says.

Sitting beside Sandi is the writer and creator of *Roman and Jewel*. Robert Christian Ruiz! What the…? When—I mean, *how* did he get here? Did he sneak in while I was in the bathroom?

I pull at my ponytail and smooth out my T-shirt. Maybe I'm literally shaking, because Mom places a hand on my shoulder and whispers, "Relax, Jerzie."

I nod in reply.

Robert Christian freakin' Ruiz studies me as I approach the folding chairs like a timid bride headed to the altar.

"Hello," I squeak as I slowly take a seat.

"Jerzie Jhames." Robert Christian Ruiz speaks. "It's nice to finally meet you."

"It is?" I reply breathlessly.

They all laugh.

"I mean." I take a moment to compose myself. "It's nice to meet you, too, Mr. Ruiz."

"God, am I that old?" He leans back in his chair. "Call me Robbie."

"And don't you dare call me Mr. Kaplan." Alan runs a hand over his bald head. "I *am* old. But I don't take kindly to reminders."

"Stop." Robbie laughs. "You're not *that* old, Alan."

I love Robbie's accent. It's super Bronx. Plus, I know from reading all about him that he was born and raised in East Tremont. I don't have a Jersey accent. Some words, I guess. Actually, when I'm visiting my aunt in Brooklyn, her friends always say, *Girl! Where you from? Jersey?* So whatever. Fine, I have an accent. I grip my water bottle and exchange a nervous glance with Mom.

Nigel is kneeling beside Robbie now, typing something into his phone as Robbie speaks softly to him. Nigel speaks to Alan. "You want anything?"

"Coffee. Black," Alan replies without looking up, deeply engrossed in his own phone. I'd guess he's typing up an email. Probably so much to do when you're a director on Broadway.

"Got it. And just the espresso for you." Nigel nods to Robbie. "Sandi?"

"I'll take an espresso, too. And one for Mae. She's stuck in traffic." Sandi pulls her long brown hair into a bun on top of her head. "Bring the raw sugar please. And stirrers."

"Copy that." Nigel stuffs his cell into his front pocket and rushes from the room.

"We have another set of auditions in a half hour," Sandi explains to us. "We're pretty much stuck in these seats till sometime tonight."

"We've got so many people to hire over the next couple of days." Alan scratches his bald head, and I notice his eyes look tired. Like he could use a nice long vacation that he's not gonna get anytime soon.

Something seems weird. Like, why is Mom in here with me? And why is the pianist packing up all her music and closing the piano? Shouldn't I be getting ready to sing again?

Alan leans back in his chair and crosses his legs. "I wanna apologize for the insane amount of auditions we've put you through."

"It wasn't bad." My voice echoes in the large rehearsal

space. "I had fun learning the songs." I twist the cap off my water bottle and take the tiniest of sips to show Mom I got this and will not injure my bladder or choke on any more ice cubes.

"I know Jewel's songs are intense." Robbie slides his baseball cap off, revealing a head full of salt-and-pepper gray hair. He definitely doesn't seem like a fancy New York type at all. Maybe that's because he's from the Bronx for real. He's dressed in simple jeans, sneakers, and a faded Journey T-shirt, and his face is showing signs that he hasn't shaved in a few days. Little sprouts of unkempt fuzz. You'd never guess he was a millionaire playwright, composer, and actor.

"Yeah. Jewel's got some tough songs," I agree.

"You make them sound easy," Robbie replies. "I watched all the recordings of your auditions. I was captivated. You're captivating, Jerzie."

"Thank you!" I scoot to the edge of my chair. "Super confession? I used to think Bernstein wrote the trickiest arrangements. Some of those songs in *West Side*? Can barely sing along to. But, man, Bernstein's got nothing on you."

"You just compared me to Bernstein?" Robbie laughs. "Bless you, child."

"And Sondheim," I add.

"Oh, now you just tryna humor me, Jerzie."

"Are you kiddin'?" I lean forward. "'Getting Married Today'? It kinda reminds me of the reprise of 'I Defy' when Jewel finds out she's not allowed to see Roman again."

Alan and Robbie both sort of smirk.

"What?" I lean back now. "I say somethin' wrong?"

"Not at all, honey." Alan smiles. "I literally said the same thing a few days ago."

Robbie holds out his phone and loads his Spotify app. "And look what I was listening to on the way here."

I squint to see what's on his screen. "You were listening to *Company*?" I grin.

"Always gotta check in to Stephen's arrangements," Robbie says. "Unspoken Broadway rules."

Did he really just call Stephen Sondheim *Stephen*? Like they were old friends or something? Were they? My cheeks are hurting from smiling so hard.

"Jerzie, I think you're a rare and amazing talent," Robbie adds.

"Voice lessons twice a week since she was seven," Mom cuts in. "Piano, too. She knows more music theory than I do. And I have a BFA in music."

I turn and blink in her direction. I was so focused on the people in front of me, I forgot Mom was even sitting here.

Alan nods. "Her knowledge of music shows. We've been searching for Jewel for a long time. We've seen hundreds of girls."

"Must make it hard, huh?" I take another sensible sip of water. Oh, God, now's the time. I think they're about to deliver my verdict.

"Yes and no." Alan runs another hand over his bald head. "Jewel's a tough character. She has to have the classic Broadway belt."

That's me. I've got the classic Broadway belt! I taught myself to belt by singing along to Liza Minnelli and Bernadette Peters when I was little. The showstopper, "Maybe This Time," from *Cabaret*? I can sing that song like nobody's business.

"She has to carry the show," Alan continues. "But also be young and innocent enough to be endearing and believable."

Young, innocent, endearing, and believable? Check, check, check, and check! "Kinda like Kim from *Miss Saigon*," I add.

"Yes," Alan agrees. "Exactly like that."

"Well, not *exactly* like that," Robbie adds with a chuckle. "Jewel's gotta be able to rap."

I can rap! I mean, I'm no hip-hop diva, but I can hold my own with the arrangements. Which are similar to Angelica's songs in *Hamilton*.

"You're the best we've seen," Alan says.

I am?

"You really are. By far," Robbie adds. But he sounds so sad when he says it. Why does he sound sad?

Robbie slides his Giants cap back on, casting shadows over his dark eyes. "You're probably too young to be a fan of Patti LuPone—"

I sit up. "*Oliver, Anything Goes, Gypsy*—"

"She's like a Broadway encyclopedia," Mom cuts in again.

"I'm up on the newer stuff, too," I say sheepishly. "Like, *Dear Evan Hansen, Mean Girls, Six...*" I trail off, and there's another moment of silence. *What* is happening here? "Is everything okay?" I finally blurt.

Now the casting director speaks up again. "Jerzie..." Sandi says. "How would you feel about joining the cast as Jewel's understudy?"

Understudy? Wait...*what*? Did she really just ask me to be an *understudy*? I look at Mom for a reassuring expression, but her face is straight-up lacking in the comfort factor. She's lookin' a mixture of shocked, confused, and heartbroken, which is probably how I look, too. My gaze shifts back to Alan and Robbie, and for a second I wait for them to say, *Sandi's just kiddin', gotcha!* But there's only silence. Painful silence.

"If it was up to us..." Robbie's Bronx accent pierces the quiet "...you'd be our girl. But there are the powers that be."

"You're not the powers that be?" Mom asks.

"In this case," Alan replies, "the powers that be are the producers who are putting up the millions it takes to fund the production. They want a big name. They're convinced the show needs it."

Is that true? I've been so excited about possibly joining the cast, I didn't think about things like ticket sales and whether or not the show would do well. To me, Broadway has always been entertainment. To them, I guess it's business. An opportunity to make lots of money.

"So I'd be the understudy for that other girl? The one who just left?" Maybe she is a big name, but *I've* never seen her before today. I force a smile, even though the thought of being that girl's understudy is making me wanna run from the room screaming *nooooooo* at the top of my lungs.

"It's not her," Alan says. "She's not our Jewel."

"She's not?" I'm not sure I wanna know the answer, but I ask anyway. "Then who is?"

"Cinny." Robbie says it with about as much excitement in his voice as the worker at the movie theater who tells you that if you get the bucket-size popcorn instead of the size you ordered, it's only a dollar more.

"Cinny?" Mom exclaims.

"*Cinny?*" I repeat. "Cinny is Jewel? Cinny the singer? *Cinny?!*"

There's a strange and eerie synchronization as they all nod their heads in reply. So this wasn't the final audition to be Jewel. This was the final audition to be Jewel's *understudy*.

"Two of the girls in the chorus will be covering Jewel as well," Sandi says. "So Cinny will have two understudies and a standby. You will, of course, be the standby."

"What's the difference between the two?" Mom asks.

"An understudy is typically somebody already cast in the show," I explain glumly.

"Right," Sandi adds. "As chorus or another small part. A standby has only one job. To stand by and replace the lead in the event something happens. Sickness or otherwise."

Exactly. Which means I'm not cast as chorus or another small part. They just wanna pay me to stand around the theater. The job shouldn't be called standby, it should be called Stand Around And Do Nothing. How do you even brag about this? *Sorry, I can't come to the party, guys.* Flip of the hair. *I gotta stand around backstage at a Broadway theater and stare at Cinny in case she* literally *breaks her leg.*

Alan sighs. When I met him during the beginning of this audition process, there was a light there. He seems dim now. Like someone blew out his flame. This is not what he wants. I sense it. I feel it. (I mean, I know it, since he did just tell me. But regardless.)

It is what it is. I didn't get the part. I'm just an understudy. Heck, I'm not even an understudy. I'm a Stand Around And Do Nothing.

I turn to my mom. "Can I do it?"

"What does being a standby entail?" Mom asks, her voice calm and composed, though her brow is furrowed.

"Rehearsals start right away for the principals. Jerzie will join the cast in a few weeks, but will practice privately right away, here, to learn the songs."

I tune out as Alan, Robbie, and Sandi explain the particulars to Mom. Nod every so often so it looks like I'm paying attention. Throw in a smile here and there so it appears I'm grateful and enthusiastic. By the time Nigel returns with everyone's coffee orders, they're wrapping up the conversation.

"This is gonna be a good opportunity for you, Jerzie," Robbie says almost apologetically.

"A lot of the Broadway greats started out as covers," Sandi adds. "You'll learn so much. You'll get your Broadway feet wet."

"Who's Roman?" I've found my voice again.

"Zeppelin Reid." Alan picks up his buzzing phone to silence it. "Don't try Googling him. He's a rare breed of kid who's not on social media. He's new. Nineteen. This will be his Broadway debut."

And it's official. My heart has shattered into a million pieces. The boy who's playing Roman gets to be an unknown, not-even-on-social-media debut, and the girl has to be an international *superstar*. How is this fair? It's not FAIR! I want to stand on top of my chair and shout, *What's happenin' here is some serious BS!*

But rather than make that dramatic proclamation, I pull my shaking hands apart, grab my water bottle, and take another sip.

"We're thrilled to have you in whatever capacity we can,

Jerzie." Robbie smiles. "You know, when I wrote these songs so many years ago, it was your voice I heard in my head. Jewel came to life because of you. Not often that happens."

I know that's a compliment. But for some reason, it just makes me wanna cry. I swallow to hold back the tears. "Thanks for this opportunity," I say as evenly as I can manage. "I'm grateful to be joining the cast." I look at Mom. Her shocked expression has been replaced with the classic, all-knowing Mom look I was hoping for earlier.

"Yes, thank you," she says. "This is *very* exciting."

Mom and I both stand.

"Welcome to the cast, Jerzie Jhames," Sandi says warmly.

"Thank you." I wave to the table of solemn faces before following Mom through the door and back into the dimly lit hallway. We move toward the elevator in silence.

"Are you disappointed in me?" I finally whisper.

"Disappointed?" We make it to the elevator, and Mom turns to me, takes both my hands in hers, and squeezes tightly. "You shot for the stars and landed on the moon. I couldn't be more proud."

"You promise?"

"I promise." She sighs.

I do, too, wiping my tears as they finally fall.

"If Love Be Rough with You"

PRESENT DAY

Who would give this place a second glance? I never have. And I've passed it before, lots of times. Simple, glass double doors. A shiny, stainless steel border. The address frosted on the front in bold white: 111 New Forty-Second Street Studios. A row of what looks like Hollywood-style vanity lights perched above the doors casts a romantic glow against the stainless steel. It's still nothing fancy. In fact, it appears to be just another storefront in Times Square. And heck, *hundreds* of people are scurrying by the way I always have before, completely ignorant of the fact that some of Broadway's best could be rehearsing just on the other side. Annaleigh Ashford, Fantasia, Jordan Fisher, Kristin Chenoweth, Hailey Kilgore! Who could imagine?

We're buzzed in. The doors slamming shut behind us quiet the brash and exhilarating roar of Times Square, which is similar to the rumble of an eternal raging storm. Like that giant red spot on Jupiter that's actually a 360-year-old hurricane.

I digress.

As we step into the lobby, Nigel pushes off a desk manned by a single attendant and makes a beeline for us.

"Nice hair." Nigel points at the curly ponytail perched on top of my head. "You are a puff princess."

I twist a curl around a finger and blink dramatically. "I wake up like this."

He slides off his cap to present his matted mess of hair. "Not me. I had to work fifteen years to look this bad."

I laugh, and we pound it out.

"Welcome to your first official rehearsal." He slides his baseball cap back on. No matter the day, Nigel always wears the same thing: a black T-shirt, backward baseball cap, khaki cargo shorts, black-and-white Chucks, and a walkie stuffed into his back pocket. I'm starting to think this is the production-assistant wardrobe. Nigel's not unattractive or anything. He's actually a nice-lookin' dude for being almost forty. He just seems to need a bath, a haircut, a shave, and clean clothes.

That aside, he's the coolest dude ever.

He waves flirtatiously at Aunt Karla, who says, "Nigel, now don't play. You wouldn't know what to do with this."

I'm confident she's right, because Aunt Karla's last boyfriend, Maximus, was about 210 pounds and worked as a roofer in Brooklyn.

But Nigel's not intimidated. He grins mischievously at Aunt Karla and whispers, "Don't underestimate me." He hands me my laminated badge and credentials. "Rashmi is tending to a tiny issue. Okay if I take her from here, Aunt K?"

"Fine by me," Aunt Karla replies.

Rashmi is the child guardian for *Roman and Jewel*. Broadway Babysitter Extraordinaire is what Nigel likes to call her. During my private rehearsals at the other studio, she was always close by. But since I'm the only cast member under eighteen, I wonder what sort of "tiny issue" Rashmi could possibly be tending to on my official first day with the cast.

"I'll see you this afternoon." Aunt Karla hugs me tight. "And try to have fun. Okay?"

"I'll try."

I take a quick moment to take in all of Forty-Second Street Studios as Nigel stares longingly after Aunt Karla while she exits the building. Though there really isn't much to take in, since we're only in the lobby. It has an industrial vibe—a sterile space with simple white walls, an elevator, and a modern set of stairs to the left.

"Ever been here before?" Nigel's walkie crackles, and unknown voices converse loudly through the speakers. He twists the knob to lower the volume, and I follow him to the lobby elevator.

"Nope. Never."

"Pretty much every musical headed to Broadway will rehearse here at some point. Our production has three rooms, but we're rehearsing big company numbers today, so most of the cast is in 7A. We can drop off your things in the classroom, say hi to your teacher and Rashmi, then I'll take you there."

This is another thing about being under eighteen and working on Broadway. Not only do I have a babysitter, I have to go to school, at least until school is out for the summer. Which, thankfully, is in two more days.

We step off the elevator and into a hallway that feels a lot like the Grand Central Terminal. There are so many people coming and going, my eyes burn from trying to take it all in. Girls shuffle down the hall in giant hoop skirts, followed by dancers in leotards, and those classic LaDuca heels that are sort of synonymous with theater productions *click clack* down the hallway as they rush past. I packed mine in my backpack in case standing around and doing nothing involves actual movement, though I'm pretty confident the heels won't actually be needed.

We make it to the end of the hallway and Nigel turns to me. "Your classroom. Fancy right?"

Small. A few chairs. Four-by-four-foot tables pushed against the walls. Two computers. Aaaaand that's it. "It's the classroom of my dreams."

My guardian, Rashmi, is kneeling beside a young girl who looks about eight or nine. The girl is sitting under one of the tables with her head resting in her hands, crying uncontrollably. Ahh. This must be the tiny issue? Literally. I wonder what production the girl could be from.

My teacher, Miss Benefield, stands beside Rashmi. Both are struggling to get her out from under the table. Rashmi gives us a polite wave that seems to say, *Sorry, I'm busy helping right now.*

I wave back and hope my wave relays a heartfelt *no worries at all!* I stuff my things under one of the chairs and turn to follow Nigel down another hallway, weaving through more swarms of performers, musicians, and crew. There's a guy dressed in full costume like he's headed to a Revolutionary-era war, and I'm thinking he's rehearsing for *Hamilton*. Is he? I freakin' love that show. My dream of all dreams is to be cast as Angelica one day. When I get older, of course.

We step inside another elevator that takes us up to the next floor. The doors slide open, and I continue to follow Nigel. This hallway isn't as busy, just a few people with cargo shorts and walkies sticking out of their back pockets passing by. Maybe Nigel's oufit *is* the production-assistant wardrobe.

At the end of the hallway, we stop in front of heavy double doors with 7A painted across the center. Nigel pulls one open, and I follow him into a massive rehearsal space.

Floor-to-ceiling windows gift us an aerial and panoramic view of a living and vibrant Times Square. The cast of *Roman and Jewel*—none of whom I've met before—is milling about. Since the show is a diverse reimagining with singing and rapping, the cast looks like a multicultural explosion. So many varieties of skin tone. So much melanin and lack thereof.

Some cast members are warming up near the piano. A few who I imagine are dancers are stretching on the floor. I make this judgment based on their perfectly muscled physiques, which look as if Michelangelo spent a few days in his studio meticulously carving their svelte figures. When they bend, muscles I didn't even know a body could have are delicately and beautifully accentuated on their thin frames. A few dressed in sexy spandex are in conversation with choreographers—at least, I think they're choreographers, since they're counting and demonstrating dance moves.

There are about forty people in the room, but I'd guess only a third account for the cast of the show. Still, it's hard to tell who is who and who does what. I should mention, it's loud in here. Conversations are roaring. Also. A portion of the floor is like…moving. Sort of like those human conveyor belts they have at airports. I think they're called moving walkways. Anyway, some of the cast members are gazing at it, watching as a technician demonstrates how it works.

To add to the roar of the room, there's a drum kit stuffed into the corner with a drummer warming up. I can feel the *thump* of the bass drum blending with the beat of my heart. It makes me want to throw caution to the wind and dance. But I'm not allowed to make a scene. I know my place. I'm here to observe. Be invisible. That's it. That's *all*.

There's also an old upright wooden piano on the opposite end of the room with a pianist banging out a song I recognize from my private rehearsals. My vocal cords are buzzing.

Too bad standbys don't get to sing.

I should probably find a place to sit, but I'm sort of frozen in place, taking in the energy of the room and also, admittedly, looking for Cinny. I'm able to spot her pretty easily, because there's a *bodyguard* standing a few feet away from her. At least, I assume he's a bodyguard. He's a big dude, dressed in all black, with his arms folded across his chest and he's looking around the room almost daring somebody unauthorized to try to talk to her.

Cinny's in deep discussion with the director, Alan, like they've become the best of friends, which I imagine they have. It stings a little. Okay, a lot. I haven't seen him since my heartbreaking final audition at Beaumont Theater, and my stomach sort of flips and flops around as I observe him in all his director glory but not directing me. Cinny nods as he speaks, and I can't help but wonder what sort of Broadway wisdom she's receiving.

She looks different in real life. Normal, I guess. She has on yoga pants, the standard LaDuca dance heels, and a white T-shirt that looks cut in half and shows off her flat tummy. We're basically wearing the same outfit, except I'm wearing black-and-white Vans instead of my dance shoes, my yoga pants aren't as fancy as hers, and the fact that I'm wearing a shirt that shows off my belly is a clear sign I'm parent-free this summer. If Dad were here, he'd probably rise out of nowhere like Storm from X-Men and shout, *Jerzie, put some clothes on!* not even caring that he was embarrassing me in front of all these people.

But back to Cinny. Her silky straight black hair hangs dramatically to the middle of her back, and her skin is like the color of cinnamon. Maybe Cinny *is* short for Cinnamon.

A tall blond boy joins Cinny and Alan's chat, and I smirk when Cinny's bodyguard gives the dude an evil glare. Clearly he's a part of the production and not a threat to Cinny. He's wearing skintight dance pants, so his manhood is like… accentuated…for lack of a better way to put it. He's also wearing an equally tight tank top that shows off his broad shoulders and muscles. His hair is slicked back, and he's nodding dramatically, as if whatever Alan is saying is the *gospel*.

Is this the guy playing Roman? I don't wanna feel disgusted, but there's something about him. A snark factor. A white-privilege air. The way he moves. The way he blinks. Like he's used to people watching him and is always putting on a show. Don't get me wrong, he's definitely got the Look. Attractive. Tall. All muscled up. Like he should enter rooms on a white horse, bow and arrow aimed and ready. But he's not *my* type. Also, he and Cinny have about as much chemistry standing next to one another as Trump and Michelle Obama.

I reach for the straps on my backpack to pull it off and realize I'm not wearing it. In the awkwardness of the crying kiddo, I left it in the classroom.

Crap. I need my script to take blocking notes. I look around for Nigel, but he's disappeared into the mass of people milling about the room.

I can be quick. I make a mad dash for the door and trace my steps back the way Nigel brought me, but the elevator is being held for some rather large scaffolding.

Around a corner I find the stairwell, yank open the door, and run down to the next floor. Once I step into the hallway, I weave around people, carts stacked with props, and musicians lugging instruments, and finally make it back to Rashmi and Miss Benefield, who have managed to at least get the crying girl out from under the table. Progress!

I grab my bag quickly and rush back to the stairwell, taking two stairs at a time. I certainly don't want to be officially late on my first day with the cast. But at the top of the stairs the door is locked. Or jammed? What the...? I pound on it.

"Hello?" I shout. "Anybody out there?" I pause to catch my breath, peeking through the crack to see if anybody is passing by, when suddenly the door is thrust open and smashes into my head. I yelp, jerk back, and wind up slamming down butt first onto the hard concrete of the empty stairwell.

"*Shit.*" Someone kneels beside me. I'm covering my head with my palm, thinking that will somehow dull the sudden, excruciating pain. "Are you okay?"

The voice is soothing, apologetic. It was an accident. Clearly. But I can only wince in reply.

"I'm so sorry I hurt you," the voice says genuinely. His voice is deep and calming. I'm not sure why, but it sends a shiver rushing up my spine. "Can you look at me?"

I raise my head. Slowly. "I can't see," I whimper. "I think I might be temporarily blinded or somethin'."

"Well, your eyes are closed." Now his voice is slightly amused.

Oh. Duh. My lids lift. A pair of blue eyes comes into view. Electric blue. As blue as the ocean was in St. Lucia when we visited two years ago. As blue as a feeling.

The boy holds out his hands. "Can I help you up?" I place mine in his, and he gently helps me to my feet. "Can't believe I did that. Who knew a human's head was pressed against the door."

"Didn't you get the memo?" I say slowly. "Human heads will heretofore be lurking in stairwells behind doors."

"I got that memo," he replies seriously. "But I didn't think it went into effect until after Labor Day."

I tilt my head up ever so slightly so that his entire face can come into clear view. And…well. He's pretty. I'm not one to swoon over pretty boys, because New York is full of them and you'd be swooning all damn day, but this one is like, cut from the pretty-boy catalog. Wild and unruly waves of jet-black hair hang over his forehead. Big, sapphire-blue eyes; full lips; wide mouth; smooth, flawless, and radiant skin with a pale, Edward Cullen vibe to go with it.

One of my hands rests on my forehead, covering the spot the door slammed into. I'm dizzy. Maybe even a little weak

in the knees. Is it because of a possible concussion? Or because of this boy's high level of *attractiveness*?

"Do you feel nauseous?" He's looking at me so weird. As
if I'm an alien stepping off a spaceship platform or something.
Or like maybe...he knows me. But I'm certain I've never
seen this guy before. He's got the sort of face you remember.

"I feel a little dizzy," I reply. *But that might be because you
smell so good.* The scent of him. It's moving through me like
a healing ointment, sort of soothing the ache in my head.

Now I lower my hand. There's blood. Just a little though.

His blue eyes widen at the sight of it. "Come with me.
We'll get you all cleaned up."

The door is propped open with a motorcycle helmet, which
I'm guessing is Pretty Boy's, since he scoops it up and stuffs it
under his arm, then he extends a hand to me. It takes me half
a second to realize he's offering to like, hold my hand. Overwhelmed with the desire to touch him again, I place mine
into his and let him lead me into the hallway, gently guide
me around a corner, and escort me into a one-stall bathroom.

At the sink, he places my hands under the nozzle, activating
a heavy stream of water that washes away all traces of blood.
There are no windows in here, but the fluorescent light flick-
ering above us makes the water glimmer like liquid crystal.
He pumps out soap and proceeds to work up a healthy lather
on both of our hands. I stare, transfixed, watching our hands
meld together. We're like living, moving, interracial art.

Our eyes meet again. What the hell, man? This boy is *fine*.
He definitely doesn't look like a Broadway type boy. Whatever that looks like. This boy looks and vibes like a rebel,
with his frayed leather bands wrapped about his wrists and

black-painted fingernails. And while I can't tell what it is, I can see a tiny bit of a tattoo, peeking out from under his long-sleeved shirt.

I bet he plays the guitar or the drums. I'd ask questions to verify, but I'm still trying to will my lips back in motion.

"I'm sorry." He grabs the last paper towel from the dispenser and lets a bit of soap and water run over it, then points to my forehead. "You mind? So it doesn't get infected."

I nod yes.

He reaches out to wipe my forehead with the wet and soapy paper towel. And even though the spot he's touching is now aching, it doesn't really bother me. His eyes. His touch. His face. My filter must somehow get shut down, because without thinking it through, I whisper, "Damn, boy, you are *cute*."

He laughs, exposing strikingly white, perfect teeth. "Says the girl with the beautiful brown skin and big brown eyes. You're pretty cute yourself."

Did he just call my skin beautiful? And cute? Really? *Me?*

"You're gonna have a nasty bruise. Want me to run and get you some ice?"

"No." I shake my head. "It's okay. I'll take my chances."

He sighs. "You'll forgive me though, right?"

Of course I forgive you, beautiful human boy!!

But rather than say *that*, I simply nod.

There's no more paper towels so he lifts his shirt to dry my hands, exposing quite the set of abs. Guys who have bodies that hint they live at the gym never really impress me. But this boy's thin and muscled physique looks effortless. He's not spending time at the gym—being cut in all the right ways is in his DNA. My God. I don't mean to stare but...*daaaaang.*

After my hands are dry, he takes them in his, warming them by rubbing his thumbs back and forth across my palms. It summons about a thousand butterflies like, drunkenly crashing into one another, deep within the pit of my belly. Is the pain in my head making me feel so all consumed? So overwhelmed? So electrified? Or is it him?

"I hope I don't have a concussion," I whisper.

"Pretty sure you're gonna be okay."

"Yeah? You an expert in concussions?"

"Didn't you know?" He runs a hand through his mess of hair, holding the silky strands off his face for a moment as we stare into one another's eyes. "Anybody can be an expert on anything these days. All you need is Google."

He leans forward so that our foreheads are almost touching, and I wonder if he can hear my heart pounding against the inside of my chest like, *Um, hello, Jerzie! What the hell is going on out there?*

"Unless you wanna go to the ER," he adds. "Where you can sit in an overcrowded, dirty waiting room for sixteen hours until a doctor tells you the same thing I did. But the doc will charge you about a thousand dollars for it. And definitely won't be as cute as me."

"You're not *that* cute." I'm lyin'. He's fine as hell. He's cute squared. He is cute to the freakin' tenth power.

"Your words, not mine." He's smiling again, presenting those pearly whites. "Say the word and I'll toss you over the back of my bike and drive you to a local hospital."

Toss me over the back of his bike? *Should* that sound enticing? Because it kinda does. Also, who am I kidding— he could take me anywhere, really. A white van with a sign that reads The Killer Is Inside? I'd probably go. Dark basement? Don't mind if I do.

He releases my hands and moves to lean against the tile wall, sighing again like he's pretty relieved I'm gonna be fine.

I take the moment to properly observe this rare concoction of supergenetics. He's tall. I'd put him at six foot two. Doesn't look too much older than me, to be honest. He's wearing *very* expensive clothes. I'm not into brands, mostly because I can't afford them, but since Aunt Karla works in fashion, I know a thing or two. He's wearing Balmain jeans. John Varvatos leather boots. His T-shirt is Play. I can tell because of the iconic red heart displayed on the front.

His phone buzzes, and he pulls it from his back pocket, glances at the screen. "One sec." He slides his finger across the glass, holds the phone up to his ear. "Hey, Ava. I'm seeing you tonight, right?"

I don't mean to pry, but it's like, dead-ass quiet with a strong echo in here, so I can easily hear both ends of the conversation.

"He's back. He won't let me," a girl with a soft, sweet voice replies sadly. "He said no."

"Don't listen to him. Please. Come anyway."

"I'm not like you. I don't know how to disobey," she replies.

"Fuck." He sighs. "It's whatever. Fine then."

"Please don't be mad."

He looks up, and our eyes meet. "I'll text you later. I'm sort of in the middle of something."

"I'm sorry. Love you." She sounds like she's about to cry.

"I know. Me, too." He ends the call.

Ava, huh? Must be a girlfriend. Probably one of many.

I watch him closely as he stuffs the phone back into the pocket of his jeans. He strikes me as that typical rich, New York City, private-school white boy. I bet he's from SoHo. Or no, correction. Those John Varvatos boots he's wearing probably cost a thousand dollars. This isn't a *rebel*. This is just a boy with rich parents wasting Mom and Dad's money on expensive clothes. I'd say he lives on the Upper East Side. That's old money.

I pull on the straps of my backpack, which probably makes me look like I'm twelve. Not that it matters. Two different households. *Nothing* alike in dignity.

"I should get going. Thanks for your help." I move toward the door.

"Wait." His voice alone stops me. I turn around to face him again. "Can I ask what you're doing here?"

"In the bathroom?"

He laughs. "You're pretty cute, you know that?"

He keeps calling me cute. I raise an eyebrow. *Is he just...messing with me?*

"I meant..." He stares at me, a curious expression on his pretty face. "What are you're doing at Forty-Second Street Studios? Today."

"Um..." *I can't tell him I'm a standby!* I decide on a diversion technique. "What are *you* doing here? Today." I smile. "Never mind. Don't tell me. I'm gonna guess you're a musician. And you play the...guitar? Right?" *Much to your parents' horror—they were hoping you'd go to Yale. At least for undergrad. Then Stanford for law. They shouldn't worry. There's still time to whip you into shape.*

"Impressive. You should consider giving psychic readings." He crosses his arms. "Now back to you."

"Me?"

"Yes," he says. "The only other person in this bathroom."

"Oh. I'm sorta here to, kinda, work on a new musical. It's my first day. With the cast, I mean."

"Your first day, huh?" Once again he runs a hand through his hair, a mess of silky strands whose complete disarray seems to be the root of their charm. I almost wanna ask if *I* can run my hands through his hair, but I know better. He takes a step closer to me, heating up the small space between us. "You excited to sorta kinda work on a new musical?"

"Sorta." I shrug. "It's Shakespeare. A *Romeo and Juliet* re-imagining. It's called *Roman and Jewel*. But this version is a fantasy. After their suicide, they both end up in purgatory and are sentenced to infinite lives on Earth until they can meet up again to, you know, right their wrongs."

"A happy Shakespeare. I love it."

"You don't tune in to Shakespeare for happily-ever-after. So don't worry. There's still enough angst and drama. Robert Christian Ruiz—he's the composer. He wrote the book, too. He most definitely captured the heart of the story."

"Which is?"

"Um." I pause. Jesus, his eyes are so bright and blue that I feel temporarily blinded. "The cycles of love and hate. In order for something good to happen, a lot of bad shit has to happen first. You know. The main theme of the original play."

"That is not the main theme." He laughs. "I think you should reread the play for fresh insight. Try *Shakespeare for Dummies*."

"Excuse me?" I shift my weight from one foot to the other, trying my hardest to play it cool, even though this boy is making my heart race so fast I'm feeling short of breath. And this time it's not because he's cute. "I've read *Romeo and Juliet* like fifteen times."

"Sixteenth time's a charm?"

I glare at him. "Are you *trying* to piss me off?"

"I'm a lover, not a fighter." Pretty Boy laughs again, holding both hands up as if in surrender. "And you're the perfect Jewel, by the way."

"I'm not Jewel." I shake my head. "I'm a *standby* for Jewel." Not that it's any of his business.

"You're an understudy."

"My technical term is *standby*. But yes, that's my story. I'm just a standby."

"Why do I get the feeling there's a lot more to the story with you?"

The bathroom door is suddenly pushed open.

I spin around and gasp. It's Cinny! Cinny is revealed in all her one-name glory. Holy hell. She looks startled to see us in here. Which. Understandable. Strangely enough, pretty-boy musician doesn't look like a person should look when a superstar singer enters the bathroom they're standing in.

"Hey, Cinny," he says with a nonchalance that makes my face scrunch up in confusion. "Don't you knock before you bust into a bathroom?"

She flips her hair over her shoulder, and I notice she has a splattering of freckles on her nose. I also notice she's even prettier up close.

"Why am I not surprised to see you holed up in a bathroom with a girl, Zeppelin Reid?" she declares.

Wait. *What?* Zeppelin Reid? *This* is Zeppelin Reid? This is the boy cast as Roman!

"Nothing funny going on," he says. "I saved this girl's life is all."

She looks at me, her expression disbelieving. "He did?"

"Not. He did not." Aaaand it's official. I am in conversation with *Cinny*. "He nearly killed me, more like it." I clumsily lurch forward and extend my hand. "By the way. Hello and greetings." *Hello and greetings? The fuck is wrong with me?!* "It's very nice to meet you, Cinny." I hope I sound mature and professional and not like the hyper superfans she's probably used to.

"Oh. Okay." She eyes me, like maybe I could be some sort of internet stalker who found her way into Forty-Second Street Studios to harass her.

"Don't worry. I'm normal. I swear," I declare.

"Fun fact…" Zeppelin moves to stand beside me, and I hold back my overwhelming desire to elbow him in his stupid, sexy six-pack. How *dare* he play some game with me? Pretending he's a musician? Letting me blab about a show he's the star of? Imbecile! "She's suffered through reading *Romeo and Juliet* fifteen times and *still* doesn't get it. Oh, and she's your cover."

"Say *what*?" I turn to him.

"Crap. Her technical term is standby." He adds apologetically, "Call her an understudy and she'll go off on you."

"That's not true!" I turn back to Cinny. "That's not true."

"*Liar.* You were all…" He places a hand on his hip and

overdramatically says, "My technical term is *standby.*" He flips imaginary hair over his shoulder.

"Is that supposed to be me?" I narrow my eyes. "Cuz that's a terrible impersonation."

"Trust me. It was spot-on."

Oh my God! Here I am meeting the world-renowned Cinny for the first time, and this pretty-boy jackass is making me look like a moron!

"Well." I shake my head. "It truly is an honor to meet you, Cinny. I look forward to watching you work and being here as a support if you need it."

"Or if you *literally* break your leg," Zeppelin adds with a grin.

I glare at him again. Maybe *pretty boy* actually is synonymous with *imbecile.* I move around Cinny, rush out of the bathroom, and hurry down the hallway.

Only seconds have passed when I hear a deep voice call out, "Hey. Wait up."

I turn to see Pretty Boy—I mean, Zeppelin—rushing to catch up with me, his backpack slung over his shoulder, his motorcycle helmet clutched in one hand.

"Forgot your guitar?" I ask as I turn to keep walking.

"Don't worry. Your psychic skills are intact. I do play the guitar. Not in this production though."

"Thanks for clarifying. Better late than never."

"What do you mean?" He laughs. "I never said I wasn't a part of the cast."

"But you should have." I stop, turning around to face him. "You just let me ramble on and on! I feel so stupid."

"Don't. It was the cutest ramble of all time. How's your

head? Seriously. I don't want you dropping dead on me in the middle of the first act. That would just extend rehearsal, and I have somewhere to be tonight."

"It's a tiny bump. I'll live."

"Good." He glances at the ceiling. "All right, Universe. Cue a *lot* of bad shit."

"Huh?"

"According to your Shakespeare logic." He smiles, electric-blue eyes lighting up the space. "In order for anything good to happen, a lot of bad shit has to happen first. So, if bad shit is my only option, I summon a lot of it." He backs away toward the doors to the rehearsal room. "Cuz I'm hoping for something *really* good. At least when it comes to you, Jerzie Jhames."

Um. Confuse me? I quickly replay our meeting. Door slammed into my head. Check. Walk down the hallway. Check. Pulled into bathroom and hands washed. Check and check. Introductions? *No.* We didn't introduce ourselves. I know *his* name only because Cinny said it.

So how does he know mine?

Before I have a chance to inquire, the adorable, annoying, and now quite mysterious Zeppelin Reid moves through the double doors marked 7A, leaving me alone in the hallway to ponder our strange and curious encounter.

"With a Tender Kiss..."

When I step back into the rehearsal space at Forty-Second Street Studios, I'm surprised to see the lights are now dim and the room mostly empty. Even Zeppelin seems to have vanished into thin air. Did I imagine him?

Standing near the piano is Robert Christian Ruiz—or, wait, he did ask me to call him Robbie. Anyway, *Robbie* is chatting quietly with Alan. There's another guy with them whom I've never seen before, wearing dance heels, spandex shorts, and a loose T-shirt. Alan is sighing dramatically with every word Robbie says while the man in heels rubs his temples. I wonder what Robbie is saying that's got both men seeming so stressed.

I feel a tap on my shoulder and turn to face Nigel.

"Hey," I whisper. "Where is everybody?"

"We have the whole floor, remember? All in different rooms. You're with Cinny, so you'll still be in here."

My eyes scan the room. There's the pianist sitting at the piano and the three men in deep discussion close beside her.

Nigel shoves his clipboard at me. "Can you sign this? It's just a formality. Your parents already signed."

I read the top line on Nigel's sheet of paper. "Nondisclosure agreement?"

"For You-Know-Who," he says quietly. "We all had to sign one."

"You-Know-Who?" I repeat.

"Yeah," Nigel whispers. "Cinny."

I scan the sheet. *Recipient will pay up to the sum of one million dollars ($1,000,000) as a reasonable and fair amount to compensate...* I look up.

"My parents signed this?"

"Yup." Nigel peels the green foil wrapper from a stick of gum and stuffs the gum into his mouth. "Just keep what happens here private. Don't talk about her, tweet about her, take pictures, look at her. That sorta thing."

"I can't *look* at her?"

"She doesn't like to be stared at. Glared at. Ogled. You get the gist."

"Nigel, I'm getting paid to look at her."

"Avoid eye contact, maybe?" He shrugs, like he's got his own problems and can't worry about mine.

And suddenly, *he* reappears. In my peripheral vision, I see the boy formerly known as Pretty Boy. Zeppelin Reid. My head swivels in his direction, and automatic body functions like breathing, blinking, swallowing—they all seem to simultaneously malfunction. My eyes water, my throat dries up, and I can't get a proper inhale. I attempt to swallow but only end up coughing like I'm about to hack up a lung.

"Full disclosure," Nigel states. "I don't know CPR."

"I'm cool." I pound on my chest. But, *ow*, a little too hard. At least I'm back to breathing normally again. And blinking. And swallowing.

Zeppelin has stepped out from behind a tall, rectangular panel on wheels. The room is actually cluttered with dozens of these panels. He must've changed behind it, because now he's wearing a pair of stylish sweatpants rolled to the knee, sneakers, and a plain black T-shirt that shows off most of the tattoo I'd noticed on his right arm. It's black and gray, but the artwork looks imaginative. Like Salvador Dalí rose from the dead and used Zeppelin's arm as a final canvas. His mess of hair is pulled off his face with a headband, accentuating those blue eyes that are now highlighted by sunlight pouring in through the windows.

Be still my heart.

Nigel follows my sight line and smirks. "Care for an introduction? He's our Roman."

"No, no." I attempt to appear disinterested by staring at the floor, but it's too late. Nigel calls out to Zeppelin. *Crap.*

He makes his way to our side.

"Zepp. This is Jerzie Jhames. She's the standby for Cinny. Jerzie, this is Zeppelin Reid. A Montague."

Zeppelin shakes my hand like we're meeting for the first time. His skin is *so* warm, but I still feel chilled, as if his hand were a solid block of ice.

"Hey, Zepp!" Robbie calls out.

"Welcome to the cast, Jerzie Jhames," Zeppelin says, then turns and heads toward Robbie.

"Sign."

"Huh?" I look at Nigel.

"The nondisclosure agreement. Sign please."

The scent of Nigel's peppermint gum burns my throat as he thrusts a pen at me. I try to read a few more lines, but I can't really discern contract speech. *Liquidated damages.* Does that have to do with water? Besides, all I can concentrate on is the fact that the hand Zeppelin touched is somehow, magically, simultaneously hot and cold. I scribble something illegible at the bottom of the page.

"Thanks, kiddo." Nigel scurries off.

My gaze shifts back to Zeppelin and Cinny as I move to the back of the room, set my backpack at my feet, and slide onto one of the folding chairs. Wait, Cinny? I didn't even notice she'd returned. She's leaning her head on Zeppelin's shoulder and holding on to his tatted arm like she never wants to let it go as they both chat with Robbie. They *definitely* have chemisty together.

Two additional cast members push through the door. A girl with sculpted legs that seem to stretch on infinitely and fire-red coils of hair piled on top of her head, and a boy with brown skin like mine. He looks familiar. In fact, it feels like I know him. Do I?

"Let's run it," Alan says. "From the top. 'I Think I Remember You.'"

"What's all that?" Cinny points.

I turn to see what's caught her attention. There are two small cameras on tripods set up in the back.

"What's with the cameras?" she asks.

Her voice. She's got the sexy raspy voice that I've always wanted. Though Judas says Cinny sounds like a chain-smoking old-lady hag. Anyway, it's surreal to see and hear her this up close and personal. It's like I've got an exclusive, all-access pass to her concert at Madison Square Garden and am watching the mic check from the front row. Her skin is all glowy, like she got an expensive body shine on the way to the studios, and even though she's wearing very little makeup, she's still so striking. She is the embodiment of celebrity. It's in her slightest move. The way her long lashes almost rest on her cheeks when she blinks. The way her ruby-red, perfectly manicured nails gleam and glisten.

I look down at my own nails. They're each painted a different color. Yellow, green, pink, purple, white—I look like human confetti. I sigh.

"Don't mind the cameras, Cinny," Alan says. "We're thinking of completely changing the number is all. The team needs to watch together to decide on a new direction."

"Thank *God*." Cinny yawns. "Hate this choreography. It's the *worst*."

The guy in the spandex shorts and heels rolls his eyes and says, "Tell me how do you really feel, Cinny?"

He's got a thick French accent, and it suddenly dawns on me who he is. It's *Elias Aubert*. Broadway choreographer extraordinaire. He's only twenty-five and is already so successful, along with his longtime partner, Nikolai. Together, they've won Outer Critics Circle Awards, Lucille Lortel Awards, and Tonys. The choreography must really be bad if Cinny is openly criticizing Elias Aubert.

"Don't be mad at me," Cinny states unapologetically. "Clearly I'm not the only person not feelin' it. Or we wouldn't be changin' it."

"We're not changing it because we don't like it though," Robbie cuts in. "It's changing because—"

"Uh-uh. Blah. Stop." Cinny shakes her head. "I'm so not the one. Not about to be arguin' with y'all. It's changing. Good. Movin' on."

Whoa. In all the interviews I've seen of Cinny, she seemed nice and gentle. Always talking about her spirituality and how Yoga keeps her super zen. Was it all an act? Or maybe she's just not a morning person.

It's now deathly quiet in the room. Though the muffled rumble of Times Square below can't be tamed, so maybe "deathly quiet" is an overstatement. In fact, either I'm hearing voices in my head, or there really is a choir of high-pitched screams coming from below.

"Do you guys hear that?" Cinny gushes.

Oh, good. She hears it, too. She rushes to the window, her mood completely flipped to cheery.

"Stop it. How cuuuuute!" She squeals. "A bunch of my fans are makin' a scene, y'all. Come see this."

Elias and Robbie exchange looks, but neither says a word in reply nor moves a muscle. The brown-skinned boy who looks familiar and the girl with the fiery red hair sigh dramatically. I also note that Zeppelin is staring at his phone as if Cinny's screeching fans are of little interest to him.

Alan only claps his hands and states, "From the top. Everyone. Places, please."

Cinny sort of smacks her lips but does move into position.

"I Think I Remember You" is one of the songs I've learned in my private rehearsals. It's when Roman and Jewel meet for the first time. I scoot to the edge of my seat as Cinny moves front and center. I'm sort of staring at her knees to avoid eye contact. It's weird. Truly. But my peripheral vision keeps all of her in clear view. And sure, I might be cross-eyed when this is all said and done, but at least I'll be in accordance with the NDA. Anyway. Cinny does have presence. She stands there so sure of herself. So poised, so confident.

Similar to Shakespeare's original play, the two meet for the first time at a party at Jewel's house. A campaign party. It starts off like a typical meet-cute. They see one another from across the room and are drawn together, almost trancelike. Then their meeting morphs into a fantasy sequence. It's a big company number. They sing a duet on the moving walkway, as time and all their past lives pass by them. In the song, they're trying to figure out why they seem so familiar to one another. Of course neither is aware (yet) that they are the reincarnations of Romeo and Juliet, meeting for the first time in hundreds of years.

Zeppelin and Cinny slowly make their way across the room to connect at the center as the pianist bangs out the complicated melody. Zeppelin wraps his arm around Cinny's tiny waist, lowers his head into the nape of her neck, and Cinny spins out of his grasp.

This move activates the moving floor, which causes Cinny to yelp, lose her footing, and fall flat on her ass, crashing into the leggy redhead in the process. There is a collective gasp from everyone (myself included) as the pianist stops playing, the floor stops moving, and Cinny rolls onto her back.

"This fucking floor!" She groans.

Alan steps forward. "How can we help, Cinny?" He's calm, as if Cinny's literal fall from grace hasn't bothered him in the least.

"One. This floor is a hazard to my *life*. How do we make it safe so I don't die?"

Since Robbie is in the back manning the cameras, Alan's gaze shifts to Elias, who is operating the floor device from the side of the room. Elias sort of tosses up his hands like, *Don't ask me!*

"What if we cue the floor after you spin." Alan asks the question, but it sounds more like a statement. "So it would be…" Alan looks back to Elias. "What would it be?"

Elias stands. "Love," he says to Cinny. "If you are counting out the move, it would be six counts to get settled with Zeppelin. Everything else would remain the same."

"Fine," she mumbles. "Also. The background girl is too close to me."

The "background girl" spins around to face Elias. She looks like she's about to speak, but Elias holds up a hand to silence her.

"Her name is Lorin," Elias says.

"And I'm not a background girl," Lorin adds. "I'm a swing."

Cinny shrugs. "Not sure what the difference is but okay."

I bite the inside of my cheek to keep my jaw from dropping. Of course *I* know what a swing is. It's someone in the chorus who learns multiple roles in case an understudy has to fill in for a lead. They're arguably the hardest workers on Broadway, having to master *their* role *and* countless other roles.

Rather than add fuel to the fire of Lorin and Cinny, Alan motions to the pianist and calls out, "From the top please. Lorin and Damon, sit this one out."

The two move to sit in a corner of the room.

Zeppelin and Cinny start from the beginning. This time, on the spin, even though the floor isn't moving yet and Lorin is nowhere around, Cinny trips over her own two feet, and she and Zeppelin clunk heads when he reaches to catch her before she falls. It's a successful (although painful-looking) save, and the two continue their duet on the now-moving walkway.

I know I'm supposed to focus on Cinny, but it's not easy. Not just because she's half-assing her way through the number, but also because Zeppelin is distracting. I can't keep my eyes off him. No wonder they wanna change the choreography. He's totally upstaging her!

Still, no matter how spectacular he is, he's essentially a Roman without a Jewel, because Cinny (the Cinny *I'm* used to seeing) has left the building. She looks bored, she's sluggish, she's barely on key. And why is she singing in her head voice when Zeppelin is belting out notes like he's the reincarnation of Freddie Mercury?

This song is worse than a train wreck. Train's derailed, on fire, and about to blow up any second. At long last, Zeppelin and Cinny make it through the awkward performance, and I've managed to jot down a few pages of notes. I exhale, and I swear everyone else in the room does, too. It's over. *Hallelujah.*

"Don't hate me," Robbie calls from the back of the room. "But we had a major camera glitch. We need to run it one more time."

"Fuckin' kidding me?" Cinny hisses. "Why do y'all care about a dance that's getting canceled?"

"Just humor us?" Alan asks dryly. "And take it from the top. The sooner we get it over with, the sooner we can move on. We have a lot to do today."

But instead of getting into position, Cinny strolls back to the window, and the Times Square screams go up to maximum hysteria volume. Whoever is down below must be able to see her, because she waves, and the screams amplify.

"They are all so cute. I gotta go say hello. Wesley?"

Her security guard stands slowly from the chair he's been sitting on near the door.

"Walk me downstairs so I can sign some autographs for these cute little kids."

She can't really think it's okay to leave rehearsal?

Clearly Alan and I are on the same page, because he says, "Cinny, you can't possibly think it's okay to leave. Right now. In the middle of rehearsal."

"Relax, *Alan*." She moves toward the door. "These are the kids who will be buyin' tickets to the show. Imma sign a few autographs and be right back up. Thank me later." And with that, she and Wesley exit into the hallway.

Alan looks so mad that I swear I can see steam coming out of his ears.

"We *have* to move on," he declares. "We're already behind schedule. We can't wait for this again."

"I didn't catch much footage," Robbie says sadly. "There's almost nothing to present to the producers. Unless you want them to see Cinny falling on her ass, we need to do it again."

"Jesus Christ, I'm getting too old for this shit," Alan mumbles.

It sorta feels like I'm intruding on this personal moment of frustration. Since there is no way to give them privacy, I try my hardest to sit as still as a stone and stare at my notes, wishing I could offer them some sort of assistance.

"Last time, she signed autographs for one whole hour," Elias complains. "Remember that?"

"How can we forget? It was yesterday," Zeppelin adds.

Hearing his soft voice makes me look up and...whoa... into his eyes. He's looking right at me. Why is he looking at me? I place my hands over my cheeks to see how warm they are. They tend to turn blazing when I'm nervous. I force my gaze back down to my script.

"How about this?" Elias calls out. "I will be Jewel for the producer video so we can move on."

I look up again. Zeppelin seems surprised to see Elias moving toward him.

"May I?" Elias asks, batting his eyelashes dramatically. "Be your Jewel?"

"You're not the Jewel of my dreams." Zeppelin laughs. "But if you're my only option—"

"I'm an option!" I stand.

Temporary insanity. I think that's what happening here. Yes. That's it exactly. I am unequivocally, without a doubt, one thousand percent, *completely* out of my damn mind.

Elias gives me a look that seems to say, *Who the hell is this girl?*

"Am I Jerzie Jhames?" I ask. Wait, why am I asking what my name is? "I mean, reverse that. I *am* Jerzie Jhames. I'm Cinny's standby."

"Jerzie?" Alan slides off his baseball cap and scratches his bald head. "Have you even learned this choreography?"

As a standby I don't get to rehearse with the cast. I learn the numbers only by watching. But I have a slight superpower that Alan doesn't know about. I learn quick. In fact, after watching only once, I know the entire dance.

"I have one of those weird minds." I knock on my forehead with my knuckles, which, *ow*. It's the spot that just got whacked with the door, and yep, Zeppelin was right. There's a bruise, all right. I'm sure it's not as big as it feels. "I memorized it already. It's pretty straightforward. Except at the key change when Roman and Jewel switch positions and Jewel walks backward for eight counts." I hold up my script. "That's what I have in my notes anyway."

"*Impressive.*" Elias claps his hands excitedly. "Très bon! Come." He moves to me, gently takes my arm, and guides me to the front of the room.

I notice Alan and Robbie both glancing at the door.

"Do not worry," Elias says to them. "She is busy being adored."

"Let's hurry anyway," Alan declares.

Elias pushes me into position as the pianist begins with the soft chords that start the song.

Okay, this is happening. It's really happening. I take a moment to compose myself by closing my eyes and taking a few deep breaths. I push aside any and all nerves and allow that magical thing to take over the way it always does when I perform. Jerzie goes away to present someone new. When I open my eyes, the piano chords are a gentle lullaby. The room is my stage. Zeppelin and I cross slowly toward one another, and I forget the cameras—I forget everything and everyone but us.

I have to admit, it's nice to stare into his blue eyes and not have to feel bad about it or quickly look away. They draw me in. If I didn't know any better, I'd swear he really *was* in love with me. Who could look at me in such a way? No one has *ever* looked at me in such a way.

We meet in the center of the room and press our hands together. There is so much heat emanating off him that when we touch, my body feels like it's been ignited. I am a flame.

I work hard to keep my knees from buckling and turning to cinder.

He steps behind me the way he did with Cinny and wraps an arm around my waist. My eyes close as I feel the warmth of him pressed against me. His soft waves of hair tickle my cheek and neck when he leans in. No wonder Cinny kept falling! How can you concentrate with this perfect human's body pressed against you? I'm getting lost in the sensation of him when I remember I'm supposed to be counting. *Oops. Focus, Jerzie!* Okay. I'm focused.

He's resting his head in the nape of my neck, and I'm not sure if he was doing this before with Cinny, but I feel his lips graze my collarbone. Damn, they're soft. It sends something pulsing through me that I've never felt before. What is this feeling? *Oh shit, I'm not counting. Count, Jerzie. Count!* I start the counts in my head, step, and spin.

The move is flawless, and the moving portion of the floor is activated. Zeppelin steps beside me and wraps his arm around my waist as we walk.

He leans closer and whispers, "A lot of touching in this scene. You're okay with it?"

I nod.

"All of it? Promise I don't bite."

His breath is warm and tickles my ear. *Bite me if you want!* I think. I purse my lips together to keep from laughing and nod again to assure him I'm okay. With all of it. Now his fingertips gently slide down my cheek as we continue to stare into one another's eyes. Just that quickly... I don't feel like laughing anymore.

"I think I remember you." We both sing. *"But how can that*

be true...when I've never seen your face before. How could I... remember you?"

I know I'm supposed to do exactly what Cinny does, so as to not throw Zeppelin off, but Cinny wasn't really doing much of anything. So, following Zeppelin's lead, I belt out some of the notes and take a gentler approach when the lyrics move me to. I'm a mezzo-soprano, although some might call me a soprano, because I can sing the higher notes with ease, too. It's just the lower notes feel perfectly placed within me. If I were to compare my singing voice to anyone's, it would probably be Sia when I'm belting. Maybe Jhené Aiko when I'm not.

Now Zeppelin and I have reached the key change. This is where we switch places. He takes my hand, and I step into the turn. When I finish the eight-count spin, I'm the one walking backward.

It's not like the floor is moving all that fast, but to add to the complexity of the backward walk and the moving floor, Zeppelin pulls me closer to him, so that we're sort of stepping in between each other's legs. I'm looking down at first, sort of nervously watching our legs, hoping we don't get tangled up and I fall splat, but Zeppelin lifts my chin so that I'm staring into his eyes again. Somehow, those eyes make me feel steady.

We continue the simple dance with the floor moving beneath our feet. He's doing all the hard work. Moving around me. Jumping from one side to the other. Making me genuinely laugh with his silly faces. At one point, he drops to his knees and falls back onto the floor. I walk over him. He chases me. Grabs me again so that I stumble into his arms. It's seriously so *fun*. It's sexy, too. Especially when the laughter quiets and our hands and bodies connect. It's exhilarating. If true love were a song and dance, it would totally be this one. I'm floating. I swear I'm soaring high above the clouds, and Zeppelin is my safety. He's the wind. He's my antigravity. My forever until eternity.

As the song nears the end, he steps behind me and presses his body to mine so that we're so close, I pretty much feel all of him. And I do mean all. *Whoa.* He turns me around to face him one last time, just as the floor stops moving and the song ends.

I step away as Cinny did. That's what's in my notes. It's the move that officially ends the number, and it's the cue for Jewel to get whisked away by the actor playing the house-keeper—Shakespeare's nurse. This is when she learns he is Roman, the son of Senator Monaghan. And he learns she is Jewel, the daughter of Senator Calloway. But as I turn to step away, Zeppelin extends a hand and draws me back to him. I sort of stumble right into his arms. He lowers his head and kisses me tenderly on the lips.

I hear a collective gasp from Elias, Robbie, Alan, the two cast members sitting in the corner, even the pianist. I'd gasp myself if my lips weren't pressed to his.

The kiss lasts for a second. Maybe two. Or maybe this kiss is lasting for an eternity. Maybe, in some alternate dimension, this kiss is pretty much the spark that ignited the big bang. It's this kiss that has spawned an entire universe. That's what's happening right now. Zeppelin and I—we're universe building.

We open our eyes at the same time, our lips still connected. I somehow manage to pull away from him, but I kid you not, my heart sort of breaks in the process. It feels like I'm saying goodbye again. I'm really Jewel in this moment, and he's my Roman, and we really did reconnect after spending so many lifetimes apart. I miss him already.

"What's happening *here*?"

I turn slowly to face the door. It's Cinny. She's back. Standing beside her scary-looking bodyguard. *Glaring* at me.

"I was helping," I offer warmly, confused by the disapproving look. "With the video."

"Well, who asked you to?" she replies.

Huh? Oh, wait. She's joking. I laugh.

"Again, who asked you to?" Cinny repeats.

Oh, God. She wasn't joking. To add to this nightmare of a moment, no one speaks. I'm not kidding. Every freaking person in this godforsaken rehearsal room has perhaps become momentarily mute.

"*We* asked her to." Robbie breaks the awkward silence. He steps around the tripod and camera setup. "Now you don't have to run the number again. Your standby did it for you."

"But I told y'all I was gonna be right back." Cinny's voice booms in the quiet rehearsal space.

"Should you not be thanking her?" Elias asks smugly. "Since you hate my choreography so much?"

"Sorry to interrupt."

We all turn to see Nigel and Rashmi standing at the door, a confused look on both of their faces. Probably wondering why I'm standing front and center in the room and not sitting on a folding chair in the back, like I'm supposed to be doing.

"But," Nigel continues, "Rashmi needs to take Jerzie downstairs to school."

"I remember where it is," I blurt. "She doesn't have to take me."

Never have I been so excited to go to school. I rush to the back of the room and grab my bag. I notice Cinny's head turn to watch me as I glide past her. I'm careful not look in return.

I literally run from the rehearsal room and race down the hall, past the elevator, and through the door to enter the dark stairwell. When the heavy door slams shuts behind me, I lean my head against it, clearly not having learned my lesson from the first time. Maybe on some level I'm hoping Zeppelin returns to bludgeon me in the head again. I need *something* to knock some sense into me. What was I thinking? Why did I volunteer as tribute? Now Cinny probably hates me.

I lift my fingers to touch the spot where Zeppelin's lips were pressed against mine. My eyes close at the memory of him. Once again, I'm floating. Floating as high as I was when we were dancing. With my eyes closed, I'm back in that magical moment where he was my safety, my wind, my antigravity—I know I can't fall down while he is here.

Only…I have to. I need to remember my place. If he's a Montague and Cinny is a Capulet, then who would I be in this story?

Ooooh. I'm the *page*. That's who I am. Mercutio's mute page, who never utters a word for the whole play. Cinny has every right to be upset. I am a standby. Her standby. And as a standby, I have my own script to follow. Out of sight. Out of mind. I'm not here to be a star.

And I'm certainly not here to fall in love.

"I'll Tell Thee Joyful Tidings Girl..."

Aunt Karla is talking. She's been talking for a long time, I think. The walk from the studio. The twenty-minute subway ride it takes to get to her street. Now we're about a block from her house, and she's *still* talking.

"You okay?"

"I'm great," I mumble.

We continue our stroll through the quiet neighborhood in Brooklyn. Aunt Karla lives in this yuppie part of town called Clinton Hill—doctors, lawyers. Those types. She's so *not* yuppie, but she's lived here since before it got all gentrified. Back when it was Bed-Stuy official. Now the edge is rebranded. I guess the white people needed it to have a different name. Anyway. It's sixteen years later, and it's like Jay-Z says in "The Story of O.J." *I could've bought a house in Dumbo before it was Dumbo.* My aunt Karla…she didn't buy a house in Dumbo, she bought one in Bed-Stuy. Crazy.

"So then what do you think about all that?" Aunt Karla finally asks, breaking the silence as we move across a pedestrian crosswalk.

"Yeah." I nod. "I get it. Yep."

"Jerzie?" She stops, turns to me and crosses her arms. "I said 'bippity boppity boo.' Then I said 'fiddle de dum and scallywag.'"

"Oh." I scratch my head. "Is there a reason why you're talkin' like the fairy godmother from Cinderella?"

"Because you're not listening!"

I stare at the dirty pavement. "Did you say anything important? Before all the nonsense?"

"Just about birthday plans. You have a birthday comin' up."

"Birthdays are lame."

"Jerzie, what's wrong? Did something happen at rehearsal?"

"I told you it was uneventful." I kick a rock off the sidewalk and watch it skip onto the street as a Tesla zooms by soundlessly.

"But I need details. You met your idol. Tell me everything, Jerzie! Was she nice?"

I kick another rock. "She was okay. I guess."

"Spill it. Right now. Something happened, and I need to know."

I sigh.

"Fine." She hands me her bags.

I fumble with them. "Why you giving me your stuff?"

She pops a squat right on the sidewalk, crosses her legs, and leans her hands back on the dirty concrete.

"Ew. What are you doing? You realize a person probably pissed there. And then died?"

"You might be right. Which is gonna make what I'm about to do even more disturbing."

"What are you about to do?"

"Jerzie Jhames. I will lick the very concrete I sit on in five seconds if you don't tell me what's wrong."

"Aunt Karla, don't do that. You'll get Hepatitis A, B, C, D. All of them."

She sticks out her tongue and leans forward. "One."

"Aunt Karla! I'm serious."

Two men with jeans, hoodies, and briefcases slung over their shoulders step into the street to walk around us. They don't even give us a second glance. Aunt K sitting with her tongue out on this street in Brooklyn is no concern of theirs. "You gonna get malaria," I whisper. "Gonorrhea. Syphilis."

"Two." Her elbows rest on the concrete now. "Three."

Oh no! Her tongue is inches away from bubonic plague.

"Okay, fine!" I grip her hand and pull her off the ground. I start talking. Fast. Beginning with me volunteering as tribute and ending with Cinny not exactly being happy about it. I leave out the kiss. It's not like she needs to know that part anyway. Besides, it's not like he kissed me for real. It was a scripted kiss. That's different.

"Look at my little niece." Aunt Karla's beaming as she takes her purse and tote bag out of my hands. "I can't believe you stood up and volunteered like that."

We start to walk again. "In retrospect, it probably wasn't the best idea."

"She's jealous. That's why she got all mad."

"Jealous? She has everything."

As we pass by, the door to a coffee shop swings open and teenagers stumble out, carrying a variety of sugary coffee drinks in clear plastic cups with dome lids. I'd ask Aunt Karla if we can grab something, but she's still mad the shop is even *in* her neighborhood. Not because she doesn't like coffee. She said it came only when the white people showed up. I guess being pissed off is her idea of a revolution. We step around the group of teens.

"It's your very presence, Jerzie. How you think Black Panther would feel if another Black Panther showed up to stare at him all day in case he can't do the job?"

"But that's the thing, Aunt Karla! Black Panther would be able to do his job and do it right. I'm not so sure about Cinny."

"Oh, please." Aunt Karla waves her hand dismissively. "You think Cinny wants to make a fool out of herself on Broadway? She'll pull it together eventually."

"Just sucks to watch her be so rude and disrespectful."

We turn a corner, moving toward the row of stoops on Aunt Karla's tree-lined street. Aunt Karla's job should not afford her to live in this part of town. At least not as a homeowner. Her neighbor is a plastic surgeon. I Googled him when he moved in. Freakin' millionaire. In fact, Aunt Karla got a bank loan for $350,000 to pay for her brownstone more than ten years ago. Last year…he paid 1.7 *million*.

"In your line of business," Aunt Karla says as we continue our walk, "people can be real assholes. Hell, assholes can be found in every line of business."

"How do you handle it?"

"I do my job, and I do it well. Today, some of the main

people who treated me like shit coming up—I'm *their* boss now. If you're patient, the universe has a way of balancing things out. Trust the process."

We're standing at the base of the stoop that leads to Aunt Karla's historic brownstone. I get to stay here for the summer, but Aunt Karla has a roommate who gets weird when company visits too long, which makes for lots of annoying run-ins and a slightly uncomfortable temporary living arrangement. But ever since this neighborhood got rebranded and property prices went up, so did Aunt Karla's property *taxes*. Now she rents out the master bedroom to make ends meet. Everybody tells her to sell. She'd be a millionaire. She justifies staying put by explaining she has every right to live in her retirement plan.

I follow her up the concrete stoop and wait while she unlocks the outside door. A few seconds later, and we're through her front door. I drop my bag on the hardwood floor, kick off my shoes, and literally fling myself onto Aunt Karla's plush brown sectional, which rests against one of the exposed brick walls.

"So is that it?" Aunt Karla moves into the kitchen and washes her hands in the sink.

I don't reply right away.

"Girl, I will go back outside and lick that utility pole across the street."

"Fine." I sit up. "Do you believe in like…love at first sight?"

"Maybe." She twists off the faucet and grabs a paper towel to dry her hands. "I loved you the first time I saw you."

"That's different. You had a nine-month lead-in. Plus, you love your brother. My dad. That's too easy. I mean like, you see someone. There is literally no connection aside from this first encounter. And you feel this thing. You maybe *love* them?"

"You mean like the plot of your musical?" She pulls open the refrigerator door, grabs a bottle of water. "Is that why you're asking?"

I contemplate telling her the truth. That I'm asking because I feel as if *I* may be a victim to its implausibility. But instead I say, "Yeah, yeah. Like the musical. Like Romeo and Juliet. Maybe they shouldn't have acted so reckless, you know. Thinking they're in love. You can't be in love after a day. And after a moment? How can that be real?"

"I don't know, Jerzie." She yanks her long braids out of the bun on top of her head. They fall down her back. "Sometimes I look up at the moon and ask the same question. How can that be real? Life is magical sometimes. I will say that *I've* never experienced anything like that. When it comes to men, they typically gotta grow on me. But I think it's cool the musical is toying around with the notion. I dig it." She crosses to join me on the couch, grabbing the TV remote from off the coffee table to flip on her flat screen. "How's the lead boy by the way? The one playing Roman?"

She hasn't even said his name, and still, the mere mention of him makes the butterflies wake from their slumber. I'm trying hard to play it cool.

"He was wearing John Varvatos boots, Aunt Karla. Balmain jeans and a Play T-shirt. To *rehearsal*."

"Oooh, he sounds fancy." She twists the cap off her bottle of water and takes a small sip.

"Right? His one outfit cost more than my entire wardrobe."

"Is this the boy we're secretly talking about?" She smiles. "Did you fall in love today at rehearsal and forget to tell me?"

"No, no. I'm not talking about *him*." I focus my eyes on the giant red NETFLIX icon that's splayed across the flat screen, hoping Aunt Karla isn't keyed in to the fact that I'm lying. Falling so hard for a boy I met just moments ago? What if she tells Mom and Dad? What if *they* tell my brother, Judas? *Uggh.* He'd never let me live it down. "Besides, I don't even believe in such a thing. Love at first sight."

"Is he cute though?"

Is he cute? Ha! He's the epitome. "He's all right. His name is Zeppelin."

"Zeppelin? I heard that name." She tosses me the remote. "Yeah, I did! I saw him and Nigel when I was coming in to pick you up."

"You did?" My heart's revving up again. *Down, girl,* I think. *Steady.*

"Mmm-hmm. Big ol' blue eyes? Dark hair? Pinkish lips."

"Oh." I fiddle with the remote. "I'm pretty sure that was him."

"Jerzie Jhames. That boy was *fine*. Woo-wee, he stepped off the elevator and I was like, hot damn, who the hell is *that*?"

"Aunt *Karla!*"

"What? Don't worry, I like my men past puberty."

"He's past puberty. He's nineteen."

"That's eleven in boy years."

We're quiet for a moment and I scroll through choices on Netflix, settling on a minimalist documentary. The show starts to play. Aunt Karla's eyes narrow at the TV screen. "Jerzie, what the hell is this?"

"It's a documentary. About minimalism. I love the concept. I think I wanna be one."

"When black people have very little, they call us poor. White people do it and they're called *minimalists*? Jerzie, don't watch this. How you get so uptight, niece?"

I playfully punch Aunt Karla on the shoulder. "I am the very antithesis of uptight."

"See? Nobody your age should say 'very antithesis.' Thus proving my point. This seems like a good time to tell you about a little surprise. I have exciting news for you, girl."

"Oh?" I perk up.

"Yep." She stands. "Follow me, little niece."

I follow her through the living room and down the hall to the master suite, where her annoying-as-shit, yuppie-in-training roommate stays. Farrah is her name. She's in law school and wants to be a prosecuting attorney. All she talks about is politics, and I imagine all she dreams about is putting people in prison.

"Why are we standing in front of Farrah's room?" I ask.

"Open the door," Aunt Karla instructs. "Don't worry. She's not here."

I do as instructed, and we both step into the master suite, which is twice as big as the room Aunt Karla sleeps in. The bedding is stripped. The closet door is open, revealing an almost empty space. I turn to Aunt K. "She movin' out? Cuz that would be the best surprise ever."

"Not quite. But she is out of town. She left this morning."

"For how long?" I cross to the large bedroom window and

stare out at the balcony. To add to the appeal of Aunt Karla's place, it's an end unit, so the master suite has this cool balcony attached. Aunt K has it set up with lights and plants and patio furniture. It's too bad only Farrah gets to enjoy it.

"She's on some sort of internship. In Amsterdam. Twelve weeks." She sits on the edge of the bed. "So we get the place to ourselves this summer."

"You're lying." I grin. "Farrah's gone all summer?"

She nods.

"Aunt Karla!" I clap my hands excitedly. "This is the best surprise ever!" I feel my sour mood beginning to lift.

"There's more." She leans back on the bed now. "Judas gets to stay, too."

"What?" My brow furrows.

"Yep. He'll be here tomorrow night. Or the day after. I can't remember. Your mom and dad are bringing him. He's gonna help out this summer. Take you to work. Pick you up. Watch you at the house in the evenings when I have to work."

"Oh my God, Aunt Karla." I groan. "Judas is my babysitter? I'm too old for that. Why can't he stay in Jersey? Doesn't he have a bunch of stuff to do before leaving for college?"

Her phone chimes, and she glances at the caller ID. "It's your dad calling. Why not ask him?"

She hands me the phone. I press the button to accept the call.

"Hey, Dad," I say glumly.

"Jerzie?" Dad's voice booms through the speakers. "Hey, honey. Why you sound so sad? Something happen?"

I look at Aunt Karla. She shrugs.

"Well," I start, "Aunt Karla told me that Judas was staying here this summer, too, and I think that's kind of...stupid."

"Stupid?" Dad replies.

"I'm just sayin'. Why can't I stay with Aunt Karla by myself? That was the original plan."

There's silence from the other end. I imagine he's taking off his glasses and rubbing his temples the way he does when he's frustrated.

"You staying by yourself was the original plan when Farrah was gonna be there," Dad replies. "You should be grateful he wants to help. He should be relaxing before college starts in the fall."

"I'm grateful, Dad. I am. But let's be real. I don't need a babysitter. He doesn't even know anything about New York City."

"Neither do you, Jerzie. And how is it gonna work when Karla wants to go out with her friends or on a date? How are you gonna manage being alone in Brooklyn when she has to work late? You're sixteen years old, and—"

"Seventeen," I correct him. "I'll be seventeen this summer. I'll be an adult in a year. Judas will be dragging me to the financial district to stare at the stock exchange building or taking selfies in front of banks. I'll be stuck with him."

"So what's wrong with that?" Dad asks.

"I don't wanna spend my summer with Judas!" I'm pacing around the room now. "Can't I just have this for myself? This one summer. I feel like I've earned it. Please, Dad."

"Jerzie. The only thing you've earned is the right to not be kidnapped or killed while alone in New York City." He's pissed off. Which is somewhat normal for Dad. When it comes to me and Judas, he's always mad about something. "Judas is coming. And you will deal with it. And if you're not grateful, pretend to be." And just like that, he ends the call.

Damn. I hand the phone back to Aunt Karla. She leans forward, her elbows resting on her knees, her braids falling over her shoulders. "Sorry, hon."

"He's being unreasonable!"

"Don't hate me, but I think he has a good point."

"Are you serious?"

"Kinda. Yeah." She stands. "I can't take you to Times Square and pick you up every day. It's too much. Take now, for example. I have to go back in to work for an emergency meeting, and I don't like the idea of you being here by yourself."

"You're leaving? Now?"

"Take-out menus are in the top drawer in the kitchen. Money, too." She crosses to the closet and yanks out a pile of fresh bedding. "You gonna be okay for a few hours?"

"Yeah. I'll be cool," I reply. "I guess."

She hands me the pile of neatly folded sheets and blankets, squeezes my shoulder, and exits the room.

I take my time making the bed. Pulling the fitted sheet so it's smooth. Making sure the flat sheet is even on both sides. Fluffing the pillows. When I'm satisfied, I grab my bag off the floor and type in the code on the keypad mounted beside the window. A second later, a soft beep lets me know I've successfully deactivated the alarm system. I slide open the window in Aunt Karla's master suite, climb through, and step onto the balcony.

It's not officially summer, but New York did not get that

memo. It's evening, so the temperature has dropped a *few* degrees, but the air still feels thick, like you could slice your way through it, and my T-shirt is sticking to my skin. I peel the fabric away and fan the shirt in an attempt to cool down. I'm mostly just blowing around hot air. I set my bag at my feet, remove my tablet, and get snuggled on one of the patio chairs. There's a string of lights wrapped around the wrought iron railing, casting a glow across the balcony. I stare up at the evening sky, tinted pink from the setting sun.

"Alexa." The light around the speaker beside my chair flashes blue. "Play *Phantom of the Opera*."

"*The Phantom of the Opera*, original London cast and Andrew Lloyd Webber on Amazon Music," Alexa says in her robotic tone.

The music begins, and I get settled into relaxation mode. I know Robbie and Alan said Zeppelin wasn't on social media. But maybe things have changed now. I Google Zeppelin Reid on my tablet. The only thing that comes up is the playbill announcement about him joining the cast of *Roman and Jewel*. His headshot is the only picture I can find online. I add Zeppelin Reid Facebook. Nothing. Zeppelin Reid Twitter. Nope. No Twitter account. He really has managed to stay off social media. Fascinating.

Next, I Google Cinny, boyfriend. I see she's rumored to be dating Shivers. He has a song called "Shiver Me Timbers," and in the video, this dude literally walks around with a peg leg.

"Alexa?"

The music pauses and the speaker turns blue.

"Um, play Shivers?"

"Shuffling music by Shivers from Amazon Music," Alexa replies.

Rap blares through the speakers.

"Cuz I'm gangsta. Not cho momma's wanksta. You mutha fuckin' pranksta!"

"Alexa!" I literally scream. The music pauses again. "Turn it off. I can't. Shivers *sucks*."

The speaker powers down and Shivers fades into the evening.

"Alexa. Play *Hamilton*."

"Playing *Hamilton*, original Broadway recording by various artists," Alexa replies.

Sensible music booms through the speakers. More than sensible. This music *fuels* me.

I should log on to Instagram. Do another live feed. My 114 followers await. We can finish our "what's in a name" conversation that got cut short this morning. I slide my phone out of my back pocket, open Instagram and study the screen.

Eight *hundred* notifications? That's like, impossible. What the hell is wrong with my account? I ignore the red icon with the hundreds of notifications. I'm sure it's some sort of glitch. I open the camera, fluff out the ponytail on top of my head, and press the button to go live.

I wait a moment for someone to start watching. Riley_Roo is the first to join the room. I grin. Riley_Roo, aka Riley Powell, aka my *best* friend. We used to go to the same school, but Riley left for a public school with a better softball team. Unfortunately the school they settled on just so happens to be Newark, a forty-minute train ride away, so I pretty much never see her anymore.

"Hey, Riley!" I blow a kiss to the camera.

Riley_Roo: I've called you twice! Tell me about the show damnit!

I lean back in my chair, holding up the phone so my face is in full view and the balcony lights make my skin all glowy. I smile. "Whatcha wanna know?"

Riley_Roo: Do all the boys on Broadway look like yours? Cuz daaaamn. I should give up sports and learn how to sing.

What is she talking about? What boy?

Only before I can comment, the room fills up. Fast. I go from one person watching to five hundred. In a matter of seconds? I've never had more than a few people watch my live feeds. I study the messages as they pop up on the screen:

Phamtasiaz: Omigosh it's Jewel! I love your voice. You're amazing!

BillyIsMyElliot112: You make me wanna be in love.

American_Idolz777: Are you guys actually dating in real life?

BreeBrums: Can't wait to see the show!

My brow furrows. There's more. The messages are scrolling so fast.

Hot_sauceLover: Sing for us right now. Sing!!

KikisBaba: I never heard of you before? Where you been?

Monkeys_Mischief: I love you Jerzie Jhames!

Ram_Butt_Booty16: You foul! Cheating on me?!
I been so loyal!

The messages are scrolling so fast I can't read anymore. And suddenly the room has one *thousand* people in it. What the holy hell is happening? I press the button to end the feed.

A call is coming through from Judas. With shaking hands I click the button to accept it. My brother's voice blares through my speakers.

"Hey yo. Sup, sis?"

"Judas." I sit up, my heart still racing from the eerie live feed. "Everything okay?"

"Yeah, man. I saw your video."

"What video?"

"The one on YouTube. With the boy. Get it, sis!" He laughs.

I sit up and uncross my legs. My bare feet settle onto the warm concrete of the balcony. "I don't have a video on You-Tube with a boy."

"Man, whatever. I watched it like three times. I stop it before the end though. Too gross."

"Judas? I swear I dunno what you're talking about."

"The video of you and the white dude. Where y'all kiss at the end."

I snatch my tablet off the chair. "What's the title?"

"Roman and Jewel."

As I type it in into the YouTube app, a crushing sensation settles in.

"Hiro told me about it when we were playing Financial Football online," Judas explains. "I thought he was joking and didn't think nothin' of it. But then Brian texted me *and* DeMario *and* Jesse and like fifteen other people from school. I guess they all saw it on Instagram."

"Instagram?" I click the link so that the video begins to play. Crushing sensation shifts into overdrive. Judas is not lying. There is a video of Zeppelin and me on YouTube. We're singing "I Think I Remember You." Our entire performance is now playing right before my eyes.

"You still there?" Judas asks.

"Judas, who could've uploaded this? This was a private thing we did earlier today. I was helping Cinny. This shouldn't be online."

I check the video's time stamp. It was uploaded exactly two hours ago. Did Robbie do this? Rehearsal ended early for everyone except Cinny and, well…me. Robbie (or anyone else for that matter) *would* have had the time to get home and get it online. But why would he do such a thing? Why would anyone do such a thing?

"It's on Twitter, too," Judas continues. "And yo, the hashtag *Roman and Jewel* is trending. Jerz, it's on *all* the social media networks. You're *viral*."

I double-check the number below the video, the one that tracks the amount of views. Two point five *million*?

I'm pacing now. Back and forth on the balcony. Me? *Viral?*

A small smile creeps onto my face right at the moment a terrifying thought occurs. *What if Cinny has seen this?* This is worse than Black Panther being watched by second Black Panther. This is Black Panther being challenged on Challenge Day and thrown over the side of a cliff! How has this happened? Who's responsible?!

"Judas, I'll call you back."

As I hang up and step back in through the window, my phone is ringing again. It's Riley. I accept the call and hold up the phone. Riley's sitting in a dugout, face covered in smears of dirt, blond hair pulled back into a messy ponytail.

"Riley? Are you at practice?"

"Nope." She blows a bubble, and it fills up the screen before she sucks it back into her mouth. The sound of a large crowd cheering blares through my phone speakers.

"You're at a game?!"

"Eh. Something like that." She blows another bubble.

"Get off the fucking phone!" a male voice cries out.

"One sec, Coach!" She leans forward and whispers, "I should probably go. But, dude! How are you viral? My best friend is viral?" More cheers. Riley stands, staring out over the phone. "Nice hit, Kaitlyn!" She looks back at me. "Not that you're any competition for Cinny's video, but I mean, yours still has *millions* of views."

"Cinny's video?" I stop pacing and stare at the screen.

"Yeah. It's obviously a publicity stunt." She snorts. "Cuz she's all over the place in her version. But it was funny. Made me laugh. Still like your version better."

"Riley Powell!" the male voice screams over the roar of the crowd. "End that FaceTime call in one second or you die."

"Coach is threatening my life. Gotta run. I'll call you later!"

She ends the call. I sit slowly on the edge of the bed. Now I type in Roman and Jewel/Cinny into the YouTube search engine. The top video to pop up has seventy million views so far, and it was uploaded two hours ago, too. I click it...and cover my mouth with my shaking hand as I watch Cinny and Zeppelin performing "I Think I Remember You."

It's actually a montage of *many* of their rehearsals. Cinny falling on her ass. Cinny messing up. Cinny missing cues. Cinny singing the wrong note. It ends with today's performance, where she trips over her own two feet and she and Zeppelin clunk heads.

Roman and Jewel Coming Soon scrolls across the screen.

"I Thought All for the Best"

After fifteen texts and twenty-something phone calls, Aunt Karla made her ride-share driver do a U-turn to bring her back home. She's currently sitting on the couch, staring at her own phone, watching the viral video. When it finishes with the kiss, she looks up and grins.

"You didn't tell me about the kiss, you little sneak." She laughs.

My video was up to 3.5 million and Cinny's was holding steady at ninety million before they were both removed from YouTube. But the videos were downloaded and reuploaded by other users, so they're still *everywhere*. Vlogger videos have them embedded in their online dialogue. News outlets are playing the footage and discussing it. Cinny is trending on Twitter, Instagram, and Facebook, too.

The comments are brutal. It's an online Cinny assassination. I'm scrolling through Twitter as I pace in front of Aunt Karla:

YogiLover: Cinny is Broadway gone K-mart #RomanAndJustStopSinging

Geranimo777: Dictionary definition of Cinny: WORST. #Ugh #GirlBYE

TaylorsSuperSwift: Listening to Cinny butcher Robert Christian Ruiz's music is like eating vomit stew. Then throwing it up. #VomitSquared #MuteCinny

JohnnyBeGooder: What do you expect? With a dumb name like Cinny. Did anybody think she could actually sing?

Brett_GameofThongs: NYC officials are on high alert. Cinny is banned from even walking down Broadway. Let alone being on one of their stages. If you see her. TELL somebody!!!

"You need to stop reading that stuff." Aunt Karla leans her head back on the couch. "It's gonna give you a panic attack."

She's right. It is making me anxious. Especially because interspersed between the online Cinny dragging is praise and adulation for…well…me. It seems the internet knows how to research, because somewhere, somehow, the trolls have discovered that I, Jerzie Jhames, am cast as Cinny's understudy:

GoGoGo_Joseph: If Cinny's falling in a forest and nobody is around. Can we leave her there so Jerzie Jhames can take her job?

PickledBeets: Joke of the day: What did the understudy say to Cinny? You STINK. #Unemployment #MuteCinny #Jerzie-Jhames4EVA

WherezCarmenSandiego: Jerzie Jhames as the understudy for Cinny would be like Beyonce being the understudy for DocMcStuffins. #BroadwayFailway

MaryJanesHurtMyFeet: Poor Jerzie Jhames. Stuck in a Broadway nightmare. #WakeUpJerzieJhames

There's more. Hundreds. *Thousands* of tweets. I toss my phone onto the couch so that it's out of reach. "It's today's news. The internet's gonna move on." I look at Aunt Karla. "Right?"

"Do you want it to?" She grabs my phone and fiddles with it. "Yesterday you were holding steady at 114 followers on Instagram. Would you like to guess how many you have now?"

"I dunno. A thousand?"

"Girl, bye. Almost one *hundred* thousand."

"Holy shit!" I cover my mouth with both hands.

Aunt Karla only laughs. I'd laugh with her, but all I can think about is Cinny. It shouldn't be #WakeUpJerzieJhames trending, it should be #WakeUpCinny. If this is my dream come true, it's her real-life nightmare.

"What's gonna happen at work tomorrow? What if Cinny makes them fire me or something?"

"Fire you?" Aunt Karla repeats. "Why? It's not your fault she's getting dragged."

The screen on my phone is lit up now. A call is coming through. I don't recognize the number, but something says to answer it. I move to the couch, grab it off the cushion, and press the button to accept the call.

"Hello?"

"Jerzie? It's Alan Kaplan. I got permission to call you from your mom."

Oh, God, no! I look at Aunt Karla with panic eyes. Worse than panic. Desperate, I'm-about-to-get-fired eyes. "It's the director," I whisper.

Aunt Karla grimaces.

"Any chance you and your guardian can meet me at my office this evening? I know it's short notice, but I'm close to Forty-Second Street Studios. Corner building. Eighteenth floor, suite 1806."

"One second. Let me see." I press the mute button and stare at Aunt Karla. "He wants to know if we can come to his office. Like, right now."

She frowns. "It can't wait until tomorrow?"

I unmute the call. "Alan? My aunt says she can bring me."

"Perfect. I'll have your names added to the list at Security."

"Is this about the videos? Am I in trouble?"

"This is about the videos." He sighs. "But you're not in trouble. We'll discuss when you get here. See you soon."

The train ride to Times Square is a somber one. At least, for me. Aunt Karla's even stopped trying to cheer me up. She does wrap an arm around my waist and lay her head on top of mine. I contemplate turning my phone off in hopes of calming the anxiety and also stopping the stream of texts coming in. When Mom messaged me and said, Wow, Jerzie was that your first kiss?! What a dreamy guy. Go daughter! I think I died a little. My entire family is watching me being kissed for the first time. On repeat.

To add to everybody and my mom texting me weird congratulations, strangers are staring at me. I kid you not. Okay, fine. *One* person on the subway is staring at me. Maybe it's because I'm wearing one of Aunt Karla's nice dresses. An orange, flowy Rebecca Taylor dress that ties in the front, with knee-high strappy sandals. I figured whatever sort of bad news I'm about to get from Alan would be better received dressed in something classy and respectable.

"That girl might be recognizing you," Aunt Karla whispers.

I slump down onto the cold plastic seat, tightly gripping the metal handrail beside me, focusing my full attention on the dirty floor of the subway car. When we make it to the Forty-Second Street stop and Aunt Karla and I stand to exit, both moving swiftly with the crowd onto the platform, I feel someone tap my shoulder. I spin around. It's the girl who was staring at me. She's holding another girl's hand, and they're both grinning at me like fools.

"Yeah?" A part of me wonders if maybe I know them from home or something. Maybe we used to go to school together. But that part of me gets proven real wrong when one of them asks, "Are you from the Romeo and Juliet video?"

I know my mouth should be moving in some semblance of a response. I blink instead.

"It *is* her," the other girl declares. "See. I told you."

"Is that your real boyfriend?" the first girl inquires. "You can tell he really loves you. You love him, too, huh?"

I blink again.

"For love!" the first girl exclaims, holding up her girlfriend's hand. They kiss on the lips, giggle, and rush off up the stairs.

Aunt Karla claps excitedly. "See? Famous!"

"Aunt Karla. I'm not famous. *Two* people recognized me."

"You're an American ambassador for love, girl. Embrace it!" She claps again. "Excuse me!" Aunt Karla calls out to a group of random strangers. "Famous niece coming through. Move."

I shake my head in embarrassment and trudge behind her, up the long flight of stairs that lead us out of the subway station.

We file into the Times Square building where Alan's office is located and move quickly through security. It's only a minute before we're stepping off the elevator and standing in front of suite 1806. I ring the buzzer mounted beside the door.

"Yes?" A male voice that sounds a lot like Alan booms through a sleek mounted camera.

"Hi," I say. "It's Jerzie. I have my aunt with me, too."

"Great. I'll buzz you in. It's the last office on the right."

A second passes and the door buzzes. Aunt Karla yanks it open, and we both step into a simple reception space.

I turn to Aunt Karla. "Would it be okay if I went in alone?" If I'm about to get fired, I really don't want an audience.

Her expression clouds but she nods in reply. "Sure, hon. Absolutely. I'll be waiting out here if you change your mind or if they need me for some reason."

I stuff my phone into the tiny leather purse slung over my shoulder. "Thanks, Aunt Karla."

I shuffle slowly, my sandals squeaking across the marble flooring as I go. When I push open the last door at the end of the hall, I'm surprised to see Zeppelin, Elias, *and* Robbie all stuffed into the cramped office space.

"Jerzie. Welcome. Have a seat." Alan's warm and friendly as he sips something from a reusable water bottle.

"Hey," I mumble and slide onto the only empty chair, right beside Zeppelin. I set my gaze on my hands, twisting my fingers like I'm trying to screw them off. The strong heat that emanates off Zeppelin warms me from the inside out. I wonder if his body temperature is higher than the standard 98.6 degrees.

"So," Alan starts. "Cinny and her manager were supposed to join us, but apparently she's feeling 'ill,' so the meeting will go on without her." He looks at me now. "We thought it would be good for all of us to be on the same page when it comes to these videos being leaked. Especially you, Jerzie. Since you've sort of been thrust in the middle of this mess."

"Did you guys upload the videos onto YouTube?" I ask.

"Absolutely not." Robbie clears his throat. "Jerzie, after you left for school, I uploaded the footage from today onto Vimeo. Password protected."

"So someone hacked into the site and stole the file?" Alan asks.

"Most likely." Robbie turns to look at Zeppelin. "But the video of Cinny has footage from quite a few rehearsals. Who's been recording her?"

"Definitely not me." Zeppelin yawns, as if this whole situation is lulling him to sleep. "And everyone knows I'm pretty much internet and social media illiterate. I've never even heard of Vimeo. Besides, Cinny's my friend. Whoever put that video online must seriously hate her."

All eyes turn to Elias. He holds up his hands.

"No, no. I do not *hate* Cinny," he declares with his strong French accent. "We disagree at times. Yes. But even if I did hate her, I love *myself* too much to give away my dances for free. A complete routine uploaded onto YouTube? When we are still weeks away from previews? Oh mon dieu. *Never.*"

Now everyone's head automatically turns toward me.

"Me?" I state incredulously. "You guys think I did this?"

"Unless she is a wizard transfiguring like Hermione Granger," Elias states smugly, "there really is no way she could have recorded Cinny in rehearsals where she was not present. As you Americans say, please give me a break."

Alan downs the rest of whatever is in his bottle before he sets it back on his desk. "So we literally have no idea who could have done this."

"Let's ask some of the cast who've had altercations with her," Elias says. "There is Lorin, Damon, Gianna, April, Justin, Angel, Walter, Zoe—"

"Stop." Robbie shakes his head. "Even if it was somebody from the cast, you think they're gonna admit it? Let's leave it to the PI."

I know I risk sounding silly, but I ask anyway. "What's a PI?"

"Private investigator," Robbie replies quickly. "We hired one to look deeper into this."

There is a long moment of silence, and I wonder what

Cinny could have possibly done to piss off a cast member in such a way that they'd seek to destroy her.

"Excuse me?" I raise my hand as if I'm in school. All heads turn toward me. "Hi. Again. So. A friend of mine called me a few hours ago. She said she *liked* Cinny's video. She figured it was a publicity stunt. She thought it was funny."

They all stare blankly, as if wondering if I'll get to a point.

"I do have a point. Basically it's this. What if you say it was Production who uploaded the video? As a promotional thing. For the show. I mean, *Roman and Jewel* is trending. This is a good thing. Right?"

Alan and Robbie exchange bemused expressions, and I get the feeling they're just now realizing that *Roman and Jewel* trending *is* a good thing.

"But then how do they explain *our* video?" Zeppelin asks.

His soothing voice sends a tingle up my spine. And did he really say "our," as if *we're* some sort of thing? I bite my bottom lip to stop myself from smiling. To be an *our* with Zeppelin Reid! *Okay, stop it! Get it together, Jerzie!*

"Well…" I pause. "Who says we have to say anything? Just have Cinny do interviews laughing about the promotional video. She could even say it was her idea. To show the world she can be fun and silly, too. It'll take the attention *away* from our video." *Omigosh now* I *said our.* "I mean, me and Zeppelin's video. And put her front and center. Where she belongs. If anybody asks her about the other video, she can say it was uploaded to give everyone a teaser of what it's supposed to be like. Since her video was meant to be funny."

It's quiet again as the men seem to mull over what I've proposed.

"You know what?" Alan says. "I kinda love this idea."

Robbie exhales. "It's brilliant." His gaze settles on me. "You're a genius, Jerzie."

Genius? Me? *Aww.* I place both hands over my cheeks and smile.

Alan drums his fingers on his desk. "We should discuss the particulars. Jerzie and Zeppelin. You guys can head home. Thanks so much for taking the late meeting. Means a lot to have you two on board."

I can sense Zeppelin studying me. It's making tiny beads of sweat form at my brow. I use the back of my hand to wipe them away before I stand. "See you all tomorrow then." I rush to the door.

Zeppelin follows closely behind and pulls the door open for me. I step out of the office quickly. I'm actually contemplating taking this hallway at a dead run to put some distance between us when he calls out my name. I stop as if under a spell.

He steps in front of me, and I have no choice but to look at him. *God, he's beautiful.* He runs a hand through his waves of hair.

"Uh. What's up?" I ask, trying my hardest not to giggle, bite my lip, and bat my eyelashes. In fact, I'm trying so hard to appear like talking to this drop-dead-gorgeous Broadway star is normal that I'm not blinking, and now my eyeballs hurt.

"I have a show tonight. Some of the cast is coming. Going there now actually. Wanna come, too?"

Over his shoulder, I notice Aunt Karla scoot to the edge of the couch in the reception area. She mouths, *Is that him?*

I take a tiny step to the left so that Zeppelin is blocking me from seeing her. "Oh, a show?" I shrug. "Things are crazy back at my aunt's pad in Brooklyn." *Did I really just say my aunt's pad?* "Probs can't make it." *What the hell is wrong with me?!*

Zeppelin smirks, stuffing his hands into the pockets of his jeans. "Well, if things die down at the 'pad' you should come. It's at Pioneerz. Let's exchange info."

"Oh, fa sho. Fa sho." *Oh. My. God. What is wrong with my vocabulary?!*

I stare into his eyes. Because his eyebrows and lashes are so dark and his skin is so pale, his eyes seem like Caribbean-blue ocean water surrounded by white sands. I can almost smell the coconut oil, hear the call of the seagulls, feel the sun on my back.

"Can I see your phone?" he asks.

"My phone? Why?"

"To give you my info."

"Oh, right. Duh." I smack myself on the forehead. Only, I *really* smacked myself hard. Right on my bruise. The loud *thwack* reverberates in the quiet hallway. *Ow.*

"You okay?" Zeppelin asks, a bemused look on his face.

"You were right. I should've let you get me ice for my forehead. Now I *do* have a nasty bruise." I grab my phone from inside my purse. His hand grazes mine during the exchange. The skin-to-skin contact lasts for maybe half a second, but a surprising surge of energy lingers at my fingertips, where we connected for the brief moment.

"'Sorry to hear it, Tuppy.'" He smiles. "'Whenever people agree with me, I always feel I must be wrong.'"

Did he really just… "Quoting Oscar Wilde?"

"Got something against Oscar Wilde?"

"No," I breathe excitedly. "I mean, *Lady Windermere's Fan,* it's one of my favorite plays. I love that scene in the play. I love that *line*."

"You just keep getting more and more interesting, Jerzie Jhames."

I was thinking the same thing about him! A wave of calm rushes through me, pushing aside the awkward nervousness. I smile at him. "It's a movie, too, you know. Have you seen it?"

"Of course I have." He slides his finger up the screen on my phone and holds it in front of my face, which unlocks it. "Don't worry, not reading any of your texts. Just leaving my info." I watch him fiddle with my cell before handing it back. "There. 'I can resist everything except temptation.'"

Wait a second. That's what Lord Darlington says to show his intentions toward Lady Windermere. Is he...hitting on me?

"I'm a big theater nerd," he confesses.

Okay. Not hitting on me. Just quoting more lines from the show.

"My mom used to take me to every play in town." He offers a weak smile. "Out of town, too. It's how I got into theater. While other kids were watching *Sesame Street*, I was watching *Hamlet, Oedipus Rex, Prometheus Bound*."

"But those are all so sad."

"She took me to see *Death of a Salesman* when I was five. Pretty sure I was the only kid there. Sitting on the edge of my seat. Feeling all depressed and shit for Willy Loman."

"Poor Willy Loman."

We both laugh.

I hear Aunt Karla dramatically clearing her throat. Zeppelin hears it, too, because he quickly adds, "Anyway. If you change your mind—Pioneerz in Fort Greene. We go on at ten. I'll call ahead to make sure you're on the list."

I watch him wave politely at Aunt Karla and push through the door that leads out of the reception area and into the hallway.

Aunt Karla rushes toward me. "Girl! He's a *nerd*."

"You were listening to our conversation?"

"Of course I was! And you two are too cute together. You guys are gonna get married and have little nerd babies and become the king and queen of nerdland."

"Aunt Karla?" I laugh. "We're not even dating. He was being nice."

"But he gave you his phone number and asked you out. Sounds like a date to me."

I don't want Aunt Karla to make a big deal of this. Besides, it really is nothing. "To be a date," I start, "I'd have to go. And I'm not going. So that's that. Besides, he said a bunch of the cast will be there. Trust me. He wasn't asking me out on a date." *Or was he?*

"But he said it's at Pioneerz. That's superclose to the house. And it's a nice place. A *safe* place."

"It's fine. I mean, thanks. But I really don't wanna go." Because how awkward would that be? Out in Brooklyn by myself? With all of Zeppelin's friends? And girlfriends, too?

"If you wanna be lame, then fine." She crosses her arms. "How'd the meeting go? What they say?"

I grab her by the arm and pull her into the hallway. Once the door to the reception area closes behind us, we move toward the elevator and I fill her in.

"See? All that worryin' for nothin'." We make it to the

elevator, and she pounds on the call buttons. The doors slide open, and we step inside. "Now can we celebrate?"

"Celebrate what?" I ask as the doors shut and the elevator jerks into motion.

"You being viral!" Aunt Karla gushes. "It's insane. Most exciting thing to ever happen to our family. Unless you count that time Uncle Roy won that hot-dog-eating competition at the county fair."

"That was pie eating. And he lost. And ended up in the hospital. Remember?"

"Oh. Well. See. This *is* the most exciting thing to ever happen to our family."

"Me getting the lead would've been more exciting."

The elevator lurches to a stop on the lobby floor and the doors slide open.

"Something is seriously wrong with you, little niece." We move through the revolving doors that lead us back into a monster crowd of pedestrians meandering through Times Square, most with their camera phones pointed up, walking slow and jamming up foot traffic on this warm and muggy New York night.

"Why? Because I'm not geeking out over some dumb video?"

"Jerzie, I'm confused." Aunt Karla grabs me by my arm and pulls me out of the path of pedestrians. We stand beside one of the many silver carts stocked with waters, sodas, and snacks for sale. "Isn't this what you wanted? A chance to shine? For it to be your turn?"

"I never wanted to be viral. I wanted my chance on *Broadway*. That's all I've *ever* wanted."

"You wanna be on Broadway?" Aunt Karla points to a street sign. "There it is, right there. You're *on* Broadway."

"You know what I mean."

"No. I don't. You've been moping around about this standby situation for weeks now, and it's startin' to get on my nerves."

"I haven't been moping!" A pair of tourists with an extended selfie stick bump into me. I stumble closer to Aunt Karla. They laugh and scurry off, oblivious to nearly bowling me over.

"The hell you haven't. You know, you and Cinny have something in common. You're jealous of each other."

I glare at my aunt. "Jealous of Cinny? How dumb would that be? It'd be like being jealous of the Queen of England."

"People can be jealous of the Queen of England. Hell, I'm jealous of Meghan Markle. The Duchess of Sussex?" Aunt Karla smacks her lips. "What*ever*. If Harry was gonna marry a black girl, it should've been me."

"Aunt Karla? Be for real."

"I'm just sayin'. Being honest with yourself is liberating. Say it. Say you're jealous of Cinny so we can all move on with our lives."

"But I'm not jealous."

"Oh, really?" Aunt Karla eyes me disbelievingly. "So you volunteering to step in while Cinny was downstairs for a few minutes had nothing to do with you trying to show her up?"

"What?" My jaw drops. "I was doing a good thing. I was trying to help her."

"For nineteen years Cinny has managed well without your help. She can handle the role of Jewel."

My eyes drift over to the swarms of happy tourists. We're

standing across the street from the famous, ruby-red, glass TKTS steps, where tourists gather to people watch or take in the festive energy where Seventh Avenue and Broadway intersect in this magical part of midtown. It feels like an odd juxtaposition, them so jovial and full of life, and me using all my strength to hold back tears.

"But they said *I* was the best out of all the girls they'd seen. *I* earned it."

Aunt Karla places a gentle hand on my shoulder. "The best for this production was someone who can insure ticket sales. Cinny was their choice. *She* earned the lead. Not you."

I know it's true. It still stings.

"I feel bad now," I say softly. "Maybe on some level, I was trying to show her up. I wanted them to see me. I knew I could do it better." I look at Aunt Karla. "All the online dragging that's happening to Cinny? I started it. It's all my fault, huh?"

"It's not *all* your fault."

"Right," I nod. "Cinny's rude and unprofessional, she acts like she doesn't care, she openly criticizes Broadway greats, she—"

"Would it be better if she was sweet as pie?" Aunt Karla asks.

Would that be better? I imagine a syrupy sweet Cinny. Working hard to make everyone happy. Having genuine chemistry with Zeppelin. Charming Elias. Impressing Alan and Robbie. Wowing everyone. *Uggh.* "Definitely not." I shake my head. "Might even be worse."

"Exactly."

"Maybe I *am* jealous then." I heave a heavy sigh. "Of Cinny. The superstar. How stupid am I?"

Aunt Karla wraps her arms around me and holds me tight. "Feels good, doesn't it? To admit it?"

"No." I lay my head on her shoulder. "Feels shitty."

"Don't beat yourself up. Being jealous is normal. Unless it turns to hate. Then you get all sorts of problems. Generations of chaos can spring from hate."

Oh my gosh. Generations of chaos *can* spring from hate. "Aunt Karla? I think I just figured out what Shakespeare was trying to say."

"Yeah?"

"Yes! It's about *perception*." I extend my arms as if presenting all of Times Square to Aunt Karla. "Look around."

She stares around at all the flashing, larger-than-life billboards. I stare at them, too.

Phantom of the Opera.

The Lion King.

Dear Evan Hansen.

Hamilton.

Ads for clothes.

And drinks.

And TV shows.

And plays.

For some reason this moment reminds me of when I was six years old. Coming into the city for the first time, somehow knowing I belonged here. Knowing I was home.

"It's proof, don't you think?" I say breathlessly. "That there's enough."

"Only infinite stars in an infinite universe could be a

better example." She guides me back into the sea of pedestrian traffic, and we walk toward the subway entrance.

"An infinite universe with infinite gifts to give." The thought warms me up inside.

"So what are you gonna do, little niece? To tap into your infinite gifts?" She wraps an arm around my shoulder.

"First thing's first. Get unjealous. Which…" I turn to her. "How do I do that?"

She laughs. "The most important step of all on the path to overcoming jealousy? Accept what's yours. Honor what's theirs."

"Right." I nod. "Even if what's yours feels kinda crappy?"

"So long as what's yours isn't physically harming you or anybody else, then yes. Even when it feels crappy. Cuz something really magical happens when you truly accept what's yours."

"What's that, Aunt Karla?"

"Well, duh. The universe gives you something new." She steps into the street, extends her arm, and yells, "Taxi!"

Within seconds a yellow taxi pulls up alongside the curb. The driver lowers the window, and Aunt Karla leans forward to speak to him.

"Pioneerz. In Fort Greene?" she calls out.

Pioneerz. Wait…huh?

"Jerzie," she pulls open the back door, "I'm headed to work from here. So you have fun." She reaches into her purse and hands me a wad of cash from her wallet. "Take a cab home." She checks the time on her cell. "It's 9:00 p.m. now. He said he goes on at ten. Come home right after, or I'll come out to find you. If you're a little past your 11:00 p.m. curfew, it'll be okay."

"But, Aunt Karla, I'm exhausted. It's been such a long day and—"

She holds up a hand to silence me. "Stop acting like a little old lady! Go out. Have fun. Make some friends. Enjoy your new internet fame. Enjoy...life."

The look on Aunt Karla's face says, *Do it or die.*

I toss back a look that hopefully covers up how terrified I am.

First time out, alone in New York City. An invitation from a boy who makes me feel like I'm Alice, plopped headfirst into Wonderland, struggling to navigate a world where nothing is as it seems, and everything that is...might not actually be.

I sigh. An unexpected "gift" from the universe, huh? Well, here goes nothin'.

I push aside my fears, step off the curb and slide into the back seat of the cab.

"Come Gentle Night"

When the cabdriver pulls up to Pioneerz, I note the large crowd of people outside, standing in line to get in. I'm not agoraphobic or anything, but everybody looks college age. I chew my bottom lip. Will I be the youngest person here?

"Thank you, sir." I dig into the purse slung over my shoulder for a tip.

"No problem." He turns and hands me his card. "I'll be in the area for a while if you need a ride back."

I slide his card into my purse and thank him again as I step onto the sidewalk and slam the door shut.

Right away, I recognize a few people from rehearsal standing among the crowd. They're all laughing. Conversing. Smoking. I approach the long line and step behind a couple locked in each other's arms, trying my hardest to avoid looking at them. People who suck face in public should be ticketed for disturbing the peace. The boy keeps moaning, and the girl keeps giggling. They seriously need a *room*.

The line is moving at a snail's pace, so I take out my cell and log on to my favorite gamer website to play *Oregon Trail*. It's this super old game I'm obsessed with. You have to create a family, give them all names, pile them into a covered wagon, and try to make it across the Oregon Trail alive in the 1800s. The game loads, and I get busy planning a trip across the Great Plains.

"Next?"

I was so busy hunting for bison to feed my virtual family that I didn't realize I'd made it to the front of the line. I slide my phone into my purse. A hostess with short pink hair holding a tablet stares at me.

"Hey." I smile. She doesn't smile back.

"We have an invite-only event tonight. Name?" she asks.

Well, I've been invited. "Jerzie Jhames."

She studies her tablet. "Sorry. I don't see you."

Maybe I got here before him? But he did say he'd call ahead. "Are you sure?" I say. "Zeppelin Reid said he would put me on the list. Can you like, call him or something? Tell him I'm here?"

The girl motions to the long line of people behind me. "I got a job to do, and getting you on the list is not a part of that job description, boo."

Bitch!

"Hey, I know you," a boy says as he's stepping out of the restaurant.

I know him, too. I saw him at rehearsal today. Damon.

"I, um. I don't think I'm on the list," I say to Damon.

He turns to the girl. "Check again. J-e-r-z-i-e J-h-a-m-e-s."

"*Fine.*" The hostess has an air of importance. Like being a hostess at this place is something real special. "Oh." Her brow furrows. "I was spelling it wrong. You're here." She looks up from her tablet. "Sorry about that. And your ticket's been covered, too."

He paid for my ticket?

"*Thank* you." Damon gives the girl the stink eye and grabs my hand. We move through the door. "Sorry that girl was being all diva. Like whatever, right?"

"Thanks for your help," I say. "You came out just in time."

"All good. My boy Zepp told me to check and see if you came. He got here about fifteen minutes before you did." Damon shouts over the noise of the restaurant. My heart flutters in my chest. Zeppelin paid for my ticket to get in *and* sent someone to check for me. Maybe this *is* a date.

"He's feelin' all sad cuz Ava couldn't make it," Damon says. "So you showing up should lift his spirits."

Oh. I deflate. Ava. That's the girl he was on the phone with earlier.

"Ava is like, the love of Zeppelin's life," he adds.

Aaaand it's official. He does have a girlfriend. I'm not really surprised by the confirmation that Ava is Zeppelin's girlfriend. I'm mostly surprised at how *officially* knowing it sort of sucks the energy from the night.

"I'm Damon, by the way. Damon Coleman. I saw you today but didn't get a chance to say what's up. Then I saw your video online. Get it, girl!" He laughs.

Wait a second. Damon *Coleman*? I knew he looked familiar! "You're from that *Sing Star* show!" I shout.

He grins. "Oh, you watched that?"

"Watched it? I was obsessed! Every week with my mom. I literally cried when you got voted off."

"I was robbed, right?" He drags me to an oversize semicircle booth with seven people stuffed into it. I slide in after him and sit awkwardly on the end. Apparently I missed the memo that I should be wearing black, since pretty much everybody else is. I look like an orange traffic cone plopped on the street next to a line of sleek, metallic black Lamborghinis. Maybe this dress wasn't such a good idea.

"You guys, this is Jerzie."

Pretty much no one acknowledges Damon introducing me. They're all too busy on their phones or in deep conversation with each other to be bothered. I notice Lorin. The leggy redhead. She's slathering hot pink lip gloss on her thin lips and using her phone camera as a mirror.

"Like, hello?" Damon says. "This is *Jerzie*. Stop being rude and say hi, y'all."

A few from the group finally look up. Lorin sets her phone down. "Oh. *Jerzie*. Not every day a standby goes viral." She eyes me like I'm a bag of trash piled on the street on trash day. "'I Think I Remember You.'"

Everyone at the table laughs. I laugh, too, even though I don't get what's funny.

"I'm Lorin," she says. "Welcome to Broadway hell."

A waitress taps me on the shoulder. I turn to face her.

"Hi, what'll it be?" She's got hair like mine. Wild. Curly.

"Nothing. I'm good."

Damon shouts into my ear over the roar of the restaurant. "Doll, it's a one-drink minimum. You gotta get a drink."

"I do? Oh, okay." I turn back to the waitress. "I'll take a grape juice."

I hear laughter from the table. Are they laughing at me? Is grape juice a lame thing to order? Am I being corny?

The waitress sort of rolls her eyes. "We don't have that."

"Um. Lemonade?"

"We have Arnold Palmers. Comes in a bottle."

"Does it have alcohol in it? I can't drink. I'm only sixteen."

More laughter from the table. Yep. They're definitely laughing at me this time. I'm sure of it.

This waitress looks so *over* me. "It's lemonade and tea. You want it or not?"

Eww. Who thought to mix those two things together? "Sure. I'll take that."

She moves off, disappearing into the crowd.

"One-drink minimum is lame, right?" Damon still has to shout over the roar of the restaurant. "Especially after having to pay to get in. But Zepp's band is blowin' up. So the restaurant knew they could make some money. Dirty capitalists."

"It's fine!" I shout back. "I don't mind."

Damon nods, then grabs the shoulder of a boy I also recognize from rehearsal. "Jerzie, did you meet Angel Aguilar?" He leans his head onto the shoulder of the striking boy beside him. Angel is sorta emo-meets-punk meets...strange. Dark eyes, bleach-blond hair with dark roots. A small hoop ring through the center of his lip. A black vest. Leather pants. His hand rests on Damon's leg. In fact, the two look *very* friendly.

"Hi. Nice to meet you." I'm talking so loud that my ears are buzzing.

Angel only nods in my direction. Viral or not, I guess I haven't earned his vocal strain. Angel plays Tyree in the show and Damon plays Mauricio. Aka Tybalt and Mercutio.

I wish I could ask them a few questions, or maybe a few hundred, but in the seconds that have passed since the introduction, Angel and Damon have entered into a major make-out session. Where is the social etiquette police when you need them? I scoot farther away. Another inch, and I'll slide right off this cushioned booth and onto the floor.

I stare at the screen on my phone like it's interesting. I could keep playing *Oregon Trail*. Would that be silly? Would they laugh at me some more? I could watch Angel and Damon make out. That would absolutely be silly. I could force the other people at this table to talk to me by asking them boring questions, like, what part of the city do you live in?

I twist my body to make sure no one can see what I'm Googling—Angel Aguilar. Right away, about a billion pictures of him load onto my screen. Apparently Angel is a slam poetry artist. Originally from Spain. Trilingual. I click on his Instagram page. Over a million followers. Insane! I look over my shoulder. Angel and Damon are still making out. Perhaps it's time for a bathroom break.

I inch my way out of the booth and skirt slowly through the crowd. Once I make it to the restrooms, I push through one of the two doors that say *All Sex* on the front and step into a quiet space with red tile walls and a painted concrete floor.

I'm alone, so I breathe a sigh of sweet relief. To think, I could be on Aunt Karla's couch watching a minimalist documentary. Why do people think going out is fun again? I step inside a stall, slide the sliver lock to bolt myself in, shut the toilet lid, and plop down right on top on it, fully clothed. Aunt Karla would be none too happy to know my night out started off stuffed inside a bathroom stall. What she doesn't know won't hurt her, I guess.

I hear girls laughing as they stumble into the bathroom. Their heels *click clack* across the concrete floor. Their voices echo off the tile walls.

"I can't believe she's wearing an orange dress. She looks like a Popsicle."

Orange dress? They talkin' about me? I hike up the possible Popsicle dress in question and step onto the toilet so they can't see my legs, hunching down *Mission Impossible* style. Tom Cruise got nothin' on me.

"She's so *young*," another girl replies. Right away I recognize the voice. It's the redhead who made the lame joke I didn't get. *Lorin.* "What is she? Twelve?" She laughs. "Cinny has a twelve-year-old standby."

"She's young. I saw her being walked back to the rehearsal room with a child wrangler."

Now they both laugh. They *are definitely* talking about me!

"Who do you think uploaded that video of Cinny?" the girl asks Lorin.

"Who knows? Maybe it was the twelve-year-old. Did you see the way she was staring at Zeppelin today? It was sorta stalkerazzi style. Then suddenly a video of her is uploaded onto YouTube?"

I wasn't staring at Zeppelin stalkerazzi style! I don't even know what that means!

"Speaking of Zeppelin…" the other girl says. "What's going on with you and him?"

"I don't know. Nothing. He's frustrating," Lorin replies.

I can hear water running now. My legs are burning from hunkering down on this toilet. I'm still careful not to move a muscle or make a sound.

"I was at his place after rehearsal. Then he had to head off to some emergency meeting," Lorin adds.

They were together? After rehearsal? At his house?! What about Zeppelin's girlfriend?

"And? Did you get a little action?" the girl asks.

They both laugh again.

"All he wanted to do was talk about boring plays from a few thousand years ago and watch YouTube videos of this old-ass singer," Lorin replies. "Leonard Cullen or something."

"Leonard Cohen," the girl corrects her.

"Yeah, yeah. Whoever the hell that is."

Her friend really cracks up at that one. "He's like super-famous. He's dead. But still."

"Whatever. It was *boring*."

"Jump his bones next time."

"If he had even one," Lorin mumbles. "The dude wanted to do nothing but *talk*."

"Maybe he's gay."

Or maybe he's a loyal boyfriend, Lorin, you skank-a-licious skank-meister!

"I asked him."

Her friend gasps. "You're rude. You asked him that?"

"Fuck yeah. That's not rude. I was like, you into dick or what?"

"Stop. What did he say?"

"He just said something about only loving the man known as his dad."

"Huh?"

"And then he went right back to his boring-ass YouTube videos."

I cover my mouth to stop myself from laughing.

"What does that even mean?" the friend asks.

"I guess it means he's not gay? I dunno," Lorin replies.

Imbeciles! He was definitely quoting a line from "Sincerely Me" from *Dear Evan Hansen*. How can they not know that?

"Well, keep trying. If you don't get that boy, I will."

"He's mine!" Lorin laughs. "Stay away. I'll try tonight. I'll probably sleep at his place again."

Sleep at his place? Again?

More giggles. Seconds pass, and I hear the door open and close. Now there is silence once again, and it's officially confirmed. *Everybody* wants Zeppelin. This isn't love at first sight that I'm feeling. It's *lust*. Besides, Damon confirmed what I already knew. Zeppelin has a girlfriend. A girlfriend who, I'm guessing, doesn't mind girls sleeping over at his apartment? Whatever. I can't do this anymore. I remove my phone and the driver's card from my purse. I compose a text: Any chance you can come back and get me? The girl you just dropped off in Fort Greene? Take me back to Bed-Stuy? Clinton Hill?

I wait for a minute. Two. Three. I'm unable to move, stuck standing on this stupid toilet like the truest form of loser.

Finally a message comes through: Be there in five.

Yes. This night can end. I'll tell Aunt Karla the universe gifted me the bestest night ever. Meanwhile, I'm gonna go home and watch my documentary, drink grape juice, and listen to *Seussical*.

I step off the toilet and groan with relief as I stretch my legs, unlatch the door, and move into the empty bathroom. After giving my hands a quick wash, I look in the mirror. Damn. My eyes are red. As if I couldn't be more pathetic? I'm near tears? *Why?* So what he's got a girlfriend. So what he's hanging out with *Lorin*. He's probably hanging out with a lot of girls. But… Jesus. It feels like some sort of strange betrayal. Why is he hanging out with *her*? She's not even interesting. Okay, fine. A beautiful, successful dancer on Broadway is interesting. But still, she wouldn't know a *Dear Evan Hansen* lyric if Ben Platt sang it to her himself. Besides, all she wants to do is have sex with Zeppelin. I don't wanna have sex with him. I mean, as a person who has never had sex, I don't really wanna have sex with anyone. I only want… I pause. What *do* I want with him? Hell if I know!

Snap out of it, Jerzie! You're obsessed. Go home.

When I push open the door and step back into the dimly lit restaurant, the room is mostly silent. Along with two other boys, Zeppelin's on the restaurant's small stage now, an acoustic guitar slung over his shoulder, wearing jeans, black leather boots, and a simple white T-shirt. Waves of black hair fall over his forehead, casting shadows under his blue eyes. He's practically perfect, if you ask me. One of his bandmates sports a massive man bun and holds a fancy purple electric bass. Super Prince vibe. The other bandmate has dark brown skin like me, with low-cut hair. He sits in front of a drum kit. Zeppelin's speaking, so I stop, my back pressed against the wall, curious to hear what he has to say.

"Feels good to be back at Pioneerz."

His voice is soothing. Deep. Calming.

"It was earlier this year," he continues. "After a set on this very stage, that a guy chased me down the street. Turned out he wasn't trying to kill me."

The crowd laughs. Zeppelin does, too.

"The guy's name was Robert Christian Ruiz. Anybody know him?"

Pretty much everyone seated at the tables and booths erupt into wild cheers.

"He said to me, and I quote, 'You're the Roman of my dreams.'" I was like, 'Huh?'" He laughs again. The crowd laughs with him. "Eight auditions later I was cast in my first Broadway musical. As the lead in his *Romeo and Juliet* reimagining, *Roman and Jewel*."

More wild cheers from the audience. The loudest of all from the table of cast members. I can't help but feel the tiniest bit of heartache. Robbie said something similar to me. *Jewel came to life because of you.*

"This song has been covered by a lot of people," Zeppelin goes on. "But the version by Lori Lieberman is the first. And it's my favorite."

Those beautiful, musician hands of his begin to lightly strum his guitar.

"Since Lori's a girl singing about a boy, I thought about changing all the gendered pronouns. But we're in Brooklyn, damnit." The crowd cheers again. Zeppelin smiles. "So yeah. Use your imagination, I guess. This is 'Killing Me Softly With His Song.'"

When he opens his mouth to sing, his voice is all falsetto.

Maybe this is how King David sounded when he composed psalms in a quiet cave so many thousands of years ago. Maybe it's what an angel would sound like if he whispered in your ear. It's serene, it's melancholy, it's hypnotic. I want nothing more than to leave this place...but I'm unable to. Not at this moment anyway. The lyrics he sings are my story right now. It's a song about a girl who comes to see a boy play. She listens to him singing and playing the guitar, and it feels like it's all about her. Like he's found her secret letters and is reading them out loud.

I wipe my cheek. I'm crying now. Officially. If I don't get out of this restaurant, I'm convinced I'll slump to the floor like a wilted flower. I will my legs into motion and turn to push through the mass of mesmerized patrons all staring adoringly up at the stage. Probably falling in love, too. I'm guessing it's an easy thing to do when Zeppelin is involved. Can't believe I said I pride myself on not being cliché. Ha! At this point, I'm pretty much the very definition.

I make it to the door and step outside into the humid, nighttime air. The lyrics to his gentle lullaby are my new soundtrack. "Killing Me Softly" is exactly what's happening here. Soft...gentle...love—the worst way to meet your demise. I see my taxi pull up a few feet down the street and run to it. Literally.

"That was quick," the driver says as I step inside and strap in.

I wipe away more tears, praying he doesn't notice. But our eyes meet through the rearview mirror.

Thankfully this is my kinda guy. He doesn't ask.

I don't tell.

"That Dreamers Often Lie"

I toss and turn most of the night. Thinking Zeppelin was asking me out on a date. Thinking maybe he might like me— a childish dream. That much is clear. But it's no use explaining that to my heart. It's like a sad puppy whose owner has yet to return home. Still it waits at the door. Tail wagging. Hopeful. My poor heart. It's the shortest love story ever told. *I'm sorry, little one.*

In the morning I awake to a text from Nigel: Rehearsal is canceled. See you tomorrow.

I text back: Why?

A moment later he replies: Damage control.

Aunt Karla knocks on the bedroom door.

"It's open." I stretch out my arms and lay my cell on the end table beside the bed.

She peeks her head inside.

"Rehearsal is canceled," I say glumly.

"I think I know why." She pushes the door open. "Come downstairs. *Breakfast Show with Sugar and Steve* is about to welcome their featured guest. You don't wanna miss it."

I slide onto the couch beside Aunt Karla as she cranks up the volume on the TV. On the screen, the bright and cheery *Breakfast Show* set livens up the energy of the living room.

"What's the *Breakfast Show* got to do with rehearsal being canceled?"

"Shh." Aunt Karla shoulder bumps me. "Just watch. You'll see."

I focus my attention on the screen.

"Welcome back to the *Breakfast Show with Sugar and Steve*! It's a fabulous morning and I'm your *favorite* fabulous host, Sugar Sanders."

"And I'm the host who gets really irritated every time she says that, because we both know it's not true, Steve Evers."

"Just accept it, Steve," Sugar sings, flipping long black hair with the signature Sugar Sanders gray streak in the front over her shoulder. "They like me more. Anyway. Exciting guest on the show today. We have R & B sensation, double platinum, Grammy Award winner Cinny with us. She is *in* this building, y'all."

I look at Aunt Karla. "They're taking my advice about the video. This is so cool!"

She smiles and we turn our attention back to the TV.

Sugar turns to Steve. "You know I love me some Cinny, right?"

"Who doesn't love Cinny?" Steve replies. "My wife wanted

to name our daughter Cinny, but I managed to talk her out of it. It would be like naming your kid Beyoncé. You can't name your kid Beyoncé. That's illegal in fifteen states!"

"What about a portmanteau," Sugar says. "Like Beyoncé and Cinny together. Beyoncinny."

"Oooh." Steve nods. "Beyoncinny actually has a nice ring to it. Too bad our daughter's already born."

The two TV hosts crack up.

"Anyway..." Sugar smiles. "Cinny's gonna talk about her role in Robert Christian Ruiz's new musical, *Roman and Jewel*. Which is coming to Broadway this summer."

"And her hilarious new viral video, in which she *purposely* makes a fool of herself," Steve adds.

"All for the love of Broadway!" Sugar says.

"All for the love of saving her career," Aunt Karla murmurs with an eye roll.

"Shhh." I elbow Aunt Karla gently on her side.

"So please welcome to the *Breakfast Show* stage..." Sugar claps her hands together "...the beautiful, talented, and fabulous Cinny!"

Cinny steps into the studio wearing a sexy red-and-gold jumper with a halter top, giant gold hoop earrings, super high-heeled stiletto boots, and her hair curled in soft beach waves that hang down her back. She looks stunning. She hugs Sugar and Steve and takes a seat on a plush green couch across from the two cohosts.

"Thank you so much for having me!" Cinny exclaims with her signature rasp. "I love the *Breakfast Show*. I literally watch you guys all the freakin' time."

She seems so comfortable in front of the camera. Like she was born to do this.

"Girl, you know we love you, too." Sugar takes a sip from her giant red mug. "I am always playing your music in the car, and my kids are like, thinkin' I'm supercool cuz I get at least *one* of the artists they like." She sets down her mug and leans forward. "But spill the tea, cuz yesterday I wake up and I'm seein' you fallin' on your be-hind, pardon my French, and I text my girlfriend." Sugar's got a superstrong Brooklyn accent. "And I'm all, Cinny has lost her *mind*?"

Cinny laughs.

Aunt Karla and I exchange knowing smiles.

"I haven't lost my mind, I swear!" Cinny explains jovially. "We wanted to wake up the internet. Think we did a good job?"

"You did a very good job," Steve agrees. "I don't think I'll ever sleep again."

Cinny laughs, crossing her legs and laying her hands gently on her lap. "Seriously though, how many times have we seen a remake of *Romeo and Juliet*? Blah. So boring, right?"

"You said it, honey." Sugar takes another sip of her coffee. "I'm not arguin' with you on that one. I think the original was written back when King Tut was alive."

"But Robbie's stuff is *different*." Cinny speaks with such passion. "It's Shakespeare like you could never imagine. Shakespeare with style. With *color*. I fell so deeply in love with the music and the book. Reincarnation? Hello? That's my jam. I wanted to do it, but only if we upped our game. Starting with the promo stuff. I was like y'all, we gotta let people know this ain't your average retelling. In fact, this ain't a retelling at all.

This is a re*do*. We're fixing all the mistakes from the world's greatest literary tragedy."

"Love it!" Sugar coos. "Cuz I'm tellin' you, it's genius. *Roman and Jewel* is trending everywhere. Even my kids are asking me to take them to see the show, and I'm all, y'all, it ain't even open yet. Stop badgering me!"

"And what about Jerzie Jhames?" Steve asks. "Is she really your understudy—because she's a phenom herself."

Aunt Karla squeezes my shoulder. "Oh my God! They just said my niece's name on national TV!"

They *did* say my name on national TV! I'm grinning so hard my cheeks are hurting.

"Isn't she amazing?" Sugar adds. "I haven't seen natural talent like that for a few decades. She reminds me of a young Whitney Houston or Mariah Carey."

I might be the only one who's noticing it, but Cinny's hands are now balled into tight fists. She's still smiling though.

"So what's the deal with her?" Sugar asks.

Omigosh. They're *still* talking about me.

"Jerzie Jhames?" Cinny repeats and for a moment I wonder if she's prepared anything to actually say about me. Did they go over this point with her?

Sugar and Steve stare anxiously at Cinny, waiting for her to continue. I can feel the energy of millions of people watching all over the country doing the same thing.

Cinny's bottom lip quivers a bit. "Jerzie Jhames?" she says again.

Aunt Karla and I exchange worried expressions.

"She's my best friend!" Cinny states excitedly.

I stare wide-eyed at the screen. *Say what?*

"When Robbie and I started chatting about the show," Cinny says nonchalantly, back in her groove, "we knew there was a real possibility of me missing a show or two or even three or four due to my erratic schedule. So we decided my understudy had to be someone very special."

"I know that's right," Sugar says. "I come to see Cinny and you're not there, I want my money back."

"Exactly my point! When I suggested my best friend, Jerzie…" Cinny pauses to smile, as if the mere mention of me makes her grin from ear to ear "…the producers were pessimistic at first, since she's *so* young and *so* inexperienced."

Inexperienced my ass!

"But…" Cinny pauses dramatically again "…I explained to them that she's basically been under my wing for *years*. I taught her everything she knows."

No she did not. Like literally. She did not. My voice teacher is probably dying a thousand deaths right now.

The screen goes black. "What just happened?" I turn to Aunt Karla who is holding up the remote.

"Sorry, but I couldn't stand another second of Pinocchininny." Aunt Karla shakes her head and tosses the remote onto the coffee table. "Cinny done lost her damn mind!"

"Aunt Karla." I place my hand on top of hers. "Listen. Tybalt killed Mercutio. You know that, right?"

Aunt Karla stares at me for a few seconds before she says, "Jerzie? What the hell are you talking about?"

"When Romeo spoke of love, Mercutio drew his sword. If he had listened, if he hadn't been so angry, things coulda turned out differently." Aunt Karla's still looking at me like she's trying to make sense of the words coming out of my mouth. I continue anyway. "I'll say to you the same thing Romeo said to Mercutio. 'Gentle Aunt Karla. Put away your sword.'"

Aunt Karla holds up her cell. "All I have is my cell."

"Your *figurative* sword."

She rolls her eyes.

"It was a little lie is all."

"Jerzie." She cocks her head to one side. "Little?"

"Okay, fine. It was a medium-size lie." I tug on my mop of curls. Since I forgot to twist my hair last night, I'm gonna spend the better part of today working hard to de-frizzify it. "But tell me this. What guided Romeo's actions after Mercutio died?"

"Jerzie? Is this a pop quiz? Cuz I graduated from college twenty-two years ago and I'm not in the mood."

"Exactly. Rage. So today, I make a vow of peace." I stand and turn to face Aunt Karla. "I'm putting away my figurative sword and from now on making only sensible choices."

"Sensible at sixteen?" Aunt Karla stands and moves into the kitchen. "Fantastic. Here's the first sensible thing you can do. Be quiet." She turns her full attention to making a fresh pot of coffee. "And please stop talking to me about Shakespeare."

"Out of His Favor, Where I Am in Love..."

The next day, as I follow Aunt Karla through the doors of Forty-Second Street Studios, I'm staring at my Instagram account, mesmerized by the growing number of followers since Cinny announced our fake best friendship. If the viral video put me on the map, Cinny has officially put me in the *limelight*. I've gone from a little over a hundred thousand followers to just under a million. In one day. I'm also watching the internet forgive her. The mob has lowered its clubs and retreated. And everybody's all best friends again.

Peter_PiperPickedYourMom: All you haters who doubted Queen Cinny can kick rocks and DIE. Cinny is the queen. Always will be.

WhoopThereitIS: Cinny and Jerzie Jhames are best friends? How cuuuute. I told y'all that video was fake. #Cinny4Eva

AbeStunner: Cinny made herself a laughing stock for Broadway? Wow. #CinnyTheSavior

BoppityBecky: Cinny is an Earth angel. Loved her on the Breakfast Show. #CinnyTheSavior

Yep. Cinny the *savior* is trending on Twitter.

"Yay, it's She-Ra and her sidekick, the Puff Princess of Power. You're both baaaack."

I look up from my phone to see Nigel and Rashmi approaching. And do my eyes deceive me? Nigel has shaved? Gotten a haircut? Not wearing his signature dirty baseball cap? Have I stepped into an alternate universe?

"What happened to you?" I ask. "Were you a contestant on *Queer Eye* last night?"

"Ha. Good one. You like?" It's impossible to ignore the fact that he's looking at Aunt Karla when he asks this.

It's also impossible to ignore the fact that Aunt Karla is gazing at Nigel sorta dumbstruck. The two stand there, staring at each other.

"Well, *I* like the new look," I say. "What do you think, Rashmi?"

Rashmi runs a hand through her long black hair. "I think he looks dashing. But perhaps it doesn't matter what either of us thinks." She takes my bag, gently guiding me toward the elevator, leaving Nigel and Aunt Karla chatting near the entrance, his hazel eyes shining as bright as I've ever seen them.

"Cinny's not here yet," Rashmi says as we step onto the elevator. "Apparently she's appearing on another morning show." She shakes her head. "Sorry. I forgot you two are best friends. You probably already know that."

My morning latte turns sour in my stomach. Will everyone now think I didn't earn my spot here? That I'm just Cinny's *bestie*?

A hand suddenly reaches through the closing doors, tripping the sensor so the doors slide back open.

"Sorry about that." Nigel rushes inside, grinning from ear to ear as the doors slide shut again.

"Where's your *girlfriend*?" I tease.

"She's not my girlfriend, silly New Jerzie." The elevator jerks into motion and he steps back into production-assistant mode. "Most of the cast is in 7A getting ready to run the opening number, so I'll take you there. Right after, we're gonna run 'Déjà Vu,' which is Cinny and Zepp. She should be back by then. If not, you can hang out with Rashmi in the classroom."

"We can play Uno," Rashmi says excitedly.

"Or *Oregon Trail*," I reply. "It's a way better game."

Rashmi's brow furrows. "Isn't that the game where people get dysentery and drown and stuff?"

Nigel's walkie crackles loudly. He twists the knob to turn down the volume. "Oh, by the way. Cell phones are now banned in all rehearsal rooms."

"Banned?" Rashmi's brow furrows. "Why?"

"You-Know-Who. That's why." Nigel runs a hand over his perfectly styled, tapered haircut. I swear he looks like he's wearing a James Bond costume.

Stepping back into the rehearsal space with Nigel at my heels, my precious cell phone stowed away in the bottom of a bucket at the door, my heart is beating against the inside of my chest like it's desperate to get my attention. I sigh. Here I am, cast in a Broadway show (sort of), new best friends with one of the biggest celebrities in the world (well...fake best friends), a million new followers on Instagram, and all my heart cares about is the cute boy in the room. The one with the girlfriend and the harem of girls after him. *This* isn't sensible.

I feel a tap on my shoulder and turn to face Damon.

"Hey, Barbie Doll." He's barefoot and wears loose-fitting jeans and a shirt that says *Stop Reading My Shirt*. His brown eyes are narrowed, eyeing me through his shiny lenses. "What happened to you the other night? You disappeared."

"Oh?" I reply. "Yeah. I got kinda sick and checked out early."

"Ew. Germs." He takes a step back and fans the air around him. "So where's your 'best friend'? She sick, too?" He laughs.

"Oh." I smile nervously. "You saw the *Breakfast Show*?"

"Mmm-hmm. And I suffered through her this morning on *Good Morning America*." He places a hand on his hip. "How did you and bestie meet? I bet it's a sweet story."

Oh, God. How did we meet?

Damon laughs again. "Never mind, girl. Tell me later. Clearly y'all need time to get your story straight."

My stomach starts to settle. Damon's not buying the "best friend" lie. Maybe the rest of the cast isn't either.

He checks the time on his watch. "Looks like your BFF is late. Again. But what else is new."

Damon moves off and immerses himself in the crowd of actors and dancers. I move to the back of the room, set my backpack at my feet, and slide onto one of the folding chairs.

The great Alan Kaplan steps front and center. He holds up

a hand to silence everyone in the room. Though he's dressed simply, almost an identical outfit from when he delivered the tragic understudy news, his faded light blue jeans and pale blue button-down dress shirt can't mask the air of importance that sort of hovers around him. He's like a rare and exotic species people pay big money to catch a quick glimpse of on safari—Broadway director extraordinaire.

"You guys." There's a twinkle in his green eyes. It takes only a few seconds for the space to quiet down. "We are *four* weeks from preview."

Everyone bursts into wild applause as the door is pushed open and Zeppelin steps into the room clutching his motor-cycle helmet in one hand, leather backpack slung over his shoulder, silky strands of dark hair pretty much everywhere.

Focus, Jerzie! Remember. You're sensible now. I force my gaze away to avoid the thirst stare. It's not a good look. Especially considering there are about a dozen girls (and boys, too) all looking at him the same way as he makes his way across the room. What it must feel like to make heads turn and hearts race.

"…which is ironic, right?" Alan laughs.

Everyone else laughs, too, and I wanna kick myself cuz I missed the joke.

There is a woman standing beside Alan now. Dark brown hair, black blazer, boot-cut jeans, Oxford shoes. It's Mae Bloomberg, the musical director. Worth noting, she's one of a very few female directors on Broadway. I watched a docu-mentary featuring her, which highlighted how the male-dominated industry hasn't exactly been kind to women. She wasn't there during my final callback, and though she never spoke to me during any of my other auditions—she mostly sat there taking notes and whispering back and forth to Alan—I was enraptured by her presence.

I glance around the room. Zeppelin's now sitting on the floor beside Lorin. She whispers something in his ear. He whispers something back. Her cheeks turn as red as her hair and she bites down hard on her lip, and I get the feeling she'd rather be biting Zeppelin's. She's in a full-on *swoon*. Damn. I wonder what they got into the other night.

"…it's *those* intricacies that will make us stand out," Mae is saying.

"Exactly." Alan claps his hands.

I notice one of the production assistants tap Zeppelin on the shoulder and bend down to talk to him. Zeppelin nods, grabs his things, and follows behind him, exiting the rehearsal room.

Focus, Jerzie. Focus. I do just that, turning my attention ahead as the cast readies to, once again, run the opening number.

In the beginning of *Roman and Jewel*, the two star-crossed lovers are facing a tribunal of judges in purgatory. The opening number is called "This Palace of Dim Night." In the scene, it's Romeo and Juliet (different actors than Zeppelin and Cinny). In song and verse, the two beg to be forgiven for their mortal sin, and the four ghostly judges in purgatory taunt them with their fate. At the end of the song, the judges settle on a compromise. Rather than be cast into hell, the lovers are sentenced to infinite lives on Earth, until they're able to meet up again to right their wrongs. It's ominous, the whole song written in a minor key. It's like Beethoven's "Moonlight Sonata" meets *Jekyll and Hyde*'s "Confrontation." I have to sit on my hands to keep myself from clapping like a little kid after they finish the run-through.

As Alan gets into a discussion with the cast, giving notes and going over particulars of the scene, I see Nigel standing near the door, waving to get my attention.

I grab my bag and step quietly toward him.

"Is it time for my last day of school?" I whisper.

"Not quite. You're going to 7B," Nigel whispers back. "Cinny has returned."

I follow him out of the room. When he shoves open a set of heavy double doors on the opposite end of the hallway and we step into a new rehearsal space, I'm completely caught off guard. There's a mattress set dead center in the room. Cinny and Zeppelin are sitting on it. Or rather, Zeppelin is straddling Cinny. Like. On top of her. *Jesus.*

"You cool, Jerzie?" Nigel asks, placing a hand on my shoulder. "You looked like you were about to faint."

"Faint? No, no. I'm good." I manage a much-needed gasp of air. "Little dehydrated I think."

"Have a seat. I'll grab you a cold water."

Nigel heads off and I move to the back of the room and take a seat on one of the folding chairs, desperately trying not to focus on the bed or the two lovers splayed across it. Cinny's hair is pulled up into a bun. Even with the less dramatic style, she's as striking as ever, wearing her celebrity like a second skin.

"The move should be quicker," Elias explains. "This is PG-13, my lovelies. Don't get too comfortable, Zeppelin."

Both he and Cinny laugh.

Zeppelin's wearing a pair of sweatpants pulled up to the knees and a blue T-shirt. Same color as his eyes. The muscles in his arms are accentuated as he straddles Cinny's waist, one arm on each side of her, so she's essentially trapped by him. With her being so scantily clad—spandex shorts and sports bra—I feel like I'm peeking in on something way over PG-13.

"So, my love," Elias says to Cinny, "Zeppelin moves to leave. On the count of four, wrap arms and legs around him. Pull him back *slowly*."

"*I'm getting déjà vu,*" Cinny sings as she reaches seductively for Zeppelin.

"Yes! Like that." Elias claps. "You guys feel good? Want to try it once or watch me and Nikolai again?"

Nikolai is Elias's choreography partner. But they're not only partners in work. I read online they got married last year.

"We're happy to show you again." Nikolai calls out from across the room where he stands beside the pianist.

Though Nikolai also has a thick French accent, the similarities between the two seem to end there. Elias is dressed in an asymmetrical dance skirt with LaDuca dance heels and a tank, his dyed white hair slicked back with so much gel that it looks frozen in place. Nikolai wears baggy workout pants, sneakers, and a long-sleeve T-shirt, and his natural brown hair is cut short and simple.

"Let's try the whole thing." Zeppelin swings his leg around Cinny and jumps off the mattress. I breathe a sweet sigh of relief. *Him off that mattress. Yes. Thank you.* His eyes meet mine. Not sure why, but for a few seconds we simply stare at one another. I break the connection, forcing my gaze down to the pages of my script. *Whoa.* Who knew eye contact could cause such intense exhilaration?

"Great. From the top." Nikolai claps.

Cinny and Zeppelin begin on the bed, lying together, wrapped in one another's arms. The pianist begins banging out the opening chords. "Déjà vu" is soft and sweet and a ton of it is verse. If the other day's performance showed the worst of Cinny, today's shows the best. She sparkles like the star she is as the two talk excitedly back and forth in rhythm with the music.

When Zeppelin makes moves to leave, Cinny brings him back onto the bed. A very seductive push-and-pull takes place between the two while they sing. She leans in to him and their lips connect.

Oh, God. I want to look away, but I can't. I literally have to watch this. Like, it's my job.

Now Cinny sort of crawls up to him in rhythm with her own rhymes. He flips her around so that she's on her back. This is where I initially came into the room. With Zeppelin in between Cinny's legs. Aaaaand. *Holy shit.* They're kissing. Again.

I pull at my hair, twisting the curls around my finger. Why should this bother me? I'm sensible. I just met Zeppelin. So I can't actually feel heartbroken right now. And betrayed. And sick to my stomach.

After what seems like quite a few eternities, the pianist plays the final chord, and I thank the Broadway gods the song has ended.

Zeppelin turns to Elias. "How was that?"

"Much better," Elias starts. "But when we run it again, this time..."

Again?! Dear God no. I get breaks. I need one. I glance around the room for the stage manager but don't see him.

Elias is giving detailed notes, so I take this moment to step quietly from the room, careful to let the door shut softly when I leave. I'm desperate for the serenity of the stairwell.

When I reach it, I go in and slip off one of my Vans, using it to keep the door cracked open, then pop a squat and lower my head into my hands. It's not till I feel moisture on my palms that I realize I'm crying. I wipe away the tears and sit this way for a while, crying into my own hands. I know I probably should head back to rehearsal. But it's not like anyone will notice I'm gone right away. It was almost time to call my break anyway. Besides, I've already memorized the stupid choreography with all its stupid kissing.

I wipe my eyes again, slide a pack of gum from my back pocket, and stuff the last piece into my mouth. I lean back on my hands just as the stairwell door is slowly pushed open. Someone steps behind me. I turn...and exhale. Zeppelin has appeared. And here we both are. Back in a stairwell together. Déjà vu for real.

"Can I talk to you?"

"Me?" I point at my chest and yelp. Too hard. *Ouch!* Why do I keep doing this to myself?

"Yes. You. The person stabbing herself with her finger." He sets the door gently against my shoe, which keeps it slightly propped open.

I'm staring down at my hands. Twisting my fingers like I'm trying to twist them right off. Hoping Zeppelin can't tell I've been reduced to blubbering over a boy in a dark stairwell.

He sits right beside me. So close that our knees are almost touching. So close that I can smell him. Of course he smells nice. Like if Warm and Sexy was a brand and had a cologne—Zeppelin's wearing it.

"Are you okay, Jerzie?"

"I'm good. Never better."

"Then how come you can't look at me?"

Damnit. I look up. With his big blue eyes dead set on me, I'm instantly aware of anything and everything that could be wrong with me. How do *I* smell? Is my hair a mess? Anything on my face? Heart beating so loud he can hear it? I quickly look away.

"You smell like strawberries." He speaks softly, as if reading my mind.

"I do?"

"I think it's the gum you're chewing."

"Oh." *Right. Duh.*

"Stage manager called break." He hands me a cold bottle of water. "And Nigel was looking for you to give you this. I told him I could find you."

"You found me." I take the bottle of water into my hands. "Thanks."

"Can't believe you're a Slytherin. I'd a pegged you for a Hufflepuff for sure."

"What?" I turn to him again, and our eyes lock. "How do you know that?"

He points to my feet, and I cover my mouth in embarrassment. Since I took off my shoe, you can see I'm wearing green Slytherin socks. "Omigosh." I laugh.

He laughs, too. "Your secret's safe with me."

"Let me guess. You're a—"

"Gryffindor."

"Daring. Chivalrous. Brave. Is that you?"

"Yes to all three. But remember, I'm a lover, not a fighter."

"Lover, huh?" I raise an eyebrow. "That sounds more Zeppelin less Gryffindor for sure."

The temperature in the cool stairwell is rising significantly.

"So why are your eyes so red, Jerzie? Looks like you've been crying."

"No, no." I wipe at them again. "It's allergies. That's all."

"Pollen count in this stairwell is pretty high?"

"Zeppelin," I stand and move to the door to slip into my shoe, which makes it slam shut. Crap. Now we're very much alone. Which feels strangely healing to my broken heart. I *like* being alone with Zeppelin. "I swear I haven't been crying."

He stands, too. "I hope not."

I could be imagining it, but it feels like he's taken another step closer to me. So I step back. Again. Only it's as far as I can go. My back is now pressed against the door.

"So, what did you want to talk to me about?"

"You came to my show."

"Oh? Yeah. No bigs." The air between us has gone from warm to blazing.

"Why didn't you stay? I wanted to see you. I wanted to talk to you."

Talk to me? Why?

"Well, you have my number. You could've texted me."

"No, Jerzie. You have *my* number. You never sent me a text so I could have yours, too."

Oh.

"Tell it to me now. I'll memorize it."

I give him my number, wondering if this is the end of our

newest random encounter, because I am starting to feel a bit faint. I think I need fresh oxygen.

"What did you think? Of my band?"

"I only heard one song before I…had to go. 'Killing Me Softly.'" *Which killed* me *softly.*

"Did I do all right?" he asks genuinely, his big blue eyes clouded with worry.

"You sounded…" *like an angel?* Nah. Too dramatic. "Like Jeff Buckley."

His worried expression shifts to cheery. "You know Jeff Buckley? I love Jeff Buckley."

"I bet I love him more." I exhale. The awkward buffoon who takes over my body whenever he is near is being replaced by the cool, calm, and collected real version of me. Yay. "His cover of 'Hallelujah.' One of my all-time favorite songs."

"See, I'm a sucker for the originals, I guess. Leonard Cohen's version makes me cry."

"Hey," I tease. "I thought grown men weren't supposed to cry."

"Well, see, that's the thing, Jerzie. I'm not a grown man. I'm a man-boy. Like Mowgli. We cry all the time." He laughs. "Tell me a song that makes you cry."

A song that makes me cry? Geez, there're so many.

The door is suddenly pushed open against my back, causing me to stumble forward, right into Zeppelin. He steadies me with his strong arms, making the butterflies deep in my belly swarm again.

"Break's over."

I spin around to see Cinny standing at the door. Her gaze darts from Zeppelin to me and back to Zeppelin before she speaks again. "Like I said. Break's over. Mae and everybody else is lookin' for you, Zepp."

Zeppelin nods. "Cool. Guess we can talk later then, Jerzie. Cuz I wanna know that song. So I can make sure nobody ever plays it." He leans forward and whispers, "Because I never wanna see you cry."

My breath catches in my throat and I stand there dumbfounded, watching him step around Cinny and disappear into the hallway. I shiver, already missing the warmth he seems to bring with him.

"Uh. Hi. Cinny." I'm careful not to make eye contact with her, twisting the bottle of water from Nigel via Zeppelin around and around in my hands.

"You don't have to do that."

"Do what?" I ask, still staring at the scuffed concrete floor.

"Not look at me."

I look up. Her face is scrubbed free of makeup. Her skin is practically perfect. Like she traded in regular skin for superstar skin. "I only have people sign that stupid NDA cuz I don't wanna be overwhelmed. You know? People can be too much. Askin' me a million questions. Tellin' me all their 'amazing' song and movie ideas. Like I'm the one who's gonna help them make it big? You strike me as somebody who understands boundaries."

Whoa. Cinny the superstar is like, talking to me?

She pulls the door open wider. "You comin' in? Or you wanna stay in the dark stairwell?"

I step into the hallway.

"Did you see me on the *Breakfast Show*?"

"Oh." *God. Do I admit I watched it? Would that make me seem pathetic?* "I heard about it."

"You're cool with the BFF thing, right?" She yanks the tie out of her hair and it falls in pretty waves on her shoulders.

"Oh, yeah. I'm cool with it."

"Good. Cuz I mean, performers gotta lie *all* the time. It's like, the media can exploit a lie. And that's cool. But when they exploit the truth? That shit hurts." She sighs. "So I try to feed them as many lies as I can. It's better that way."

Who knew celebrities lied to protect their truth? "I get that." *But did you have to lie about me?*

We stand quietly in the hallway. Awkwardly.

"I'm sorry about the video," I say.

"It's cool. All worked out for the best. Now the show is trending."

More awkward quiet.

"Hey." She finally speaks again. "Maybe we can have lunch sometime soon. You down?"

"To have lunch with you? Am I down? Holy shit. Yes!"

She laughs. "You're funny, Jerzie."

"I'm sorry, it's just…" I take a deep breath. "I was being such a poser when I first met you. Honestly, I'm a total super-fan. And of course you're among the other one-name greats. Like. Duh. Who the hell am I kidding?"

"I have no idea what that means." She laughs again.

"Could we be real friends?" The words feel silly coming out of my mouth. Like I'm a character on *Sesame Street* talking to one of the colorful monster puppets instead of the world's most famous pop star. "Because," I add softly, "I don't want us to be enemies."

"Then stay away from Zeppelin."

Wait. *What?* "I'm sorry?"

She places a perfectly manicured hand on her hip. "I dunno what's going on between you two, but he's been acting mad weird since you showed up."

"I just met him. How could anything be going on?"

"I dunno. You tell me."

"There's not," I state firmly. "I swear."

"Good. Because there *is* something going on with us. Me and him."

There is? What about Lorin? And… "What about Ava?"

"Who the hell is Ava?"

I shake my head. I really should mind my own business. Zeppelin's harem is not my concern. "Nothing. Never mind." I plaster a smile onto my face, even though it feels like Cinny stabbed me in the heart with her Zeppelin confession. "I promise there is nothing going on between me and Zeppelin."

"I believe you, Jerzie." She extends her arms. "Hug."

She's pretty much the last person I wanna hug. Ever. But she leans forward to hug me anyway.

"Who says warring families don't know how to get along? Right, Jerzie?"

"Right," I reply softly. "Who says?"

"Wherefore Art Thou Romeo?"

"Here you are, madam." Aunt Karla places my cell in my hands. "Rashmi gave it to me when I got here to pick you up."

I lift it to my lips, kiss it, and say in my best Sméagol imitation, "My *preciousss*."

"You do know studies show cell phones to be dirtier than public urinals, right?" Aunt Karla steps onto Forty-Second Street, raising her arm to hail a cab.

"We're taking a cab? How come?"

A yellow taxi quickly pulls to the side and stops in front of us. Aunt Karla yanks open the door and motions for me to step inside.

"Gotta make a quick run to a store in Bay Ridge. The subway would take forever."

I climb into the cab and slide all the way over so that Aunt Karla can climb in, too. I click on my seat belt as she gives the older male driver an address. He types it into his GPS and pulls into heavy traffic.

"Sorry I gotta drag you along, little niece. But this is exactly why I need help with you this summer. When Judas gets here, you won't have to tag along for this kinda stuff."

"It's cool. I don't mind. Not like I have anything better to do. All good."

She pulls her seat belt over her shoulder. "Tell me about rehearsal. I wanna hear every detail."

I tell her *most* of the details. About how good Damon and Angel Aguilar are as Mauricio and Tyree. Or Mercutio and Tybalt.

"Angel won the National Slam Poetry contest last year. He was so good today. The rap battle between him and Damon? Omigosh. This musical is gonna win sooo many Tonys. Oh, and Robbie treated the whole cast to ice cream sandwiches from Big Gay Ice Cream right before we finished for the day."

"Yeah, Nigel brought me one when he saw me waiting for you. So good." Aunt Karla grabs her cell phone from her purse.

"He did?" I grin. "Did he put a dollop of vanilla on your nose?" I bop her on the nose.

"Oh, you got jokes?" Aunt Karla laughs. "You just worry about *Vampire Diaries*. How's *he*?"

"Who?"

"You know. Zeppelin? Did you guys record another kiss?" Aunt Karla teases as we bump along in traffic, horns outside blaring, car and truck engines roaring. "Still think you've fallen in love at first sight, Juliet?"

"I told you that wasn't about me!" Except it was. "I didn't even talk to him." Only I did.

"As cute as he is? I bet all the girls want him."

"Not *all* the girls." I lean my head back and stare out the window. "It's ridiculous how people get so excited over someone because they're attractive. I've never had a boyfriend before. But when I get one, I wanna make sure he's smart. I don't care what he looks like."

"How noble of you," Aunt Karla chides. "I know a one-toothed cyclops genius, if you want his number."

"He sounds perfect. Have him call me."

She laughs. "So Zeppelin didn't even talk to you? After that steamy kiss y'all had? And then you went to his show. Wait." She turns to me. "How was that? You never gave me the details."

"He likes Cinny, okay? They're dating."

"Cinny is not dating Zeppelin."

"Why is that so hard to believe?"

"Because I would imagine Cinny to be dating a version of herself. A famous narcissist. Plus, I've seen the way that boy looks at you. He *likes* you."

"Well, you're wrong. She told me today that they're a thing and warned me that I need to stay away from her man or else."

Aunt Karla twists in her seat so she's facing me. "And what did you say?"

"Nothing really. I just assured her I'll stay in my lane and nothing's going on."

"Good for you, Jerzie Jhames! You really are trying to be sensible. I woulda told her to go straight to hell. But that's just me."

"Yeah." I sigh. "You're a Shakespearean tragedy waiting to happen."

Her phone buzzes in her lap, and she stares down at the screen and quickly jumps on the call. A few seconds later she's yapping away about data entry and low product quotients and blah blah blah.

I focus on my own cell, happy to have the Zeppelin conversation cut short. I study my screen. I've missed quite a few texts and phone calls from it being quarantined all day. Judas. Riley. Mom. Dad. A bunch of kids from show choir have sent me happy summer texts. And like seven of my theater friends have sent me text freak-outs about my new internet fame. I click my Instagram icon. One point one million followers? Holy geez. Should I post something? Do a live? What do you say when 1.1 *million* people are listening?

A new text comes through as I contemplate. It's from My-Romeo. Huh?

Who is *that*?

MyRomeo: You left so fast. Didn't get to say goodbye.

I stare at the message, remembering Zeppelin was the one who programmed his own number into my phone. Did he seriously save himself as MyRomeo? I glance at Aunt Karla. She's still yapping away on her work call. My hands are shaking a bit, but I manage a text back:

Me: Romeo? Thought you drank a vial of poison.

MyRomeo: We're back from the dead, remember?

I smile at the messages. Then quickly remember I'm ca-
vorting with the enemy from the house of Montague!

Me: Phone's about to die. I'll see you tomorrow! Bye!

I click the side button to lock my screen and stuff my fully
charged cell into my bag.

It's well over an hour since I last texted Zeppelin. Maybe
he got the hint, because he hasn't texted back. Good. It's for
the best.

The taxi pulls up in front of a small boutique on a busy
street in Bay Ridge. We both push open our doors and step
outside. I stretch my legs on the sidewalk, checking out the
evening view as Aunt Karla hands the driver a wad of cash
through the window. Even though Bay Ridge is Brooklyn,
it's a section of Brooklyn I've actually never been to before.
I can see a massive bridge that stretches over the bay. Lots of
cute shops, restaurants, too.

"You wanna come in with me? You can find a spot in the
back of the boutique and relax while I take my meeting with
the owner."

Across the street, I notice a tiny little Italian restaurant and
bakery called Belle Torte. They have a sign outside: Home-
made Gelato! Fresh Every Day!

Yum. "I'll head over there." I point.

She turns. "Jerzie Jhames. More ice cream?"

"No, no," I lie. "Gonna sit and relax. You know, have a
coffee. Scroll through the Gram. My one point one *million*
followers await me." I pop an imaginary collar.

"Sounds good." Aunt Karla laughs. "I'll join you when I'm done."

"Cool."

I wait for a few cars to pass, then race across the street. When I push into the tiny, dimly lit restaurant, I see it's got a cool vintage vibe, with red leather booths and white table-cloths. There's a chalkboard sign at the hostess podium that says Seat Yourself! It's mostly empty in here, so I slide into a booth near the front. A waitress approaches. Short hair cut into a bob with blunt bangs. Bright blue eyes that strike me as familiar. Do I know her?

"Hi. Welcome to Belle Torte."

"Hey. How's it going? Uh…" I stare at the menu on the table. "Can I get a slice of your chocolate truffle cake? And a scoop of vanilla gelato? And a scoop of strawberry? And a scoop of chocolate?" I hand the menu to her. "And one of your amaretti cookies?"

"An order is two." She takes the menu. "It's cheaper that way."

Cheaper is good. Since Mom and Dad are making me put most of my *Roman and Jewel* money in a CD that I can't touch until I turn eighteen, leaving me only a small allowance to get by on. "That's fine. I'll take two then. Oh!" I grab the menu back out of her hands. "Sorry." I study it for a second. "And one zeppole. Did I say that right?"

She smiles. "You said ze-pole. It's ze-po-lee."

"Ze-po-lee," I repeat.

"Yes. Very good! The zeppole, they come in an order of two as well. Is that okay?"

"That's maybe more than I want but…" I study the menu.

"Yeah, sure. And can I have pistachios on the chocolate ice-cream?"

"Not pi-stash-yo. Say pi-stah-kio."

"Pi-stah-kio?"

"Molto bene! You learn quick. And yes. You may. Anything for you." She stuffs her notepad into her smock and reaches out to retrieve the menu.

"Can I keep it? If you don't mind. My aunt might join me later."

"Of course you can. Girls with big appetites. I love it." She heads off toward the back of the store.

I've been so consumed with all this Broadway drama in the house of Montague and Capulet that I haven't been eating. I swear I could eat everything in here. I inhale. The scent. It must be what Roald Dahl imagined Willy Wonka's chocolate factory would smell like.

A man with a beautiful Italian accent is chatting loudly in the back of the restaurant. "Luciano!" He laughs heartily. "Stop checking on us. We are fine."

"I can't help it," someone else says.

Do my ears deceive me? I spin around. Holy cannoli. The "someone else" is *Zeppelin.* I twist back around and slide down into the booth seat so that I'm almost under the table. *Please don't let him see me!*

"Go home. Rest. I insist. We don't need help," the man says.

"Fine," Zeppelin replies. "Tomorrow?"

"No. Go play. Do what young boys do. You'll give yourself high blood pressure." The man laughs again. "Luciano, stop worrying so much."

"I'll check in tomorrow. You know I will."

I use the menu to hide my face as I hunker down. Zeppelin walks past me, and thankfully, I go unnoticed. I peek over the top of the menu. It's definitely him. He's holding his motorcycle helmet as he pushes through the front door.

His name is *Luciano*? After he's disappeared down the street, I twist around again. The waitress with the bright eyes is counting money at the register.

"Excuse me?" I say. "Miss?"

She stuffs money into her smock as she makes her way to my table. "Yes?" she says. "Sorry, I was just about to check on your order."

"Oh, no worries. I. Uh. Had a question about that guy who was just in here?"

"Oh?" She eyes me suspiciously. "What's your question?"

"I thought his name was Zeppelin."

"Ahh." She smiles, softening. "You know Zeppelin?"

"Yeah. We sorta work together."

"In the show? How nice!"

"Yeah. But I heard that guy call him Luciano?"

"Okay…don't tell him I told you this. But when he was a kid, he would eat the zeppole like a cow." She laughs. "Always with zeppole in his sticky little hands. So we started calling him Zeppolini. Somehow, over the years, it became Zeppelin. He says it's after the band." Even though she rolls her eyes, I can tell she has nothing but love for Zeppelin. "*We* all know it's because of his love for fried dough." She laughs. "He's my cousin."

Ahh. Now I see why her eyes look familiar.

"He's a lot like his mom. My aunt. Francesca Ricci. Google her. You'll see. Most beautiful voice you ever heard."

"I just so happen to be fluent in Google." I hold up my phone and grin, then type the name into a YouTube search. The first link features a photo of a woman with the same eyes as Zeppelin and the waitress. A rare beauty with thick waves of long black hair and lustrous ivory skin. No wonder Zeppelin's so pretty.

"That's her! That's my aunt." She slides into the booth and sits across from me. "Press the link," she says excitedly.

I do. The video features only the audio of an aria from *The Barber of Seville*. I sit, enraptured as I listen. "Wow," I breathe. "Her tops notes are *effortless*." I tap the screen to stop the audio. "I swear I've never heard 'Una voce poco fa' sound so perfect."

"You like opera?" Her blue eyes shine as bright as Zeppelin's.

"Sure. Some operas are pretty dope. Especially *The Barber of Seville*."

"Fantastico! You know, Zeppelin won't admit it, but I think performing is his way of staying close to his mom. You know?"

"Well, she's my new favorite for sure."

She smiles warmly. "I'm Marta by the way. What's your name? I'll tell him I saw you."

Oh, God. Do I really want Zeppelin to know I was here? "It's Patti. Patti...LuPone."

"Patti LuPone?" She gives me a curious look.

I swallow nervously. "He's probably mentioned me."

"Yeah." She nods. "Maybe. Okay, Patti LuPone. So nice meeting you."

"You, too, Marta."

★ ★ ★

Nothing wrong with a little white lie. Okay, it's a blatant lie. But I can't have Zeppelin knowing I stumbled upon his family in Bay Ridge. So surreal. I whip out my phone and Google Francesca Ricci as Marta heads to the back of the restaurant.

This time, a Wikipedia link pops up on my screen. I click the link and scroll quickly through all the information. I cover my mouth with my hand.

After a boating accident in Florence, Francesca Ricci was grievously injured and could no longer perform. She later drowned herself in the Arno.

No. Zeppelin's mom died by suicide? That's devastating. Poor Zeppelin.

Speaking of the man formerly known as such. I Google the name Luciano Ricci. I have...hits?

Luciano Ricci has an Instagram, a Facebook, Twitter, too. He *is* on social media! I check out the Instagram account first, scrolling through all the photos. He looks a lot younger in these pics. Some of them look like they're from photo shoots. Him with his shirt off. Him on a runway. There's a video. I click the button to activate the sound.

"Paris is cold." Zeppelin is speaking directly into the camera he's holding. "I'm not sure why anybody would say this is the lover's capital of the world, cuz mostly I wanna stay in the hotel, crank up the heat, and drink hot tea."

I hear a girl laughing off camera. "You sound like an old lady, Lucio."

He looks at the camera. "In Paris, I *am* an old lady." He widens his eyes dramatically. "Somebody take me to Hawaii."

He looks young in the video. I'd say he was fourteen or fifteen. Paris at fifteen years old? I hit the back arrow and continue scrolling through his pics, noting all the different locations. Rome, Milan, Prague, London. *Wow.* Zeppelin's a world traveler. Was Cinny telling me to stay away even necessary? I'm way out of my league with this guy.

I feel a hand on my shoulder, look up, and...oh shit... I am looking into the face of little Luciano himself.

"Hello, stalker," he says.

"Pronounce It Faithfully"

I fumble with my phone, pushing the side button to lock the screen. "Zeppelin?"

He slides into the booth, directly across from me, folding his hands and placing them gently on the white tablecloth. "Please. Don't let me interrupt your stalking."

"I'm not *stalking* you."

"Oh? You live in Bay Ridge?"

"No. I'm here with my aunt. She's across the street working. And." Ugh. How can I make this okay? This must look so bad. To add to my woes, Marta has now shown up with my food. *All* my food. Why did I order so much food?!

"I thought you left," she says to Zeppelin, setting down the ice cream first. Then the cookies. The donuts. And finally the giant slice of cake.

Zeppelin eyes the smorgasbord of treats. "Are you expecting the rest of the cast?"

"Funny you should come back, Lucio," Marta says. "Patti LuPone was asking about you. She said you guys work together."

Zeppelin's eyes grow wide. "Patti *LuPone*?"

Oh no. This has gone from bad to worse.

She speaks to Zeppelin. "Come la conosci?"

"Non si chiama, Patti LuPone." He looks at me and shakes his head. *"Dio Santo."*

"Chi è Patti Lupone?" Marta asks wide-eyed.

"Un'attrice molto famosa. *Evita. Les Misérables. Sweeney Todd.*"

"Ahhh. I remember now. Of course." She laughs and turns to me. "Well, let me know if you need anything else, *Patti*." She sets the check on the table.

"Wait." Zeppelin grabs the check and reaches into the pocket of his jeans to retrieve his wallet. He slides out two twenties and hands them and the check to Marta. "Tieni il resto, va bene?"

"Grazie." She playfully ruffles his mess of hair and moves off.

"Thanks for that."

"You're welcome, Patti LuPone."

"Don't judge me. Your name's not exactly Zeppelin Reid. It's Luciano Ricci."

"Reid is my middle name. Zeppelin is what everyone has always called me. Now. Please explain how you're here right now? Stalking me. With a phone that's clearly not dead."

"So, uh." I stare down at the plates of desserts. "The short version of this is that my aunt really is working across the street. Me being here is totally random."

"Riveting. Go on."

There's not a ton of light shining through the window because of the setting sun, but the amusement in Zeppelin's eyes seems highlighted for some reason.

"So I came here," I continue. "Randomly."

"Yeah. I get that."

"I heard you and that guy in the back."

"My uncle."

"Yeah. Him. Anyway, I asked Marta about you."

"My cousin."

"Yeah. She told me your name and stuff like that."

"Stalker."

"I was just curious!"

"I think 'I was just curious' is in the stalker oath." He leans back. "Are you gonna eat all this?"

In fact, my appetite has gone completely out the door. "I'm not hungry."

"Could've fooled me." He takes a fork from off the table and digs in to my cake. I watch the muscles in his jaw as he chews. He even looks good when he eats. "Find out anything interesting about me?"

"Only that you lie."

"You found out I'm a liar?"

"Well, you're on social media. You said you weren't."

"Haven't been on social media for years. That's the truth. Those accounts are all old."

"Are you a model or something?"

"Used to do runway. Hated it. A lot. I quit a couple years

ago. It wasn't like I was very good at it anyway." He takes another bite of cake. "My uncle's the best baker in New York City. You should eat some of this food you ordered."

I grab a fork and decide to do just that. I dig into the tiniest section of the slice of cake. It basically melts in my mouth. Forget the city, his uncle might be the best baker in the state. I haven't tasted a cake this good since we got invited to a fancy wedding in the Hamptons two years ago, and the cake was made by that spiky-haired guy from all the Food Network shows.

Zeppelin switches to the gelato, using a clean spoon he grabs off the table to taste the strawberry. "Anything else you find out?"

I take my own spoon and dig into the strawberry gelato as well. It's ice-cold and creamy. I can taste tiny bits of crushed strawberries. It's like somebody picked the fruit this morning from a nearby farm. So incredibly fresh. I relax a bit. "I read about your mom."

Zeppelin exhales.

"I'm really sorry that happened."

"Would you like to know why she threw herself into the River Arno like something out of a Gianni Schicchi opera?"

"We don't have to talk about it. It seems very personal. I only wanted you to know I saw it. It felt like I should admit that."

"I don't mind talking about it," he says. "When I was twelve, we were on a family holiday in Tuscany and there was a boating accident. Afterward, she couldn't work anymore. At least not doing what she'd always done. She was an opera star in Naples."

"Is that where you grew up?"

"I like to say I grew up in the backstage of an opera house." He digs his spoon into the chocolate gelato now. "But yeah, Naples was home."

I lean back in the booth. "Do you miss it?"

"Not really. Being there just makes me sad. Without her career, my mom was depressed. It got pretty bad. Meanwhile, my dad had a work opportunity in the States. He's a lawyer. He moved us all here, to New York. A lot of our family was already living in Bay Ridge, so it sorta made sense for us to move. It meant he'd get more help with Mom. With us." He pauses to heave a heavy sigh. "She did start to get better. Her doctors were amazed. She was gaining mobility. Singing... a little bit anyway. But it didn't take long for my dad to get real tired of being her caretaker. He was cheating on her when he filed for divorce. But that's not even the worst part. When the divorce was finalized, Dad won full custody of me and my sister."

"You have a sister?"

"Yes. Ava."

Ava—the love of his life. It's his *sister*.

"After losing us, Mom flew home to live with family and in a rare moment when no one was with her, she drowned herself."

I've suddenly lost my appetite again. I set down my spoon and search for words, but none seem fitting or adequate.

Zeppelin continues. "He married the girlfriend, now known as my evil stepmother. They have two terrible children together. Anastasia and Drizella."

"Anastasia and Drizella?" I smile. "Seriously?"

He laughs. "Okay, fine. They're not named after the evil stepsisters in *Cinderella*. But they should be." He pauses to stare out the window and I realize the laissez-faire attitude he seems to maintain isn't laissez-faire at all. It's a weight. It's…sadness. "But then there is Ava." He sighs.

"You guys must be really close."

"We always have been, yeah." His eyes darken. "But I haven't seen her in a year. He monitors her every move. She's fifteen now. Not allowed anywhere near me."

"Why?"

"It's kind of a long story."

"Zeppelin. I'm so sorry."

"Me, too, Jerzie." He sets down his spoon, and in an instant, the cloud that suddenly appeared is gone and he's back to having the charming glint in his eye. "Anything else I can clear up?"

Hmm. Is there? "Not really, I guess. What's it like dating Cinny?"

"You'd have to ask someone who's dating her. Try Shivers."

"Wait." I study his expression. Eyebrows raised. Jaw clenched. "You're *not* dating Cinny?"

"Do you think we're dating because I was kissing her today? You do realize that's in the script, right? Like, I'm contractually obligated to kiss her."

I think back to my conversation with Cinny at the studios. She said they were a thing.

Zeppelin leans forward. "Cinny's not my type."

I eye him suspiciously. "If beautiful, rich, successful, and talented isn't your type, then what is?"

"How tall are you?"

"Huh? I'm five-five."

"My type? Girls who are five-five." He smiles. "With beautiful brown skin, pretty curly hair, and a voice like an angel. And if they're named after the state they live in? Bonus."

I cock my head. "Whatever, Zeppelin."

"I love how you say my name. With three syllables. Most people call me Zep-plin. You with your Jersey accent, you call me Zep-pa-lin. It's kind of adorable."

I nervously pull at my ponytail. "Stop messing with me."

"I'm not messing with you. I like you."

I place my hands over my cheeks to cool them down. He really *does* like me.

"You put your hands on your cheeks when you're nervous." He puts both hands on his own cheeks, imitating me. "It's cute."

Oh my God. Now I place a hand over my stomach. Butterflies. They're swarming again. I'm gonna need insecticide for these things. I'm *sick*.

He runs a hand through his hair, holding it off his face for a moment. "I do like you, Jerzie. I liked you from the moment I first saw you."

"Maybe you just felt sorry for me," I whisper. "You know, after clobbering me over the head."

"No." He shakes his head. "That wasn't the first time I saw you."

"What do you mean?"

"I had to meet up with Nigel about a month ago. He was at Beaumont Theater."

Beaumont was where I had all my private rehearsals to learn the songs. Sometimes Nigel *would* be there. Doing whatever production assistants seem to always be doing. Running here. Running there.

"When I got there, I saw you," Zeppelin says.

I don't know why this story is making my heart beat so fast. Zeppelin saw me? "What was I doing?"

"You were standing next to the piano. Singing 'I Defy.'"

"Can't believe I didn't see you."

"I watched you for a bit. You didn't know I was there, standing at the door. I even came in and sat in the back until you finished."

And I never saw him? How could I have been so blind?

"You never saw me," he says, as if reading my mind. "Afterward, I asked Nigel who you were. He told me. So when I saw you in the stairwell the other day, I was so happy. I'd been waiting for you to show up. I missed you. Silly, huh? How can you miss someone you don't really even know? But I did."

This can't be real. I press a finger against my wrist. Pulse is intact. I'm alive. Good.

"Jerzie." Zeppelin's gaze causes me to shift nervously in my seat. "Don't tell me I'm alone in what I'm feeling. I'm not. Right? You like me, too?"

There are so many things I want to say in return. But I don't know how to say them! *I've been ordered to stay away from you.* That would be a good opener. Followed by, *I think it's for the best.* I nod. Yeah. That says it all. *Besides,* I'm Mercutio's mute page and he was never an integral part of this story! Mostly, *this isn't sensible, Zeppelin. Because I promised Cinny I'd stay away from you and I'm a woman of my word.* That's what I need to say. *I, dear Zeppelin, am sensible.* I mean, I really am. So, *I'm sorry.* Like, *I'm so, so sorry.*

"Jerzie." Zeppelin's expression clouds with worry. "Say something. Please."

Here goes nothing. "Zeppelin." I pause, reaching up to touch the bruise left on my forehead from when the door hit me and he magically appeared in my life. I heave the heaviest of sighs. "It was really, really hard watching you kiss Cinny today." *Wait. That's not what I was supposed to say!*

He slides out of the booth and into the seat beside me and takes both of my hands in his so that I turn to face him. "It was really, really hard to do that today. I knew you were watching, and it was making me sick to think it might be hurting you. That's why I came looking for you." He lifts his hand to touch my cheek, long enough to make my heart flutter in my chest. Maybe it skipped a beat. Maybe it's not beating at all. "You were crying in the stairwell, weren't you?"

I nod.

"I'm sorry it hurt you."

I reach up and push a strand of hair away from his eyes. It feels soft, like threads of silk.

He smiles. No, it's more than a smile. He's basically beaming like a ray of sunshine. "What are you doing right now? Come spend the night with me."

Say what! "Spend the night with you?"

He laughs. "I mean. Spend *time* with me. Hang out with me."

"Zeppelin." I chew on my bottom lip, contemplating the best way to say this. Finally I settle on the one word that can properly articulate the big problem here. *"Cinny."*

"She said something to you today?" He rests his hand on my knee. Of course his hand feels so warm. So comforting.

A sensation is growing in me that I've not felt before. It's intoxicating. I've never had alcohol, but I imagine being drunk feels a little something like this. "Tell me what she said."

"Basically, to stay away from you. She said there was something between you two. Why does she think there's something between you two if there's nothing?"

"Honestly?" He shakes his head. "Who the hell knows? Cinny liking me feels a lot like you two being best friends."

"Which we aren't."

"Exactly. We've been working together for weeks, and suddenly she's into me? I've never been anything to Cinny but professional and friendly. Let me talk to her. I'll tell her how I feel about you."

"No. Zeppelin, I wanna keep peace."

"But I want her to know—"

"Please, Zeppelin."

"Fine." He sighs. "We'll keep peace, Jerzie."

"Promise you won't say anything?"

"I promise." He squeezes my hand. "And you still haven't told me what song makes you cry. I need to put the city on alert."

There are so many sweet melodies that bring tears to my eyes. But maybe one song rises above all the others. "'Maybe This Time.' But only when Liza Minnelli sings it."

"I like *Cabaret*. It's a cool musical. But now I shall never watch it again."

"Alan was wrong." I smile. "You're not new."

"Alan called me new?"

"After they told me I was Cinny's standby, I asked who was Roman. Alan said, 'Zeppelin Reid. He's new.' But you're not

new. You grew up onstage. You know music. This is like…
your destiny."

"Destiny." He leans forward, resting his forehead against
mine, taking both my hands into his, warming me with his
touch. "I like that word."

We sit this way for a few seconds, the temperature between
us rising with each passing second, until we hear someone
clearing their throat and look up to see Aunt Karla standing
in front of the booth, her eyes open superwide at the sight
of us together.

"Well, okay then. Hello, Jerzie and *Zeppelin*."

"Oh. Hi." I pull my hands away from Zeppelin. "I sorta
ran into him."

"Yes. My vision is intact. I can see that." Aunt Karla smirks.

"My family owns this restaurant," Zeppelin adds, sounding
nervous. "Would you like something? It's on me."

"That's awfully sweet of you, but I can't stay." Aunt Karla
motions to me. "I was coming to tell you it's gonna be a long
one. The buyer's insisting I stay for dinner to 'hear her out.'
I feel bad you having to wait." She looks at Zeppelin. "But
apparently you know how to keep yourself entertained."

"Could she come with me?" Zeppelin asks.

"Come with you where?" Aunt Karla asks. "Your apartment?"

"No. I was thinking we could walk across the Brooklyn Bridge," Zeppelin replies respectfully. "Look out at the
water. Superchill. Totally innocent. Very far away from my
apartment."

"Brooklyn Bridge, huh?" Aunt Karla sucks her teeth. "Jerzie has an 11:00 p.m. curfew."

"I'll make sure I'm home before curfew," I blurt. *Wait. What is wrong with me? I'm agreeing to this?!*

Aunt Karla seems to relax. A bit anyway. "How are you two getting to the Brooklyn Bridge from here?"

"My...motorcycle?" Zeppelin asks.

"Nope." Aunt Karla makes the noise a buzzer makes when a contestant on a game show gets the answer wrong. "Try again."

"Ride share," Zeppelin says definitively.

"More like it. All right. Sounds like a safe enough date." Aunt Karla studies Zeppelin. "Don't let me down, okay? Take good care of her, or I'll put a hit out on you. I got people in low places that aren't afraid of a life sentence. They got nothing to live for. Remember that."

Aunt Karla isn't lying about that. She points to me.

"Outside, Jerzie. Let's chat before you go."

"I told you that boy liked you," Aunt Karla says as we stand on the busy street corner.

"I guess you were right."

"And you trying to pretend you didn't like him, too, was your worst acting to date."

I bite my lip. Didn't realize I was such a bad actor.

"But are you sure you wanna spend the summer fighting with Cinny over a boy?"

"Aren't you the one who said you would've told her to go straight to hell?"

"I'm different than you, Jerzie. I've never been afraid of a little controversy. But if Cinny finds out you were with him tonight, you gonna start an all-out *war*. For some reason, she's staked her claim on him."

"She won't find out. We're gonna make sure of it. Zeppelin wants to keep peace, too."

"If y'all say so," Aunt Karla says. "And please do what you're telling me. Don't lie to me. He seems nice and all, but he's a boy. With a penis."

"Aunt Karla!"

"I'm serious. Keep it all PG, and it'll be better for everyone involved. I'll text your mom and let her know I'm letting you go." She bops me on the nose. "And, Jerzie."

"Yes, Aunt Karla."

"Have fun, okay?"

I smile for real. I'm about to spend an evening with Zeppelin Reid. How could I not?

"Give Me My Romeo"

Walking down the busy street in Bay Ridge, alone again with Zeppelin, I'm reminded of the fact that I've never been on a date before. Are we supposed to hold hands? Walk arm in arm? I swear he can read my mind, because out of nowhere he grabs my hand and interlocks his fingers between mine as we approach a lime-green and black street bike that's parked down the block from his family's restaurant.

"This is my bike. I can't leave it here though. It'll get towed." He turns to me. "What if you stayed at the restaurant? My family will get you anything you want while I take it home and change into something I didn't wear to rehearsal, and then I'll come back to get you. That cool?"

I pull on the straps of my backpack, wishing I had a change of clothes, too. I'm still dressed in my yoga pants and T-shirt, and no doubt Zeppelin's about to get all fancied up in designer clothes.

"I have something you can wear if you wanna change, too. I'll bring it back."

I look up at him. "I swear you can read my mind."

He laughs. "I've known you for a few million years is all."

"Are you about to dress me in your ex-girlfriend's clothes?"

"Nothing that salacious. I have some gifts I've wanted to give my sister for a while. You guys are about the same size."

I take the helmet he's been gripping in his hand. "I'm coming with you." I move toward the bike.

He rushes in front of me, taking the helmet gently from my hands. "Jerzie. I promised your aunt—"

"It's just a quick stop-off, right? Then we'll catch the ride share from your place. I'll text her. It'll be fine."

I can tell Aunt Karla put a proper fear in Zeppelin because he looks more than a little worried. Still, he says, "Okay. Text her. Yeah. That'll work," and hands me the helmet.

Riding on the back of Zeppelin's motorcycle, pressed against him, my arms wrapped around his waist, the only thing that's missing is being able to share with the world how happy I am to be reunited with my million-year-old love. Post pictures on my social media. FaceTime Riley. But no one can know about this. Like, no one.

We're riding alongside the shore promenade, right by the beautiful blue suspension bridge. The city lights reflect in dark waters like a life-size oil painting stretched from here to the horizon. I rest my head on Zeppelin's back, enjoying the warmth of his body as the bike coasts through the cool breeze. When we come to a stop at a light, he takes a hand off one of the handles to interlock his fingers with mine.

"Almost there, Jerzie."

I'd say something back, but the helmet sort of makes that impossible. So I squeeze him a little tighter in response.

The light turns green, the bike revs up, and we take off again. A few minutes later we're pulling up to an older brick apartment complex. A gate opens, and Zeppelin slows to a stop in the private parking and yanks the key out of the ignition. I pull the helmet off and try to put my mess of hair back into a neat ponytail.

"Can I help?" Zeppelin asks. "I'm a pro at fixing helmet hair."

I laugh and he places his two hands on top of my head and ruffles my hair so that it flies in every imaginable direction.

"Zeppelin, you lied." I'm laughing so hard as I force my hands through my wild strands of hair. "You're terrible at this."

"What? Now it's perfect."

Zeppelin helps me off the bike, and I think maybe I'm now addicted to this way of travel. We move to a private side entrance, where he uses a key card to open the door and we step into the lobby of his apartment building. He uses the same key card to access the elevators.

As soon as we step inside, Zeppelin leans against one wall and pulls me close so that I step between his legs. He lifts my chin so that I'm looking up into his eyes. He stares at me with such intensity, I could seriously get lost in him. If he's a drug, I'm already addicted. I hold my breath, thinking he's about to kiss me, but the elevator dings and the doors slide open. Holding my hand tightly, he guides me off the elevator.

At the end of the narrow hallway, he uses his key card again. The door beeps like a hotel room and we push into a studio apartment that overlooks the bay. I guess there are some advantages to living farther away from the city, because the closer you get to midtown, the smaller the apartments get. This place is huge.

The studio has an eclectic bathroom with frosted glass doors, a tiny kitchenette, a walk-in closet, and a Murphy bed sitting against the wall. Also worth noting—it's *clean*. I'm talking not a speck of dust in sight. I guess I figured Judas was the only meticulously neat and tidy teenage boy with everything in perfect order.

"Love your place, Zeppelin. It has everything."

"Except a balcony. A few units have them. Might trade up if I can."

"The room I stay in at my aunt's has a balcony attached. They are kinda nice." I step farther inside. "No roommates?"

"At first. Yeah. I shared this place with my bandmate, Kenyon. We split the rent for a year. Don't worry. We didn't share a bed. He slept on a blow-up mattress on the floor. But then he got a place with his girlfriend in Crown Heights right around the time I booked the show."

He pulls open the door of his closet, and I peek inside. It's stuffed to the brim. Of course I recognize a lot of the brands. Play, Gucci, Ralph Lauren, Tom Ford—wait—is that a Burberry *umbrella*? He even walks in the rain in style? There are also racks of expensive sneakers, designer boots, and shoes lining the floor.

Dozens of hanging belts and a shelf with a few designer watches. I note a Breitling among the collection.

"So runway modeling must pay...pretty good?"

"It pays shit," he admits. "The main perk of it was the travel. Most everything here, honestly, I stole."

"You did not." I laugh. "You're lying."

"I'm serious." He reaches up to pull a hanging string in the closet. Dim light casts a glow on all the neatly organized items of couture clothing and accessories. "When a runway show would end, I'd stuff shit in my bags. I wasn't exactly the greatest kind of kid."

I'm sort of frozen under the archway of his closet. My eyes must look some kind of horrified, because he quickly adds, "Don't worry. I'm reformed." He takes my arm and gently pulls me into the closet. "Feels like I should ask permission before I touch you. May I?"

I nod and he wraps his arms around my waist and rests his chin on top of my head. "At least I stopped holding girls prisoner in here. That was a really bad phase."

"Zeppelin." I playfully push him, and he stumbles back. "Not funny."

"Kidding about that last part." He steps forward to kiss me softly on the cheek. His lips feel warm on my skin. "Do you think badly of me now?"

"No. I mean...so you stole...thousands of dollars worth of clothes. And jewelry." *I guess when I put it like that... Yikes.* I look up at him. "You seriously never got caught?"

"Well. Yeah."

"And what happened?"

"I got arrested."

My jaw drops.

"But my dad's a lawyer. He got the charges dropped to a misdemeanor. I had to take some classes. Do some community service. My dad still hates me for it though."

"Is that why he hasn't let you see Ava?"

"That," he says, "and my friends are a 'bad influence.' His words, not mine. Technically I can see her as long as he's around to supervise. At their house only."

"That doesn't sound so bad."

"I haven't stepped foot in that mausoleum for years and don't plan to anytime soon."

"Why though? At least you'd get to see her and—" I pause. "You know what. It's none of my business. I'm sorry."

"Don't be. I like when you ask me questions. But the truth is…" His expression turns dark. "Seeing his 'happy' life, after mom suffered so much…shit seems unfair. Hurts too much to be there."

Of course that would hurt. Hurts me just thinking about it.

"Your turn, Jerzie." He smiles now. "We're in a closet. So skeletons are coming out. What's your secret story? I mean. You are a Slytherin, after all."

Do I have any salacious stories? "I'm not a Goody Two-shoes if that's what you're thinking."

"Wasn't thinking that at all."

"I've done bad stuff." That's a lie. I've never been arrested. Never stolen anything. Never done drugs. Never had sex. Never, never, never. "Does jaywalking count?"

"Across a freeway? Yes." He reaches to grab a black T-shirt from off the top shelf of his closet. Then, he basically yanks off the one he's wearing and tosses it into a clothes hamper. Aaaand now he's standing half-naked in front of me.

I can't help but stare. First at his tattoo. When I saw it in rehearsal, I thought it looked like something by Salvador Dalí. Now I can see that it *is* Salvador Dalí. It's *The Persistence of Memory*, sort of reimagined in black and gray on his arm. *Sexy.* And then there's the issue of his body. I've never stared at a guy with his shirt off before and thought the sort of things I'm thinking now. Like, I wonder what it would be like to touch each individual muscle on his stomach. Yeah. I've pretty much never thought that before.

"You like this, Jerzie?"

"Your...body?"

He pulls the T-shirt over his head. "Sure. But I meant the shirt."

Oh my God, how embarrassing! "Oh. The shirt. Duh."

"*This* shirt I didn't steal."

"Zepp. It's fine. I'm not judging you for your past. I promise." I shrug. "Sorry I'm short on skeletons though. Guess I'm boring."

"Jerzie." He reaches behind the rack of clothes and pulls out a decorative gift bag. "I think you're perfect. Just hope I don't fuck things up. I have a way of fucking things up. At least, according to my dad." He reaches in the bag to remove a beautiful purple-and-black flowy tank dress. Supercute. Totally hipster. "Didn't steal this either. You like it?"

I *love* it. "I can't take your sister's gift."

He hands it to me. "It's forever yours now. I'll get her something else." He pulls a pair of dark jeans off a hanger. "Change now if you want."

I swallow. "In here?"

"You can have privacy in the bathroom."

"Oh." I sort of deflate. He wants me to dress in the bathroom. He doesn't want to see me nearly naked. Good thing, too, cuz I don't look anything like a sculpted statue the way he does.

"After you, bella." He motions for the door. "Promise not to barge in on you."

Changing in Zeppelin's bathroom, I keep waiting for the door to slide open and him to see me half-dressed and stare in awe at my body the way I stared at his. But the door remains tightly closed. We're alone in his apartment, and he hasn't even tried to kiss me. Not for real anyway. He even asks permission before he touches me. It's because he thinks I'm a Goody Two-shoes. I did gape at him in judgment when he confessed his felonious past. God, why did I do that? I once took a mechanical pencil home from school. It was the teacher's pencil. And actually… I brought it back the next day and apologized for it accidentally ending up in my bag. *Two-shoes!*

I step back into my boots and redo my ponytail, using water to smooth the edges, which I'll pay the price for later when it all frizzes up on me again. The gifted dress is one that can be dressed up to look superchic or down to look casual. It looks casual on me now, but still nice enough to make me feel like I'm going on a real date. When I slide open the bathroom door with my backpack slung over my shoulder, Zeppelin is waiting by the door.

"Sei bella."

I raise an eyebrow.

"That means you look pretty."

"Oh," I say. "You look pretty, too."

He laughs. But I'm not kidding. The dark skinny jeans, the boots, the hair now wet and brushed back off his face. His eyes bright. His skin so pale. He looks like a painting. If he were mounted on a museum wall, I would study him. I would never want to leave his side.

He pulls open the door. "After you, Jerzie."

The door's open. The lights are off. My first time in a boy's apartment, and I am leaving completely unscathed. How do you say *ugh* in Italian?

"Hey." I stop when I make it to his side. "Let's take your bike. My aunt doesn't have to know." I'm surprised these words have come out of my mouth. Zeppelin must be surprised, too, because he eyes me inquisitively. "You have an extra helmet, right?"

"I do. Yeah. But—"

"Great. Let's do it then."

"Jerzie." Zeppelin's holding the door open with one hand, and his other hand grabs mine. "I don't want your aunt's friends killing me and then serving a life sentence after. Ride share's cool. It's actually already here. It'll give us a chance to talk. Okay?"

Great. My first attempt to rack up a skeleton has failed miserably. I'm even turning the bad boy good.

I force a smile. "Okay."

Zeppelin and I don't get a chance to talk, because we're stuck with a ride-share driver who must have a disorder where he can't stop his mouth from moving.

"And then we moved to Nigeria, and then my wife and I opened up the first church in Nigeria to have a full-time school and then my wife taught school and I preached the good word."

"Wait, you're a *pastor*?" Zeppelin asks. "I thought you were a security guard."

"*I* thought you worked in construction," I add.

"Yes, yes. All that. Plus, I run a church in Nigeria."

Zeppelin and I exchange amused expressions as the Brooklyn Bridge comes into view. Even from the car I can see that the bridge is jam-packed with foot traffic. I don't want Zeppelin to think I don't wanna cross the bridge, it's just that... well... I don't wanna cross the bridge. It's such a Jhames family thing to do, plus it'll be arm-to-arm, shoulder-to-shoulder pedestrian traffic. Not exactly my idea of a good time.

Zeppelin's phone buzzes in his pocket. He checks the screen. Studies it for a second.

"Everything all right?" I ask.

"Kenyon and Thomas are watching live music at Washington Square Park."

"Who's Thomas?"

"He plays bass in our band." He quickly types a message. "Don't worry. Told them I was busy."

"Let's go." I sit up.

"You don't wanna walk across the bridge?"

"I mean." I shrug. "I do." *Not.* "But we can do that any day. When's the last time you got to hang with your friends? Unless you don't want me to meet your friends."

"You kidding? My friends would love you. But full disclosure, this is Greenwich Village on a Sunday night. I've done this with them before. All they do is smoke and drink."

"So. I've smoked. I drink, too." I'm lying. I reach into my bag like I'm searching for something, hoping this time he can't read me the way he always does.

Zeppelin leans forward, speaking to our driver. "Could you actually take us *across* the bridge. To Washington Square Park?"

"Oh. Yes. I can do that," the man says. "And we will drive past the ferry. I used to drive the ferry."

"Wait. You're a sea captain?" Zeppelin asks.

"Ferry master. Yes."

"I bet you used to pilot airplanes, too," Zeppelin says.

"No, no," the man responds seriously. "I only fly the airplanes when I'm in Nigeria. No license to fly in America."

"And we think we're important, with our fancy Broadway jobs," Zeppelin whispers.

The park is packed. People are eating, drinking, and relaxing as they listen to the live music. Some lie out on blankets. Kids run barefoot through the famous Washington Square Fountain. The Empire State Building in the background and the night lights of the city just starting to flicker on, it's a perfect moment to whip out the camera and snap a quick selfie.

"Zeppelin?"

He turns to me.

"Quick pic?"

He rests his head on top of mine, and I snap the shot. I laugh at the picture. "We look like a Gap ad."

"We're fucking adorable," he says.

I laugh again.

The live band is playing underneath the Washington Square arch. An arch that, with its intricate designs cut into the pristine white marble, makes me think it should be somewhere in London instead of Lower Manhattan. The band is covering old Motown songs, so tons of people are dancing, while others lounge on the few rows of plastic chairs they have set up, bobbing their heads along.

Zeppelin points. "There they are."

I recognize the boys from Zeppelin's band. They're sitting on blankets with two girls, surrounded by drinks and snacks, like bags of chips and cookies. All four look seriously thrilled to see Zeppelin approaching.

"Zepp!" The boy with the man bun stands to wave us over.

Zeppelin wraps an arm around my shoulder. "That's Thomas. I apologize in advance for him. The other guy is Kenyon."

Kenyon is dressed simply in jeans and a T-shirt. Thomas... he sorta looks like Jesus. Like, I'm not kidding. At least, he looks like the guys that get to play Jesus in the movies. Where Jesus is a ridiculously attractive blue-eyed British man.

"Kenyon kills on the drums. And Thomas is the best bass player I know. They'll both be famous for sure someday. They're like my brothers. Known them for forever."

"And the girls?" I ask as we approach.

"Girlfriends. Tanya is with Kenyon and has been for years. You'll like her. She's a love-and-light type person. Always positive and saying shit that makes no sense. And Thomas's girl. They've only been together for a few months, but she's good for him. Her name is Melissa. You'll like her, too."

I'm greeted by a warm chorus of hellos as Zeppelin and I make it to the group's layout. We pop a squat on the corner of the large blanket.

"Oh my gosh, it's *Jerzie*." Tanya's grinning at me. She's sitting between Kenyon's legs, leaning back against him as if she doesn't have a care in the world. "We saw your video. So many good vibes. I felt the chemistry like *whoa*." Tanya's kinky curly hair is cut supershort but so stylish. She's wearing one of those boho summer dresses with gold bangle bracelets and rings. She's also got a septum ring through her nose. It suits her.

"Very good to know you're not a figment of Zeppelin's imagination." Thomas hands me a beer. "I was starting to worry."

Thomas has a British accent, too? He really *could* play Jesus in the movies.

"He's been obsessed with you for a while now." Thomas shakes his head. "A very unhealthy infatuation."

Zeppelin literally takes the beer out of my hand and laughs. "C'mon, dude. Don't fucking rat me out."

I frown. Why did he take the beer away from me? Okay, sure. I don't drink. But maybe I want to. It's just a beer.

Thomas sorta looks me up and down. "You're much smaller in person. You're practically miniscule."

"How's *Cinny*?" Melissa is the polar opposite of Tanya. Dark hair pulled back into a messy ponytail. A T-shirt with an emoji sticking its tongue out that says Sit On My Face. Baggy jeans and dirty Chucks.

"Cinny hasn't changed." Zeppelin flips the tab on the can of beer and downs a big gulp of the drink.

Melissa places a hand on my shoulder. "I saw her on the *Breakfast Show*. How did you guys become best friends? How cool is that?"

Zeppelin nearly chokes on his beer. He sets it down and wraps an arm around my shoulder. "Yes, Jerzie. How *did* you guys become besties?"

"Boring story," I say. "Family friends is all."

"That's a *terribly* boring story, isn't it?" Thomas whines.

"Where were you guys headed before we derailed you?" Kenyon takes a long drag from something he's smoking. It looks like a cigarette. It smells like something else.

"We were gonna walk across the Brooklyn Bridge." Zeppelin takes another swig of beer. "And then hang out by the water."

Kenyon laughs. "How incredibly cute. Were you guys gonna skip rocks afterward and then carve your names into a tree?"

Tanya turns to face Kenyon and pinches him on the arm.

He blows smoke in her face when he yelps. "Ow. The fuck?"

"Don't tease," she scolds. "We want Jerzie to like us."

"It's not my fault Zeppelin's corny-ass date got canceled." Kenyon takes another drag from his "cigarette." "We saved Jerzie. Trust me. She should love us now."

"Ignore him." Tanya's brown eyes are warm and friendly. "We're just happy to see what a Zeppelin girl looks like. We've not seen one for a long, long time."

"You're so rude, Zeppelin." Melissa reaches into a cooler they have and hands me another beer. "Jerzie has nothing to drink."

Zeppelin takes the drink out of Melissa's hand. "Jerzie wouldn't drink this cheap shit you guys buy anyway."

I sorta glare at Zeppelin. He turns to me, not aware of the scowl I have on my face as he leans to kiss me on the cheek.

"I can kiss you, right?" he whispers in my ear.

Still asking permission to touch me. Another kiss on the cheek. Won't kiss me for real. Won't let me drink. If I grab a bag of chips, will he snatch those out of my hands, too? Doesn't want me to eat fried food?

Now Tanya takes a hit from what I've deduced is weed in a cigarette roller. She reaches across Zeppelin's lap to hand it off to Thomas, but I intercept, snatching it from her before Thomas can. Now that it's in my hands, I realize how foreign it feels. What exactly do I think I'm doing here? "Sorry," I say to Tanya. "You don't mind, do you?"

"Uh." She looks nervously at Zeppelin. "*I* don't."

I can feel everyone's eyes on me. I can also sense Zeppelin's overwhelming desire to take it from my hand and scold me like Aunt Karla would.

"Like this." Melissa scoots over to me to demonstrate. "Inhale. Hold in the smoke as long as you can and then exhale. It's easy."

I feel Zeppelin's whole body tense beside me, but I ignore him and do as Melissa instructs, bringing the "cigarette" to my lips and inhaling. Smoke fills my lungs.

It *hurts*.

"Hold it as long as you can, boo," Tanya calls out.

I can hold it no more. I exhale. A puff of smoke surrounds my face. I fan it away.

"Good job!" Tanya claps excitedly.

"What a rotten influence you are," Thomas states. "You're tainting Zepp's little flower."

I'm coughing now. Zeppelin sets his beer down and places a hand on my back.

"Breathe deep, Jerzie." He sounds upset. *Really* upset.

But I suppose I'm in full-on Slytherin rebellion, because rather than listen to Zeppelin, I take another hit. It actually hurts worse the second time and makes me cough even harder. A water bottle is offered to me. I look up to see Jesus, or Thomas, extending me the lifeline, a goofy grin spread across his face.

"Drink, little flower."

I happily accept the bottle of water and down about half of it. It calms the burn in my chest. When I move the bottle away from my mouth and the cough subsides, all of Zeppelin's friends start cheering. It makes me laugh.

Melissa takes the "cigarette" out of my hands. "Remember. Puff, puff, *pass*."

They all look so happy and free. Well, everyone except Zeppelin. He doesn't speak at first. He downs the rest of the beer, sets the empty can beside him, and sits there, seething. Finally he turns to me. "Please don't do that again, Jerzie," he whispers so that only I can hear. "What were you thinking?"

I roll my eyes and whisper back, "You forgot to *ask* me if you could whisper in my ear."

Now Tanya and Melissa stand, move off the blanket, and dance to the music, which has kicked into high gear with the Jackson 5.

I take a moment to stare down at the blanket, gathering

my thoughts. Or maybe just one thought. Something along the lines of:

What the hell was *I thinking?!*

I don't exactly feel any different though. I don't feel "high." Whatever that means. But what *does* that mean? What's going to happen to me? What if the smoke destroyed my vocal cords? What if I'm allergic to weed? Did I ever think that I could be allergic? *Stupid Jerzie! Idiot, imbecilic move!* Smoking weed to prove some sort of point, to create some stupid skeleton, and now I'm on the brink of an allergic reaction.

When I look up, Zeppelin is chatting with Kenyon about something, but I can't make out what they're saying. Mostly because my heart is beating so fast. Is that the first sign of a weed allergy? *Shit.*

I grab Zeppelin's leg and attempt to sound as calm as possible. "Hey."

He looks at me, his blue eyes narrowed.

"My aunt Karla called. I'm gonna call her back superquick."

Before he can reply, I hop off the blanket and walk a few hundred feet to the fountain. I sit slowly on the ledge. My heart is beating so fast. God. I look around me. There are so many people. All oblivious to the terror about to unfold. Anaphylactic weed shock. I look at my hands, doing that thing where I'm trying to twist off my fingers. But they are not budging. Why are my fingers screwed on so tight? Why am I so stupid? I try to take another deep breath to slow my heart rate. I might be the very first girl ever to be allergic to weed. How do you say *what terrible luck* in Italian? I lower my head into my hands.

A few seconds later I feel someone sit beside me. Close.

Too close. I look over, about to bark at them to move the hell away from me, when I realize it's Zeppelin.

"How do you say *bad luck* in Italian?" I ask.

"Are you okay?"

I shake my head. "No," I reply honestly. "I think I'm allergic to weed."

"Jerzie, that's not a thing."

"How do you know?" I wail.

He rests a hand on my shoulder. "You're panicking. It probably hasn't hit you yet. But if you're flipping the fuck out when it does, you're gonna stay like that for the next hour."

"Oh my God, Zeppelin!" I whisper. "I *am* flipping the fuck out. I'm so scared. I want out of my body. Help me." I lower my head into my hands again. "Help me, help me, help me."

"I'm here." He rests his hand on my back. "You're fine. I promise."

"I shouldn't have done that. I didn't mean to. But you were treating me like a kid."

"I was *what*?"

"Not letting me drink."

"You're *sixteen*."

"So what? I'll be seventeen soon."

"Jerzie."

I look up at him now. "And why do you keep kissing me on the cheek?" Oh, God. It's getting hard to breathe. "If I die from weed overdose. Please remember me well."

Zeppelin's eyes go from worried to amused real quick. "Jerzie, give me your hands." He takes my hands in his. "What calms you? We gotta get you calm."

"Uh, raindrops on roses? No. Wait. Oh, I don't know!"

I'm about to burst into tears when suddenly Zeppelin leans forward and presses his lips to mine. It starts off sorta like the way he kissed me during the dance. But this time, he doesn't pull away. I sort of gasp when he rests one hand on my knee and his tongue slips into my mouth.

"Holy shit." Somehow *I* manage to pull away. I stare into his eyes.

But he only draws me closer to him, pressing his lips on top of mine again. I realize what he's trying to do. Because this—*this* is calming me. Zeppelin must sense it's working, because his lips stay connected to mine. His mouth is soft and warm. His kisses gentle, tender. And since I've never really been kissed before and don't know what the hell to actually do, I decide to speak and say something really dumb:

"I've never kissed anyone before you."

He pulls away, his forehead resting against mine. "*No.* Our YouTube kiss was your first kiss? Seriously?" He sighs.

"It's okay," I say. "I didn't mind it."

"I never imagined it would feel so real," he whispers. "That we'd feel so connected. I hope I didn't embarrass you."

"You didn't embarrass me. Is that why you've been kissing me on the cheek?"

"I'm trying to be respectful is all. I've never dated a girl like you before."

"What's a girl like me?"

"Hmm." He leans back and stares up at the sky, like he's searching for just the right words. "Voice like an angel. Insanely talented and yet…so sweet. And humble." He laughs. "And funny. Mostly on accident."

"I'm accidentally funny?"

"You're accidentally *hilarious*." He turns to me now. "And then I watch when you get teary eyed at rehearsal. You get so moved by everyone's performances and you don't want anyone to notice, so you pretend to look for something in your bag."

"You notice that?" I cover my cheeks with my hands. "I can't help it. Everyone is so good."

"But most importantly, you wear Slytherin socks." He laughs. "And care so much about the meaning of an old piece of literature, that you would take the time to read it fifteen times."

"So that's a girl like me, huh?" I smile.

"Jerzie, a girl like you is the one you meet maybe once in a lifetime. Where everything you ever wanted fits into the prettiest person you ever saw."

He leans forward to kiss me again. First on the lips. Then his mouth moves slowly down to kiss me gently on the neck. My eyes open enough to realize I am one half of that couple I despise. Kissing in public like they've no decorum. But who knew those couples were having so much fun! And suddenly it feels like I'm floating. I look up at the sky. It's *moving*. Slightly. Like, I can tell the Earth is spinning through space. I can literally *see* it moving. This is a giant spaceship. *Whoa.*

"We're on a spaceship!" I laugh. Now Zeppelin's appeared. Out of nowhere. His blue eyes looking especially freaky. Alien eyes. "Dude. You magically appeared and your alien eyes are terrifying." I reach out to touch his face. "Don't scare me like that."

I place my hands over my ears. There is something revving like a motor. A very loud motor. What *is* that? I look up at the sky again. Searching for the strange sound. Why isn't everyone else freaking out about this?

"It's a helicopter." Zeppelin's doing that mind-reading thing. "You're high, Jerzie. Sounds are gonna seem louder than normal."

"I'm high?" I burst into laughter. Why is everything so *funny*?

Zeppelin smiles. "Let's head back over. We can sit and relax."

I wrap my arms around Zeppelin's neck and pull him closer to me. "Why? Am I boring you?"

"Jerzie…" he whispers. "There's this thing that happens when you're high. Your filter gets sort of shut down. *I'm* kind of curious to see how this is gonna play out." He runs a hand through his hair. "But there're a lot of *kids* around. And I'm not gonna lie, you seem a bit on the verge."

On the verge of what? And talk about filter being shut down. I move my hands into Zeppelin's hair. Push it off his face the way he does all the time. It's like feathers! I love the way it feels on my fingers. He closes his eyes and sighs heavily. "Will you teach me things, Zeppelin?"

"Careful, Jerzie."

Careful? "What do you mean?"

"It's just…that part of me has been shut down for a long time. I don't wanna turn it back on until I know you're ready."

"But I am ready. I *do* want you to teach me."

He takes my wrists and pulls my hands out of his hair, staring into my eyes. "What shall I teach you?"

"Everything."

"Shit." He shakes his head. "Don't say that to me."

"Why?" I ask sadly. "You don't wanna teach me?"

"I do. I just want you to mean it is all. Right now you're out of your mind. Literally."

"No. I've liked you since you clobbered me over the head." Now it's my turn to bare my soul. The way he did in Bay Ridge. "Luciano Lucio Zeppolini Sticky Fingers Reid Ricci."

He laughs.

"I do like you," I whisper. "I've liked you from the moment I first saw you. *I've* been waiting for you to show up, too. Like, my whole life. I missed you, too. Silly, huh? How can you miss someone you hardly know?"

"I want you to say all of this to me when you're not high. Then maybe it'll fully sink in and I won't think I'm dreaming."

"Okay. When will this fade? I'll say it again then."

"You took two hits? Never smoked before?" He shrugs. "An hour maybe?"

"Yay!" I wrap my arms around his neck again and rest my lips on his ear. "I love having no filter."

"Is she okay?"

We both look up. Jesus is standing in front of us. Barefoot. Or wait. Never mind. It's just Thomas.

"Eww!" I point to his bare feet. "You're barefoot in New York City. Disgusting!" I burst into laughter.

Thomas laughs, too. "She's high, man."

Zeppelin nods. "She's fine. We'll join you guys in a second. Taking a few minutes so she can get her bearings."

"Better hurry. The girls are requesting a dance with Jerzie. We all saw the video. We know she can dance." He moves off.

"His feet are gonna fall off."

Zeppelin laughs. "I *love* high Jerzie. But I'm never letting you get high again. You know that, right? Better enjoy the next hour."

"You're not the boss of me. I do what I want. I'm a Slytherin!" I press my lips to his. "Teach me how to kiss," I murmur. "Teach me everything."

"Oh, God." He moans. "Somewhere Aunt Karla is calling the police on me. Please stop. I wanna live."

The sound of the water fountain behind us is like Niagara Falls, it's *so* loud. But it's also soft. Which is weird. The people beside us. The conversations. Their laughter. It's filling up all the space in my ears. But it's also so deathly quiet, I can hear my own heart beating. I can hear the blood gushing through my veins. I can hear *everything*.

"All right." Zeppelin's whispering in my ear again. His deep voice is so soothing, it quiets the rest of the noise. "The lips have one of the thinnest layers of skin on the body. Which is why they're so sensitive." He moves to gently kiss my lips, and I shiver. "One million nerve endings in your lips." He kisses me again. "So I just touched one million parts of you. How does it feel to have one million parts of you touched at the same time?"

I want to answer him. But it's like my brain has lost control. Somehow signals aren't reaching their destination. Wires are crossed. Brain waves completely shut down. Thankfully Zeppelin must not need an answer, because he continues.

"Now most of the time, less is more." He kisses the corners of my mouth. "And sometimes." He kisses my lips again, tilting my chin up so my mouth parts. I feel him gently bite down on my bottom lip. My eyes pop open. "Sometimes you can do that. Soft at first. But it can also be nice when things aren't so soft."

"Why don't you guys get a fucking room?"

We turn to see a disgusted teen girl on her phone, sitting beside us.

"He's *really* good at this," I say. "You wanna have a turn? You'll see I'm not lying."

"God, I hate this city." She stands and storms away.

I turn back to Zeppelin and he's laughing so hard. He grabs my hand. "Come on, Jerzie."

I stand and whoa…too fast. My knees buckle, and Zeppelin wraps an arm around my waist.

"I got you, Jerzie."

He's holding me so tightly. Everything really is better when you're in love. Even almost passing out. I rest my head on his chest. "Zeppelin." He gently massages my shoulders. "I think maybe you're Romeo and I'm Juliet and we really are back on Earth. Trying to get it right this time."

"How do we get it right this time, Jerzie?" he asks, still gently massaging my shoulders.

"This time?" I pause. "I guess we make sure nothing comes between us."

"Nothing can come between us. I'll make sure of it."

I look up into his eyes. "I've really missed you."

"I've missed you, too, Jerzie."

We spend the rest of the evening dancing and singing along to Motown hits with Tanya, Thomas, Melissa, and Kenyon. It's not till a silvery moon is high in the night sky that Zeppelin shows me the time on his cell phone.

"I scheduled a ride share."

"Aww," Tanya whines, wrapping her arms around my waist. "Stay."

"Yeah, we can stay a little longer, can't we?" I ask.

He shakes his head. "No way. What if we run into traffic? We should go."

I know he's right. We've pretty much done none of what we told Aunt Karla we would do. The least I can do is be home on time.

I hug all of Zeppelin's friends goodbye, feeling like they're my friends now, too.

"Text me when you get home," Tanya orders. "And follow me back on Instagram!"

"Me, too," Melissa echoes. "You're stuck with us now. Forever!" she shouts.

"To forever!" Tanya echoes.

I'm all lit up inside.

When Zeppelin and I climb into the ride share, I collapse onto his chest.

"Let me take you somewhere special tomorrow," he says.

"I'd like that." I wrap my arms around his waist. I can hear his heart thumping so slowly. So steady. "And hey, guess what?"

"What?"

"I'm not high anymore."

He rubs my back. "I'll miss high Jerzie."

"Guess what else?"

"What's that?"

"I don't wanna be high anymore."

Zeppelin's fingertips lightly graze my neck. "Welcome to my world, Jerzie. Let's just be high on life. Together."

I sit up and stare into his eyes as the car bumps along in traffic. "I still meant everything I said though."

"So say it again then." Zeppelin slides his hand gently down my cheek. "So I can believe you."

Oh, God. The filter is back on. My cheeks feel hot so I place both my hands on top of them. I asked him to teach me things. I told him to teach me *everything*. How am I going to say that again?

"It's all right, Jerzie. You don't have to say it again. I can teach you anything you want to know, okay?" He rests his hand on my thigh. "And if I go too fast, you can ask me to slow down."

"Slow down?" I repeat. "It's been a billion years. How much slower can we go?"

"You're right." He wraps his arms around me, like he never wants to let me go. "Guess we've waited long enough."

"So Shalt Thou
Show Me Friendship"

Someone is knocking on Aunt Karla's master bedroom door.
Or, actually, pounding on the door more like it. I rub my
eyes and swing my legs out of bed, snatching my cell off the
end table to check the time.

"Aunt Karla?" I call out.

The door is pushed open to present not Aunt Karla, but
Judas. His short fade looks like he left the barber a few seconds
ago, leather messenger bag slung over his shoulder, wearing
Dockers and a crisp white shirt like he's headed out to a job
interview, which I imagine he is.

"Yo. Sis. I thought you had a job. Why are you still asleep?"

I hold up my phone. "Judas Jhames. It's 7:00 a.m. Rehearsal
starts late today."

He frowns. "You still need to wake up. I've been to the
gym. Got a haircut. Traded stocks. Made breakfast. And

picked up your early birthday present, and you haven't even stepped outta bed."

"Oh, God." I tighten the silk scarf wrapped about my head, stretch out my legs and stand. "A present? I hope it's not another savings bond. I still can't redeem the one you got me for Christmas."

"That's because the point is to not redeem it, dum-dum. But to *save*. Thus the name s*avings* bond."

"Whatever. Who gets somebody a gift they can't open for a year?"

"How are we related?" He shakes his head. "It makes no sense. Anyway. Tell me I'm the greatest big brother to ever live and I'll tell your gift to come forth."

"It has *consciousness*? Is it a guinea pig? Cuz you can take it back. I don't got time to be raisin' no pigs."

"Say it." He clears his throat. "I'm the greatest big brother."

"You're the most annoying human on the planet. Now what is it?"

"Whatever. Just know you owe me. Big. Oh, surprise?" he calls out. "You may come forth."

I stare at the door. Waiting. "Judas? What the hell, man?"

"I swear she was right there." He moves toward the door. "Riley?"

Riley? "What?!" I literally push Judas out of the way and run into the hallway. I can hear Riley downstairs laughing with Aunt Karla, Mom, and Dad.

"Riley!"

I rush down the stairs and see her sitting cross-legged on the couch, slurping a giant iced coffee drink, her long blond tresses pulled back into a ponytail. She looks at me. "Dude! You went on a date and didn't tell me?"

"Ahh!" I scream. Riley does, too. I rush into her arms, and we jump up and down, hugging. And screaming.

"Well, hello to you, too," Mom says, laughing.

"And who went on a date?" Dad asks. "You went on a date? When?"

I pull away from Riley and run to Mom, hugging her tightly. "Missed you, Mommy." I cross over to Dad and wrap my arms around his waist. "You, too, Dad. And it wasn't really a date." I look up at him. He stares at me over the rim of his glasses. "Just hanging out with a friend from the show is all."

"A boy?" Dad and Judas are so similar in style. Dad stuffs a hand into the pocket of his Dockers, using the other hand to unbutton the top button on his dress shirt as he eyes Mom disapprovingly. "You knew about this?"

"They walked across the Brooklyn Bridge." Mom waves Dad away. "It was totally innocent."

Dad grunts.

"I'm offended." Judas moves into the living room. "Riley got screams. Mom and Dad get hugs. I got insults." He pulls his messenger bag off his shoulder and sets it beside the couch.

I turn my attention back to Riley. "What are you doing here?" I ask excitedly.

"Tournament upstate," she explains. "Flying out of JFK by myself, and we were in New Brunswick visiting Grams, so Mom let me ride into the city with your family."

"And now *I'm* stuck headed to midtown later today with Jerzie." Judas groans. "Since Aunt Karla can't go."

"What?" I spin around to face Aunt Karla. "Nigel's gonna be devastated."

"Nigel?" Mom smiles. "Who is *Nigel*?"

"Yeah. Who's Nigel?" Riley grins.

"He's one of the production assistants at work," I explain. "I think Aunt Karla likes him."

"I do not! Will y'all stop?" Aunt Karla laughs as she scoops coffee into her coffeepot. "Anyway. It'll be good for Judas to see how things work. Plus, I need a break. I'm sick of catching the train to Times Square."

"Wish your mom and I could stay. We're gonna miss all the fun this summer." Dad groans. "Why did I sign up to teach summer school? So many things we could all do. We could walk across the Brooklyn Bridge. Or go see the Statue of Liberty on the river walk." He pulls open Aunt Karla's fridge door and takes out a cold bottle of water. "Remember we used to do that?"

"Which decade?" Judas rolls his eyes. "We have way too many pictures of that rusted thing."

Mom sits beside Judas on the couch. "You excited to spend the summer at Times Square, son?"

"I hate Times Square." Judas grabs the remote. "It's like stepping into a real-life infomercial. So much useless crap for sale. People wasting money. And time. Ahh." He nods. "Now I finally get why it's called Times Square."

"What about Riley?" I turn to my friend. "Can *you* come with us to rehearsal? How long do you get to stay?"

"Flight leaves at eleven. Today."

"Nooo. I only get to see you this morning?" I whine.

She makes a pouty face. "I know. But." She moves to the

counter, picking up a giant iced coffee. "Your vanilla sweet cream cold brew is joining us."

I snatch the coffee right out of her hands and take the biggest sip. "Bless you, woman." I grab her hand. "Let's go upstairs."

"Were you seriously not gonna tell me you have a boyfriend? Shit like that'll get you kicked out of the Best Friend Club for life."

Riley and I are sitting on the balcony, sharing the same lounge chair, my head resting on her shoulder as we watch the sky brighten with the sunrise. "It's all so new. And secret. Cinny can't find out."

"Oh, hot damn." Riley sighs dramatically. "Better take her off my favorites list so I don't accidentally butt dial her."

"I know. I'm paranoid. I get that. It's just that I like him *so* much. I don't want anything to ruin it."

"You don't like him." Riley downs the last bit of her coffee. "You loooove him. You wanna have babies with him. A girl named Jerzepplin and a boy name Zepperzie."

I bump her playfully with my shoulder.

"Still…" she goes on. "Cinny's like the queen. On the cover of all the magazines. A trillion followers on Instagram. And you have the man she wants. That's cray cray."

"She has the job I want. I'd say we're even."

"*Ouch.*" Riley winces. "Tit for tat!" she roars like a lion. "Glad I'm on your good side, *Venom.*"

"Sorry." I sit up. "I shouldn't have said that. I really do accept she got the part over me."

"Look, don't apologize. I'm competitive, too. I get it."

"That's different, Riley. You never lose."

"You're oblivious, woman. I lose. All the time."

I give my best friend a look. "Headed into your senior year of high school. UCLA bound."

"Unofficially."

"Still. You could go to any D1 school you want. First team All State. All American Games. MVP, Player of the Year. No one has stats like you."

"Wrong. Try again. It's true, I'm one of the best pitchers in Jersey." Riley pauses to brush imaginary dust off her shoulders. "Don't hate the playa."

I laugh. "So modest."

"But on a *national* level? It's different. Lots of girls are better than me. Broadway is national, baby. Competition is stiff."

I guess she's right. "Yeah."

"Question for you." Riley sets her empty coffee cup beside the chair. "I mean. Don't get me wrong. I freakin' love *Hamilton* like nobody's business. When I listen to that soundtrack, I am pretty much a professional rapper. But my Broadway knowledge sorta ends there. What makes you want Broadway so bad?"

I'm surprised by the question. Nobody has ever asked me that. Not even my own parents. How come no one's ever asked me this before?

"Well," I start. "I've always loved musical theater, you know that much."

"True, true," Riley replies.

"But it was this musical I watched called *Cabaret*, with Liza Minnelli, that officially sealed the deal. I saw it for the first time when I was seven."

"Never heard of it. Tell me *all* about it."

I smile. Riley has this way about her. Even though she's such a stud—I mean, her parents moved her entire family to Newark so she could play for a better high school softball team—she has this way of making you feel like *you're* the most important and amazing thing in her life.

"It's about this eccentric cabaret singer who falls for a guy who's sort of confused about his sexuality. And they end up in a weird love triangle with another guy."

"Both of them?"

"Yeah. With the same guy. And there's like, a Nazi side story."

"Wait," Riley laughs. "You saw this when you were seven?"

I laugh, too. "In all fairness, my parents had no idea I was watching it."

"Did you understand it?"

"Some parts. I was a pretty intuitive kid. For me, it was mostly about the music though. The music in *Cabaret* made me *feel*. When Liza Minnelli sang a song called 'Maybe This Time,' I cried. Not because I was sad. I thought, I dunno, I hope I can make people feel someday."

"Hmm." Riley leans forward. "Alexa," she calls out, and the speaker Aunt Karla keeps outside on the balcony lights up blue. "Play 'Maybe This Time' from *Cabaret*."

"Playing 'Maybe This Time' from *Cabaret* by Liza Minnelli from Amazon Music," Alexa replies.

The song begins to play. Riley and I listen for a while. I stand and move to the railing and lean my back against it, watching Riley as she lies on the lounge chair, staring up at the morning sky.

"Look at my arm, Jerz." She presents her arm to me. *"Goose bumps."*

"See?" My eyes are welling with tears. I blink them away. "You can feel it, can't you?"

"I can relate, too. 'Everybody loves a winner, so nobody loved me.' Those *lyrics*. Is this at the heart of every competitive person? Striving so hard to be validated, you know? To be loved. To be a winner. It's like a warped mindset of, if I could just win, everything will be okay."

This is another thing I love about me and Riley. We can laugh and joke about boys, gossip about celebrities and school stuff—but we can also contemplate the meaning of life together.

"You can do this, you know." She sits up. "Make people feel. You don't have to wait for Broadway per se. I know only one other person whose singing gives me goose bumps, and that's you. If you wanna make people feel, do it. Sing. You have over a million followers on Instagram now. Sing for them."

"But what if nobody's listening?" I ask seriously. "On a Broadway stage, everybody is listening. It's this magical storytelling that people from all over the world come to see. It matters. My crummy old Instagram account doesn't matter."

"Says who? I'm following sooo many celebrities. But wanna know my favorite Instagram account?"

"Selena Gomez?"

"No, silly. You!"

"Knock, knock." Dad peeks his head out onto the balcony. "Riley, dear, we'll be leaving in about fifteen minutes."

"Copy that, Mr. Jhames," Riley replies respectfully as Dad disappears back inside.

"Wish we had more time."

"Me, too." She stands. At five foot ten, Riley sorta towers over me. I kinda miss how people always look twice when they see us together, her at 150 pounds, so tall and blond. She's like a new age Viking warrior princess.

"I'm bummed I haven't been to any of your games lately. I'm the worst."

"Nah, you're the best." She slings her arm over my shoulder. "Besides. It's my turn to watch." She lays her head on top of mine. "And please believe me when I say, I will be watching, Jerzie. So show me somethin' good."

"Do Not Say Banishment"

Standing outside on the stoop, I'm waving as Riley climbs into Dad's SUV and Mom moves down the steps, clutching her purse and her cell phone.

"Jerzie, honey, I feel bad about missing your birthday. You sure you don't want us to come back up for the big day?"

"Mom, it's fine. I gotta work. You guys gotta work, too. It's seriously not a big deal."

"If you say so." Her phone buzzes in her hand. She glances at the screen, then slides her finger across to answer the call. "Hello?" I study her worried expression. "Right. Yes. Right *now*?" She pauses, her brow furrows. "No, no. I would have to say no." More silence. More brow furrowing. "Yes. Absolutely. Can you at least give me some sort of hint as to what's going on?" She shifts. "Right. See you then."

"Mom? What's wrong?"

"That was weird." She slides her cell phone into her purse. "It was a cryptic call. There's a meeting this morning at your director's office. They asked if I could be present."

"But you're headed back with Dad."

"I was. I'll have to take a car back later." She crosses her arms. "They suggested we bring a lawyer."

My chest tightens so suddenly that I feel short of breath. "Do we even *have* a lawyer?"

"Do we need one?" Mom turns to face me. "What did you do, Jerzie?"

"Nothing, Mom. I swear. At work, I sit. I watch. I go home."

"Something about that call wasn't right. I better tell your dad. Ask what he thinks."

Mom rushes down the stairs, and I stare up at the sky. The clouds have turned dark and menacing this morning. I expect rain. Maybe even a storm. My head is suddenly throbbing, my heart pounding. I'm Alice, back in Wonderland wondering what lies beyond the bend *this* time.

Mom and I take a car to Times Square. Mostly cuz Mom doesn't know the subways as well as Aunt Karla, and we always end up on the right train heading in the wrong direction. Plus it is raining now. I'll admit, it's nice to be dropped off in front of the building, as a long walk from the subway station in the pouring rain would prove difficult when I'm this distraught. Something's not right. I can sense it.

Mom places an arm around my shoulder and kisses me on the top of my mess of hair as we approach the building. We quickly check in with Security, make it up the elevator, and

are back into the office reception area fairly quickly. This
time, there's a boy sitting at a desk.

"Hi," Mom greets him warmly. "We're here to see Alan
Kaplan?"

"Around the corner in conference room C. That's where
everyone is." He points the way.

Everyone? Mom and I exchange worried looks as we walk
together down the hall. We move past Alan's office, where
I met with him the other day. Around the corner, Zeppelin
pushes through the double doors of a conference room, trailed
by a man dressed in a gray suit, with dark waves of shoulder
length hair and dark eyes.

"Zeppelin?" My mood soars. Like the sun unexpectedly
showed up on this gray day. But…something's not right. His
face is flushed, his mess of hair is truly that—a mess. Pointing
in every possible direction. He runs a hand through it, but that
does nothing to tame the beast of unruly waves. He's dressed
in sweatpants, dirty sneakers, and a wrinkled T-shirt. It's the
first time I've seen him looking less than couture. Still, even
though he looks like he fell out of bed and rolled all the way
here, he's a beautiful sight. At least to me. "What's going on?"

"I'm sorry, Jerzie." His eyes are so red, I'd swear he's been
crying. "Know that I'm sorry, okay? Forgive me."

"*Zeppelin,*" the man says sternly. "Let's go. Now."

He steps forward and whispers in my ear, "*Trust* me, Jerzie.
Please."

And suddenly the sun is gone. Covered by dark stormy
clouds once again. Thunder seems to roar. Lightning seems
to flash. I want to call after him. I want to run into his arms

and tell him I forgive him already, even though I don't know what he could possibly be apologizing for.

Instead, I follow Mom as she pushes through the conference room doors. Inside are Robbie, Alan, and a man I've never seen before, sitting at a large conference table. Cinny is here, too. Why is *Cinny* here? She's accompanied by a woman who I'm guessing is her lawyer. *Should* we have brought a lawyer? Cinny looks quite fragile in this moment, not standard Cinny for sure. Her shoulders are slumped, and when she looks up as Mom and I enter, I see her cheeks are streaked with tears.

"Please, have a seat, Jerzie. Mrs. Jhames," Alan instructs.

We sit, sliding into individual high-back swivel chairs that surround the large conference table.

The man who I don't know passes along some sort of contract and a pen to Mom and me.

"Read and sign this NDA," he instructs. "Have Jerzie sign, too. Right underneath your signature."

Mom signs. I do as well.

"So." Robbie twists a pen in his hands. "We've gotten Zeppelin's side of the story. Jerzie, we'd like to get yours as well."

"Can you all tell us what's going on?" Mom asks.

"Garret Webb here." The man sitting beside Robbie speaks. "I'm one of the producers for *Roman and Jewel*." He looks directly at me. "A private investigator was hired to look into the video uploads. We found out the YouTube account responsible was created in Bay Ridge, at a residence where Zeppelin resides."

Black spots flash in my vision. *No. It couldn't have been him. It wasn't.*

Garret continues, "We've also been able to confirm that the Vimeo hack happened at the same residence."

"We were under the assumption," Robbie says to Mom, "that since Jerzie joined the cast just days ago, she and Zeppelin were not acquainted. However, the private investigator confirmed that Jerzie was at his residence last night. *And* at his family's restaurant. In addition, they were together at Washington Square Park." Robbie speaks to me now. "We'd like to know how long you two have known one another. And if, in fact, you had anything to do with the video uploads."

Holy hell! My gaze darts to Cinny. She's not making eye contact with me, just staring down at the table, looking like she'd very much like to wake up from this nightmare.

I look at Mom, whose expression is a mixture of anger and confusion.

"Jerzie?" she says in disbelief. "What on earth?"

"Mommy, I *swear* I just met him." I turn to Robbie. "I met Zeppelin on my first day of work. I was in the stairwell and he accidentally hit me in the head with the door. Look." I point to the bruise that's still visible on my forehead. "I have the bruise to prove it." I'm trying so hard to hold back my tears. *Zeppelin uploaded the videos?* "In a very random coincidence, yesterday, my aunt had to work in Bay Ridge, and I went along with her. I ended up at a restaurant Zeppelin's family owns. On accident. Because my aunt had to work late, he invited me to hang out with him and his friends. We never even discussed the videos. I had no clue he was the one who uploaded them. Are you *sure* it was him?"

"He confessed, Jerzie," Alan replies sadly.

Why? Why would he do something like this?

"But did he say *I* had something to do with it?"

"He said you did not," Robbie replies.

Well, thank God for that. "I didn't. I swear on my life I did not know." I look at Cinny now. "Believe me, Cinny. I had no idea."

"I believe her." Cinny finally looks up.

I breathe a sigh of relief.

"I'm sorry this happened, Jerzie," Alan says. "And I'm sorry Zeppelin dragged you into something so potentially destructive by uploading the video that was recorded with you."

"We're honestly at a loss for words," Robbie adds. "Zeppelin…" He shakes his head glumly. "He's like family to us."

"What happens now?" My eyes must look panicked as I gaze from Robbie to Alan.

"Zeppelin is no longer with the show." Alan says it so softly that I think for a moment maybe I misheard him.

"I'm sorry, *what*?" I ask.

"It's a major breach of confidentiality," Robbie explains despondently. "We had no choice. One of his understudies will take over the role for now. We may find a suitable replacement. We're looking."

No! God, no! It's as if the world has stopped spinning and come to a screeching halt, and I'm being hurled off the planet at a thousand miles per hour. Tsunamis are destroying the coastlines. Trees are being uprooted. The world is ending. Today is the last of all days.

I don't even realize I'm crying until Mom whispers, "Jerzie. *Please*, honey. Pull yourself together."

She removes a wad of tissues from her purse and thrusts

them into my hands. "Is he going to jail?" I say out loud to no one in particular.

"He should," Cinny states harshly, wiping away her own tears.

"He's not going to jail." Alan leans back in his chair. "We're not pressing charges or anything like that. I think we're happy to sweep this under the rug."

"Jerzie," Robbie says, "I think we're done with our questions. Sorry to have disturbed your morning. Thank you for being so accommodating." He smiles, and I can sense he wishes he could reach over the table and give me a big hug.

"And again. We apologize that you were dragged into this in the first place," Alan adds. "Hopefully things will settle down now, and we can all get back to work."

I stand. Or rather, Mom pulls me up, because I'm pretty sure I don't quite have control over all of my muscles just yet. Not to mention all the blood must be rushing to my brain, because my head is pounding as if I should be going to the ER instead of back to Aunt Karla's. Mom must sense that I'm in danger of a head gone full-on firework, because she places a hand on my back, leans toward me, and whispers, "Breathe, Jerzie."

I do as instructed, taking a long, deep breath, then exhaling. It slows my heart rate a bit and makes my hands stop shaking. I follow Mom out of the conference room. Once we've traveled down the hallway, she turns to me.

"You are never to see that boy again. Do you understand me?"

"*What?*"

"Don't 'what' me, Jerzie. He could've gotten you fired. Secretly recording that girl all this time and then uploading videos onto YouTube? That poor girl. Seeing her sitting there crying like that? Heartbreaking. What was he trying to do? Ruin her career? He doesn't have the right to do that. And please believe he could and would easily do the same thing to you."

"Mom." My hands are shaking, my voice cracking. "I'll talk to him and he can explain. He owes me an explanation. He's my friend."

"You barely know him. He's not your friend."

"But he is! Let me talk to him. I—"

"Jerzie Jhames, so help me God!" Mom places a hand on her hip. "If I learn you've spoken so much as a word to that kid, I will personally pull you out of this musical and take you back home for the summer. Are we clear? You will have *nothing* to do with him. Give me your phone."

Tears are streaming down my face. "Mom. You can't take my phone. I need it."

"I sure as hell can. You'll be with Judas this summer. He has a phone. Borrow his if there's an emergency. Until I feel I can trust you again, you won't be getting it back anytime soon. What were you doing at his *house*?"

"It was nothing. Aunt Karla said we could hang out. So we stopped at his apartment to drop off his motorcycle."

"His *motorcycle*?" She draws back, nostrils flaring. "And Washington Square Park? The message I got from Karla said you were walking across the Brooklyn Bridge."

"We were. It was a last-second change of plans is all. It's not a big deal."

"Not a big deal? Did you text Karla and ask her if it was okay?"

I shake my head.

"*Unbelievable.* Give me your phone. Now."

I don't know Zeppelin's number by heart. I don't have his email. I know where he lives but have no clue how to even get there. This can't be happening. Never see Zeppelin again? Never speak to him?

"I'm sorry to interrupt."

We both turn to see Cinny, standing alone in the hallway. I wipe my eyes.

"Cinny, I'm sorry," I offer. "About all of this."

"Jerzie, stop. So not your fault." She steps forward and extends her hand to Mom. "I'm Cinny. Nice meeting you."

Mom beams. "Oh, Cinny. It's a pleasure to meet *you.* We're all big fans. Honored. Truly."

Cinny turns to me. "I'm glad we found out the truth about Zeppelin. Aren't you?"

I'm not sure *glad* is a word that should be attached to how I'm feeling right now. Besides, *have* we found out the truth about Zeppelin?

"Why do you think he did it?" Mom asks.

"Revenge," Cinny tosses out casually. "We were on a break. Zepp and I had been dating since the show started. Secretly. Nobody knew. When I tried to slow things down, he got upset. He's intense like that. I think he was trying to use Jerzie as a way to get back at me."

I'm stunned. Speechless. Last night? Our time at his family's restaurant? At the park? By the water fountain? I refuse to believe that none of it was real.

Cinny leans forward and hugs me tightly. It makes me feel like itchy little bugs are crawling all over my skin. I resist the urge to push her away. Hard. "I hope we can get to be friends, Jerzie. Real friends. I'd like that." She turns to Mom. "I'd better get back to my lawyer. Calm her down. She's begging me to press charges, but I agree with Alan. We should all move on. As much as we can anyway." She smiles weakly. "I'll see you guys soon."

She moves down the hallway and pushes back through the conference room doors.

Mom extends her hand. "Phone, Jerzie."

"Mom, she's a confirmed liar," I whisper.

"And so is the boy. Phone. *Now.*"

I reach into my backpack and retrieve my cell, checking the screen to see if he's sent a message. None are there. She snatches it out of my hands.

"Don't invade my privacy," I say sullenly.

"I wouldn't do that, Jerzie, and you know it." She presses the side button to power down the phone and wraps an arm around my shoulder. "Now let's get you back to Brooklyn."

I heave the heaviest of sighs and trudge after Mom. Zeppelin *did* say he has a way of fucking things up. He practically warned me. But he also asked me to trust him.

Trust me, Jerzie. Please.

But can I? Should I?

I already miss yesterday, when I was a girl in love. Today I discover I could simply be a pawn in a very clever game Zeppelin's been playing. Knight takes rook.

Zeppelin takes all.

 ## "And This Is Wisely Done"

There's sleep. And then there's the kind of comatose, depths of despair, Sleeping Beauty type, Maleficent cursed slumber, and that's what I've been in and out of for the past week. In fact, where the hell is Maleficent when you need her? I would happily sleep for a hundred years if I could.

Rehearsals have been painful. Literally. Watching Zeppelin's understudy, Tag, take over the role of Roman makes my chest feel like it's caving in. It makes my stomach twist into knots and my head pulse like a beating heart. Will this eternal migraine never end? And if Zeppelin is the Roman of Robbie's dreams, I imagine that Tag is the Roman of his most boring days on Earth.

"Tag." Alan waves at the pianist and the drummer. The room turns quiet. "There has to be more of a dramatic shift. And remember, you're giving the cue for the transition. Pause.

Take your time. *Notice* your parent on the television. Give yourself adequate time to take it in. Everyone moves *after* you do."

"They do? Oh, sorry." Tag uses the back of his sleeve to wipe away the sweat dripping down his forehead.

I shift, bored. Sitting on this metal chair. Watching Robbie's show die a slow death. It feels like I'm serving a sentence. I mean, Tag does bring a certain boyish charm to Roman. But Zeppelin's interpretation was darker, pained, and if I'm being honest…better. Like, way, way better.

The stage manager announces a ten-minute break and I remind myself that soon I'll be home. Under the warm covers. *Sleep.* The thought makes me smile weakly. The days are too long anyway. Come, Maleficent. Come soon.

"Hey, hon." Aunt Karla's standing at the stove stirring something in a large pot as Judas and I step through the front door. "I'm making chili. You guys hungry?"

"Maybe later," I mumble. I toss my bag onto the floor and move as quickly as I can to the master suite, shutting the door behind me and throwing myself onto the bed. I can hear Judas and Aunt Karla laughing and chatting as I crawl under the covers and rest my head on the pillow. It doesn't take long for sleep to take over.

My eyes have fluttered open. The digital clock on the nightstand says it's 11:00 p.m. I yawn. I can hear the TV blaring downstairs. Two dudes are arguing about market shares. I'm sure Judas fell asleep watching *Wall Street Warriors* or something equally boring.

As I swing my legs out of bed, a strange sound outside on the balcony makes me imagine a giant black raven is perched on the windowsill, come to torment me. I hear it again. It kinda sounds like a tree branch is being blown about by the wind. I wonder if Aunt Karla accidently left the Alexa speaker outside. When it's raining, she brings it inside, and it was raining pretty hard all day. I move slowly to the window and pull back the curtains to check.

Eeep! I yank them shut, heart pounding in my ears as loud as a hammer pounding against a steel nail head.

"Jerzie." Zeppelin's deep, muffled voice calls to me softly. "Please. Can we talk?"

"Are you tryin' to give me a heart attack?" I ask as softly as I can. If Aunt Karla knew Zeppelin was standing on her balcony, the shit would really hit the fan.

"You won't answer my calls. I didn't know what else to do."

I run to a mirror. I look a whole mess. I pull the bedroom door open, race down the hall and into the bathroom. I splash water on my face, brush my teeth at lightning speed and smooth out my hair, then tiptoe back into my room, type in the code to turn off the window alarm and pull back the curtains. I slide open the window as quietly as I can. Zeppelin is now sitting on one of the chairs, head in his hands.

I'm breathing so hard. Holding back my overwhelming desire to rush into his arms and stay there forever. I step onto the balcony and keep my distance instead. The concrete feels cool on my bare feet even though the night is warm and humid from the rain. "How did you know this was my room?"

"You mentioned a balcony. I took a gamble."

"Okay. So, what do you want?"

"You won't reply to my texts or calls, Jerzie." He looks over at me. "Why?"

"My mom took my phone. It's currently quarantined in the bottom of her purse in New Brunswick."

"Oh." He runs both hands through his hair. "Well, I've texted you about a hundred times. And I've been calling you nonstop."

"I'm not allowed to see you anymore."

"*What?*" Zeppelin shakes his head. "Because of a *video?*"

"Not just a video, Zeppelin. I think what you did is like… illegal. Just leave, okay? I could get into a lot of trouble with you being here. My mom's threatening to pull me out of the show if I even speak a word to you. Clearly I'm already in violation."

"Can I talk to her? Can I explain my side of the story?"

An explanation *would* be nice. "Maybe explain it to me first." I swallow nervously, not sure if I'm ready to know the answer to the question on the tip of my tongue. I ask it anyway. "Were you using me to get back at Cinny?"

"Is that what she told you?"

I nod.

"And do you believe her, Jerzie?"

"I don't know what to believe anymore."

He groans. "Can I come in?"

Can he? I look back at the window. Aunt Karla could hear us. Or worse, Judas. He's as snitchy as his namesake. But then again, they could just as easily hear us or even see us out here. Maybe inside is better. "We have to be quiet, Zeppelin."

He stands and follows me as I crawl back in through the window. Once again, I'm reminded of the heat that emanates off him as the space between us swiftly warms. I move to the bedroom door, lock it, and turn to face him. He's dressed in a pair of old black boots, jeans, and a faded sweatshirt, his hair pointing in all directions. A beautiful mess is what I'd call him. He sits on the edge of the bed, resting his elbows on his knees as he stares up at me.

"Why didn't you tell me you and Cinny actually were dating?" I ask softly. "You straight-up lied to me."

"Jerzie." Zeppelin's eyes narrow. "I didn't tell you we were dating because we're *not*. She's a liar."

"Then you're a liar, too. You said you had nothing to do with those videos. Turns out, it was you who uploaded them."

He's quiet for a moment. "It was never my plan to put Cinny online. That's the truth."

"So then why did you?"

"Jerzie." Zeppelin anxiously rubs his hands together. "It's complicated."

"What's that supposed to mean?"

He looks up at me. "Just know that it was never my plan to put her or you online. Especially you. That's the truth."

I glare at him. "This is what you came in here to tell me? This is your side of the story? That it's complicated? I need more than that. I need the whole story."

"It's all I can tell you right now. It *is* complicated. Trust me."

"You used me in some revenge plot, and I don't get to know the truth about why?"

"I would never use you, Jerzie." Zeppelin's not looking at me now. He stares glumly at the floor instead, and for the first time since I met him, I feel a painful distance. Like we're on opposite shorelines of a raging river. "And I haven't lied to you. That I can tell you. I swear I haven't."

I move to the window, staring out at the lights wrapped around the wrought iron balcony bars. I want so badly to believe him. "Who was the guy with you?"

"My dad."

I spin back around to face him. "That was your dad?"

"I was afraid they were gonna arrest me. So I called him. Told him what happened. He knew all the right words to say to calm everyone down."

"Well." I sigh. "Seems like he's there for you. Seems like he cares."

"Doesn't erase what he did to my mom. Nothing will ever erase what he did."

Even in the darkness of my room, I can see the sadness in his eyes. Sense the pain. Feel it…as if it's mine, too. I want to reach across the room and hold his hand. Rest my head on his chest. Lie next to him. But the secrets now between us—they're like a strong force, determined to keep us apart.

"Jerzie." He stands. "I've lost the best job I ever had. If I lose you, too, then I've lost everything. Know that it's you I care about." He steps toward me. "Trust me. Please."

"You keep saying to trust you." I take a step back, not sure I can handle him being much closer. Not sure I can resist reaching out to touch him. In spite of everything, I care, too. "But how can I trust you when you won't talk to me?"

"What else do you want me to say? I'm standing here baring my soul. Why can't that be enough? This week has been pure hell without my job. Without *you*." He pulls at his hair. "In fact, screw the job. I want you more."

My heart leaps inside my chest like it's mad at me. Like it's saying, *Damnit, Jerzie, if you don't run into his arms right now, I'll break free and do it myself!*

"There's never been anything between Cinny and me. How could there be? She's a fucking liar and a maniac. She's incapable of liking anyone but herself."

"That's harsh, Zeppelin." Instead of listening to my heart, I turn back around to stare out onto the balcony. "She's been nice to me."

"Cinny's been nice? To you? How?"

"I dunno. She says hi now. She even invited me out. To have lunch with her."

"And I bet it'll be at some fancy place where a horde of paparazzi can take pictures to fuel the lie that you two are best friends. Trust me when I say this—Cinny only does what benefits Cinny."

I remember her at the conference table. Looking so broken. I've seen Cinny act. She's not *that* good. Those were real tears.

I feel the most gentle touch on my shoulder and turn to see him standing in front of me now. I stare into his eyes. In the darkness of the room, it's like staring into the night sky. It makes me want to cry.

He takes my hand in his, waking the butterflies from their slumber, and places it gently on his chest. "What do you feel, Jerzie?"

I feel his heart.

I feel it beating so slow. So steady.

I feel the warmth from his skin.

I feel love.

There's a knock at my door. "Jerzie?"

It's Aunt Karla. Holy shit! I push Zeppelin toward the window. "Yeah. One second!" I call out. "You have to go." I whisper.

"No," Aunt Karla calls out. "Let the boy stay right where he is. Let me in this room. Now."

Omigosh. *I'm screwed!* I move to the door, twist the lock, and pull it open. Aunt Karla steps inside and locks the door again behind her.

"Jerzie." Aunt Karla is speaking very softly. "You do realize I have a security camera on the balcony, right?"

I shake my head. I, in fact, did not realize that.

She looks at Zeppelin. "It's too bad I can't have you arrested. But based on the video footage, my idiotic niece *let* you in."

"She didn't know I was coming. It's not her fault. All me, ma'am."

"Boy, did you just call me ma'am? Do I look like my grandma to you?"

"No, ma'am. I mean. Miss. Or… Aunt Karla?" I've never seen Zeppelin look terrified before. He runs both hands through his hair. "Sorry. Shit. What should I call you?"

"Call me nothing." Aunt Karla moves to the window. "And leave the same way you came in. Try not to break your ankles on the way down. But if you do, it would probably serve you right."

Zeppelin looks back and forth between Aunt Karla and me, and for a moment, I imagine him defying her. Dropping to one knee to declare his love for me. Begging for her to have mercy on him. But instead, he backs away slowly, turns, and crawls back out onto the balcony.

Aunt Karla stands at the window, watching. After a moment, she slams the window shut and reactivates the alarm. She turns to me.

"You better thank whoever you pray to that your nosy-ass brother is asleep."

"You're not gonna tell Mom and Dad on me?"

"*This* time." She crosses to the bed. Sits on the edge. "Jerzie, you realize what's at stake here? Don't throw away a lifetime worth of work for some boy. He's not worth it. You know how many young, beautiful girls like you, with their whole life ahead of them, have had their plans sidelined for 'love'?

"Your parents—they spent years and years dedicated to making your dreams come true. Driving you around to this piano class and that voice teacher and this music theory instructor and dance classes, theater troupes, and, and, *and*. I remember one summer your mom drove an hour and a half, *every* morning, to Rowan University so you could take an advanced music theory class. I told her she was out of her damn mind and should let you swim and watch cartoons so she could enjoy her summer. She never wavered. You were and still are her top priority."

She pauses, leaning forward to rest her elbows on her knees, the same way Zeppelin did just moments ago. "You have two options here, Jerzie. Option one. Enjoy your well-earned spot as a part of a Robert Christian Ruiz Broadway musical. Who knows where it can lead. Option two. Defy your parents for a boy who *used* you in some twisted revenge plot and risk losing it all."

"But, Aunt Karla…" My eyes are welling with tears. "What if there's more to the story?"

"Is that what he said?"

I nod.

"Well." Aunt Karla places a hand on her hip. "Let's hear it."

"He…" I shake my head. "Didn't actually get a chance to tell me."

"Of course he didn't." Aunt Karla rolls her eyes. "Don't be so gullible, little niece. He's a boy. They *lie*."

"All of them?"

"Most of them. Especially the ones that look like him."

"But, Aunt Karla…" I say again as evenly as I can, not wanting her to hear any of the desperation I feel in my voice. "What if there really is more to the story?"

"It still wouldn't matter. It makes no reason *why* he did it. He did it."

"Okay, fine. So what if he did?" I throw my arms up in exasperation. "So what? So he uploaded a video of a girl to—"

"Ruin her life? Jerzie, listen to yourself. You sound ridiculous."

"Aunt Karla," I cry. "What if he's the great love of my life?"

"Jerzie, please. What do you even know about love?" She sighs. "Listen, this choice you need to make is not for nothin'. It's for *everything*. There are a million guys just like Zeppelin. There is only one opportunity like this. *He's* not your destiny."

I wipe tears as they slide down my cheeks. "This is really what you believe?"

"I'm speaking from my heart and my soul. And half the women in New York City would tell you the same thing." She adds, "You know the poem, 'The Road Not Taken'?"

I nod. By Robert Frost. We had to memorize it for a

seventh-grade English project. *Two roads diverged in a yellow wood. And sorry I could not travel both…*

"People throw away so much for love, Jerzie. And usually, they live to regret it. Don't live to regret. Take the road less traveled." She hugs me tight. "I promise you, little niece. It'll make all the difference."

"O Juliet. I Already Know Thy Grief"

The current scene in rehearsal room 7A takes place at the high school. The students are divided, their inherited hatred for one another is boiling over into all-out war. Tyree and Mauricio (aka Tybalt and Mercutio) get into a fight. Or in this case, a battle of the spoken word. Roman tries to intercede, but Tyree has a gun in his backpack.

The entire scene plays out while, on an overhead projector, their parents are participants in a political debate. It's an odd juxtaposition. As an enraged Tyree aims his gun, the parents stand so poised and eloquent on a debate stage.

Thus begins Roman's big solo, 'Let's Rewrite the Story,' a song-and-verse number where he convinces his best friend and greatest school rival to change the narrative.

"Become allies instead of enemies!" Tag screams. And boy, do I mean scream. *Ouch.*

"Tag, why are you screaming?" Mae waves at the pianist to stop playing and moves toward Tag. "This should be a tender moment. You've got their attention already. You're the only one singing. Plead with them."

"I need a break." Tag uses the back of his sleeve to wipe away the sweat dripping down his forehead. "Please."

Mae sighs and turns to the stage manager, who quickly announces a ten-minute break. There's not a lot of chitchat as the cast disperses to drink from bottles of water or head to the bathroom. Mae, Alan, and Tag have a hushed conversation in the corner.

"Hey you."

I look up to see Damon slide into the seat beside me, trailed by Angel. Angel has violet eyes today. Last time I saw him his eyes were brown, so I'm guessing he's wearing contacts, because...nobody has eyes that shade of purple. At least no one I've ever seen. His hair, which he has pulled into a low ponytail, hangs almost to the middle of his back, and a small hoop is pierced through the center of his bottom lip. He's dressed in all black. I think if you ran into Angel in the dark of night, you'd swear he was there to suck your blood and leave you for dead. He rests a hand on Damon's leg. I get the feeling these two are an official couple, but I don't ask. Mostly because, at the moment, happy couples make my heart hurt.

I sit up in my seat. "Hey."

Angel leans across Damon's lap. "You're too good to be sitting on a plastic chair looking bored."

"They pay me to sit here," I explain. "I don't mind."

"Don't worry about her." Damon smiles. "Jerzie's gonna audition for *Black Barbie the Musical* after this."

"That's not a thing," I say.

"No," Damon agrees. "But if it was, you'd be the lead black Barbie and you know it."

"Then you'd be Ken." Angel laughs.

"You know..." I say softly, hoping to divert the conversation away from me. "You two are seriously brilliant. It's a really good scene. I got lost in it."

"It could be better," Angel declares. He and Damon exchange looks, but neither says a word about the elephant in the room, i.e., the less-than-stellar replacement Roman.

"So where's your phone?" Damon asks. "You know we get to keep them now, right? People were complaining. Missing calls from kids and shit. I don't have kids." He looks up at the ceiling and folds his hands in prayer. "Thank you, Lady. Keep them away forever, please." He looks back at me. "But I do need to check my Instagram every five minutes." He holds up his phone. "Where's yours?"

"Oh. I don't have it. Don't really need it." Lies, lies, lies! My phone was my third arm. How dare my mom take it away from me! *How dare she!*

"We were gonna see if you wanted to come out with us tonight," Angel says. "I know we have work tomorrow, but it is Saturday."

It *is* Saturday. So many days since I've last seen or heard from Zeppelin. So many long and arduous days on the proverbial road less traveled, where the thorns and thistles and random rattlesnake sightings are a constant reminder that people steer clear of this road for damn good reasons.

"It's in Chelsea," Damon adds. "It's a cute little karaoke spot. You in?"

Karaoke? In Chelsea? Uggh. Wouldn't that interfere with

my plans of pulling my blanket over my head and crying myself to sleep in the dark? "Who's all going?"

"Me." Angel poses as if he's pretty much the only person needed on a night out. "And Damon."

"And Lorin," Damon cuts in.

"Lorin?" I remember the night at Zeppelin's event, when I overheard her talking about me to her friend. "I don't think she likes me very much."

"Lorin's harmless," Damon says. "Besides, she does like you. She told me so."

She did?

I scan the room, searching for Lorin, and find her sitting against the back wall, head slumped in her hands, looking like she lost her best friend. I wonder if the missing Roman is what's got her looking so glum.

"So, what do you say, Jerzie?" Damon asks again. "You in?"

"If I do come, my brother probably has to come with me. He's my..." I pause. *What is Judas exactly?* "Human tattletale?" Both Damon and Angel laugh. I smile. If I'm being honest, it's my first smile in days. "My parents have to make sure I don't do anything stupid." *Like fall for a convicted felon.* Oops, too late!

"Is your brother the cutie who drops you off in the mornings?" Angel asks, a glint in his purple eyes. "Cuz God *yes.* He can totally come."

Damon shoulder bumps him. "I'm gonna kick you in the shin."

"Violent, violent Mauricio." Angel laughs.

"You're the one holding the gun." Damon turns his attention back to me. "Bring your brother. But does he even like karaoke? He doesn't seem like the type."

Judas Jhames? Like karaoke? I think he would rather die.

"He'll be happy to get out of the house and away from Times Square." Note to self. Bribe Judas with a thousand dollars' worth of savings bonds.

"Nice. If this rehearsal ever ends." Angel sighs. "We can't wait to see you there."

"See you where?" Cinny is standing behind the boys now. They both turn and stare blankly at her. "I wanna come. Where you guys goin'?"

"To an *Exorcist*-themed escape room in Bedford Park," Damon replies quickly, giving me a look like, *Please play along.* "You *should* come, Cinny!"

"Yeah. Totes!" Angel echoes. "Pleeeease?" he sings.

"*Exorcist*-themed escape room?" Cinny shakes her head. "You guys are lying."

"No, we're not." Angel pulls his long ponytail over his shoulder. "It's fun. Last time we went, Pennywise put me in a choke hold."

"Didn't you lose consciousness for a few seconds?" Damon asks.

"Did I?" Angel scratches his head. "Everything's a blur when horror movie demons are involved."

"And be prepared to sign a death waiver," Damon says. "They make everyone sign one."

Cinny turns to me. "Jerzie. Where are they *really* going?"

"Um." I look back and forth between Cinny and the boys. "Karaoke. In Chelsea. Sorry, guys. I'm a terrible liar."

"It's whatever anyway." Cinny rolls her eyes. "An *Exorcist*-themed escape room sounds way more fun than boring-ass karaoke."

Angel stands. "You'll be missed."

"How do we get a hold of you, Jerzie?" Damon asks. "What's your number?"

I look at Cinny, not wanting to hurt her feelings, but also not wanting to miss an opportunity to hang out with Damon Coleman and company. I quickly give them Judas's number.

"Sweet. We'll hit you later, Barbie Doll," Damon says. He and Angel move across the room.

"See how rude they are to me?" Cinny hands me a bottle of cold Gatorade as she slams onto the seat beside me. I twist off the cap and take a sip. It tastes sour. Like all food and drink does lately. "Are you really hanging out with those witless wonders?"

I shrug. "I have to make friends, don't I?"

"I'm your friend." She wraps an arm around my shoulder. "But I haven't been a good one. That's changing. Starting today. We have an hour break today. Come have lunch with me. I owe you lunch anyway."

Lunch with Cinny? I guess that would be all right. But there is the issue of Judas. Today he's roaming about Times Square waiting for me. "Could...maybe...my brother come, too?"

"Sure. Bring him." She claps her hands excitedly. "And let's go to Gush. You down?"

I frown. Gush. I know that spot because Aunt Karla goes out of her way to avoid the area. Dozens of paparazzi camp out on the street outside the restaurant waiting for celebrities to show up, and traffic is always a nightmare.

"Can we try a place not so busy?" *And not swarming with paparazzi?*

Cinny sighs. "I sorta had my heart set on Gush. They have the best avocado toast. Besides, we break for lunch at two. Gush won't even be busy at that time. I'll call ahead. Okay?"

"Yeah. I guess."

I look over Cinny's shoulder and see Nigel approaching. He kneels in front of Cinny and me.

"So," he says. "We'd like to run the balcony scene with Tag. But we need to run 'I Defy' with Rob in 7C. Alan and Robbie are trying to work out some particulars with the song."

My stomach churns. "I Defy." The song Zeppelin first heard me sing. Or maybe Zeppelin never even heard me sing the song. So much of what he said to me could've been a lie.

Cinny yawns. "So is Tag gonna run the balcony scene by himself? Cuz I can't be in two places at once."

"Well…" Nigel pauses. "One of the understudies can mark your movements for 'I Defy,' since it's more about Robbie figuring out arrangement stuff. It's important you and Tag get into a groove."

"Why?" Cinny rolls her eyes. "He's not actually gonna be Roman, is he? Please tell me you guys are in the process of hiring a real actor."

"Jesus, *Cinny*." It's the first time I've ever seen Nigel angry. "Give the kid a fucking break."

"It's not my fault he sucks." Cinny is oblivious to Nigel's enraged expression.

"Can I help?" I blurt. "I mean, if it's okay with you, Cinny. I can run the balcony scene with Tag. That way you can work with Robbie and Alan."

"Brilliant." Nigel exhales. "Thank you, Jerzie."

"Wait." Cinny holds out a hand. "*I'll* work with Tag. No offense, Jerzie, but if he's gonna be my leading man, *I'm* the one who should be working with him."

"No doubt," I say quickly. "Was only trying to help."

"So do we have your permission to use Jerzie to help *Robbie*?" Nigel's not really trying to camouflage the anger in his voice. "Cuz if not Jerzie, we can use Kiara or Genevieve. Your other covers."

"You don't need my permission. Use who you want. I don't care what you do." Her cell chimes in her lap. "I gotta take this." She places the phone to her ear and walks off.

Nigel turns back to me. "7C, Jerzie. You can head there now."

I grab the pocket of Nigel's cargo shorts as he tries to rush away. "Wait."

He turns back. "What's up?"

"I have a randomly weird question."

"I love randomly weird things." He sits beside me. "Talk to me."

"Did Zeppelin ever come to the Beaumont Theater? While I was rehearsing there?"

"Not that I recall," Nigel replies swiftly.

Zeppelin was lying. He never saw me rehearsing alone at Beaumont. Those rehearsal spaces were tiny. Of course I would've seen him come in.

"Wait a second," Nigel says. "My memory gets fuzzy sometimes, but I remember now. We did have a payroll issue, and he had to come to Beaumont to pick up some paperwork from me. It was about a month ago. In fact..." He turns to me. "He must've seen you."

"Really?" I breathe. "You think?"

"Yeah. Cuz he asked me what's Cinny's standby's name." Nigel nods. "Yeah. I remember now."

That's how he knew my name when I first met him. The

day is still so vivid in my mind. Him backing away toward the doors to the rehearsal room. A smile so big it lit up the entire hallway when he said,

"*I'm hoping for something* really *good. At least when it comes to you, Jerzie Jhames.*"

He *wasn't* lying. He really did see me at Beaumont.

I stand and pull my backpack over my shoulders. "No big deal." I'm hoping Nigel can't hear the quiver in my voice. "I was only curious."

"When she goes upstage, you come down." Alan holds a worn copy of the *Roman and Jewel* script, looking over the edge of his glasses to stare at the pages. "But it's in a strange rhythm. Is that what's making it seem so disconnected?"

"Hmm. I wouldn't call syncopated strange, but I do see what you mean." Robbie's staring at his own copy of *Roman and Jewel*. I'm actually standing on my mark—well, Jewel's mark—as they talk out the particulars, trying to be as still as a stone and as quiet as a mouse. Not that mice are quiet. In New York City they're downright rowdy. Freakin' gangster mice.

Alan sets down his script. "Is it the key change?"

Robbie shakes his head. "There's definitely something about it that's making me dislike it, but I really don't think it's the key change."

It *is* odd. I've watched Cinny and Robbie perform "I Defy" quite a few times, and each time Jewel begins her solo, her desperate plea to Professor Lawrence, or Friar Laurence, as he's known in Shakespeare's version, it feels off to me. And Cinny's not to blame. The song is right in her range, and she sounds really good when she sings it. But like, I can't connect to it the way I want to either.

The rehearsal door is pushed open to reveal Linda, one of the music assistants who helps during rehearsals. She's an older woman with gray hair. "Hi." She's fumbling with a massive music folder. "Sorry I'm late."

"No worries, Linda," Alan calls out. "We were about to take it from the top of 'I Defy.'"

Linda sits at the piano and begins laying out her sheet music. I watch Alan and Robbie continue their discussion as Linda warms up on the keys. My ears focus on her as she lightly taps out the chords for "I Defy."

It suddenly dawns on me. Like, call me crazy, but I think I figured it out.

"Excuse me?" I raise my hand. Linda stops playing, and Robbie and Alan look over at me as if realizing for the first time that I'm here.

"Yes, Jerzie?" Alan replies, brow furrowed. "Do you need to run to the bathroom? You don't have to ask permission."

"No, no. It's just…" I pull nervously at my hair. "Can I show you guys something real quick? It'll take like twenty-five seconds?" I don't wait for an answer. I rush to the piano and stand beside Linda. "Hi. Could I borrow your piano?"

Linda nods. "You should know it's not my piano, dear."

She stands, and I take her place at the bench, studying the music as Robbie and Alan cross to me.

"Okay." My hands are sweating now. Two Broadway greats have paused their rehearsal to listen to me? Holy shit. "So when Jewel and Professor Lawrence are chatting in the beginning. The verse stuff has all this chaos, right?" I play the beginning of the song, reading Linda's sheet music. "Then, when the verse conversation morphs into Jewel's solo, it turns into a pattern." I pound out the repeated chords.

Robbie folds his arms under his chest. "I get that, Jerzie. I did write it."

"Right, and it's brilliant," I say. "But listen." I play the chords and sing over them. But rather than sing "I Defy," I sing Journey's "Open Arms." Then I morph into Queen's "Bohemian Rhapsody."

Robbie and Alan laugh.

I point to the music. "It's a B-flat seventh chord resolving to C major. It feels weird to you guys, because it suddenly sounds similar to a bunch of really popular songs, and the melody line isn't distinct enough to stand out above it."

"How do we fix it?" Robbie sits beside me, snatching off his baseball cap and running his hands through his hair. "Are you suggesting we rewrite the—"

"Melody line. Yeah. The common cadence is fine. But if Jewel could do some *improvisations*... Like this..."

"Wait. Can I record this?" He holds up his cell phone. "Just the audio?"

"Sure. Of course."

Robbie hits the record button and sets his cell on top of the piano. I sing as I play the chords, dramatically changing the melody line and feeling connected to the words in a way I haven't before. A defiant Jewel. No longer wanting to be a pawn in her parents' divisive game. Wanting desperately to *love* her adversary. Adamant that's exactly what she plans to do. When I feel my eyes start to water, I rush through to the end, then slide my hands off the keys.

"That's all." I look at Robbie and smile brightly. Thankfully the smile stops the tears from brimming to the surface.

Robbie looks up at Alan. "Well?"

"Fucking brilliant." Alan looks at me. "Excuse my language. I shouldn't be cursing in front of a sixteen-year-old."

"Actually, I'm seventeen. Today is my birthday."

"Well, happy fucking birthday." Alan looks at Robbie. "I'm gonna get Mae. She needs to hear this. Now."

"I'm coming with," Linda says. "Left my glasses in 7A and I can hardly see a foot in front of me."

I watch the two exit the rehearsal space.

"Not too many kids understand music theory, Jerzie." Robbie retrieves his cell phone from the top of the piano. "You could compose. Like, for a living. Have you ever thought about that?"

I slide my fingers across the keys, careful not to make a sound. The quiet of the room feels comforting for some reason. "Yeah. I take all sorts of composition classes."

"What kind of stuff do you like to write?" Robbie stands and leans against the piano, looking down at me.

"I dunno. Love songs mostly." I look up at him. Just the mention of love, and my chest feels like it's caving in. "How are you liking Tag as Roman?"

Robbie takes his time before he answers. "I think he brings something interesting. He'll get there."

"You miss Zeppelin?"

"I do." He sighs. "But the show's always gotta go on. Regardless of what happens backstage. That's Broadway. Things have a way of morphing into something you'd never expect.

I've learned to roll with it. But he was my perfect Roman. And I considered him a friend. Still do."

"Have you talked to him? I mean, since, you know."

"We've chatted through email."

Once again my fingers glide silently across the piano keys. "How is he?" I'm trying to sound nonchalant. "He okay?"

"He's sad. About the show. But mostly I think he's a little lovesick."

"Oh? Yeah, I heard he was dating someone."

"Yep," Robbie replies. "He confessed it all. Thinks maybe he's lost her forever though. He was more sad about that than losing the show."

"Well, he should reach out to her."

"Apparently her parents took her phone?"

I look up now, my eyes wide with surprise.

"And they banned her from ever speaking to him again." Robbie winces. "That's harsh, if you ask me. But he's a good kid. He doesn't wanna get her in trouble. So he's keeping his distance."

The tears I was holding back have freed themselves from captivity and are now sliding down my cheeks. I wipe them away.

"I'm sorry I'm crying in front of you." I cover my face with my hands. I feel Robbie sit down beside me.

"Jerzie. You're not the first one of my actors to break down crying in a rehearsal. You won't be the last."

"I'm being sensible," I explain. "I'm taking the road less traveled."

"Remind me. Which road is that?"

"Where young love doesn't ruin my life."

"Ahh. That road." Robbie's quiet for a moment. "You

know, when I was in high school, I was a terrible screwup. Ask my parents."

I look over at him, wiping tears away. "No way. Not you."

"Yep. It's true. I was always listening to music. Terrible *rap* music. I was writing songs when I should've been learning calculus. Which, by the way, is very important. I was in rap battles with my friends on the street corners after school instead of studying. Also, I had such below-average grades that I didn't get into any universities or win any scholarships and instead had to..." he pauses, places a hand over his heart "...go to a community college," he whispers. "Where I..." He sighs. "Oh, God, Jerzie. This is bad. I studied *music*."

I smirk. "Robbie. None of this is bad."

"Oh, you haven't talked to Mr. Ruiz. Also known as my father. He'll tell you the truth. I was too busy 'tinkering with music toys' instead of being serious about my academics. I was wasting my life away. Doomed to fail."

"What does he say now?"

"Now?" He leans back. "He says, 'Roberto, my son. When are you going to get a real job and make your papa proud?'"

"That's unbelievable."

"In his defense, he says it from the deep blue metallic Model X I just bought him."

I smile. "Well..." I'm staring down at the piano keys now. "*My* parents say they will take me out of this musical if I pull a Jewel and defy them. I can't risk that. This means too much."

"What you just showed me..." he taps the piano keys "...is that you know music. Like, you *know* it. And I'm guessing you didn't learn it by listening to top forty on Spotify. I'm guessing you learned music by taking music theory and composition classes. I'm guessing your parents had something to do with that."

"Piano since I was four. Theory every summer."

"See, unlike my parents—God bless them in their fancy matching Teslas that their screwup of a son bought for them—your parents are all in. They want what you want."

"So what are you suggesting?" I watch Robbie as he slips his baseball cap back over his mess of hair. "I can't go against them."

"No, no. God no. Don't do that. Parents know it all. I'm suggesting this. There is the main road. The road less traveled. And then there is a secret third road that not too many people know about. I've been on it for decades."

"There's a secret road?" I perk up.

"Oh, yeah. You don't even need a metro pass for it."

I laugh. "I *gotta* know where this secret road is. Tell me."

"That's the thing. I can't tell you. Because the secret road is a road you personally build. You are the architect, the construction crew. You do it all. And this road? Jerzie, it can be whatever you want it to be. Lead to wherever you wanna go. It can be twisty and turny or straight and narrow. It can travel over the ocean. It can soar high into the sky or delve into the depths of the ocean."

I frown. "That sounds scary. Like a secret road that could lead to my ultimate doom."

"That's what you're building? A road that leads to your ultimate doom?"

"You know what I mean."

"Here's the thing." He turns to me now. "The main road? The one a lot of people choose? Booooring."

I nod. "So boring."

"The road less traveled? That road is a *nightmare*. It's less traveled for good reason."

"Yeah," I agree. "There's rattlesnakes on it."

"And poisonous spiders and skunks and all sorts of random shit that'll make you run for cover. Steer clear. But the third, secret road?" Robbie whistles. "That road is the ride of your *life*."

The ride of my *life*? Am I ready for that?

"And, Jerzie?"

"Yeah?"

"I'm gonna use your new melody line. I love it. And since I plan to use it, I'm gonna give you writing credit for 'I Defy.'"

I'm momentarily speechless.

"Are you okay with that, Jerzie?"

"*You* wrote the song. Not me."

"It takes a lot of cooks in the kitchen to construct a song. You rewrote the melody line in less than a minute and I think it's wonderful. You deserve credit. And would you look at that?" He crosses his arms under his chest. "Now your parents couldn't take you out of this musical even if they tried. You're in the Playbill regardless."

I can only stare into his brown eyes, shaking my head in amazement. This cannot be happening.

"I'd say you *just* started laying the foundation for your new road. And if I were you, I'd keep that toolbox open. Keep building, Jerzie Jhames."

I'm crying now. But these are happy tears. The happiest tears I've ever cried.

"And happy birthday, kiddo."

"Here's Drink. I Drink to Thee"

When Cinny's driver pulls up to Gush, a dozen paparazzi with their cameras pointed at the car stand on the street screaming her name, and all *I* can hear is Zeppelin's soft voice. The words he spoke to me at Aunt Karla's house in the dead of night. It's on repeat in my head. Scrolling and scrolling:

I bet it'll be at some fancy place where a horde of paparazzi can take pictures to fuel the lie that you two are best friends. Cinny only does what benefits Cinny.

"Dang." Judas gazes out the window. "All this for some damn avocado toast?"

I elbow him in the side. *"Judas."*

He motions dramatically. *"What?"*

It's not like Cinny heard him anyway. She's been on the phone for the entire seven-minute car ride.

"Okay, Chance. I gotta go. We're pulling up to Gush."

Judas pokes me in the side. I look at him and he mouths, *Chance the Rapper?!*

I shrug.

Cinny stuffs her cell into her purse and, at last, acknowledges Judas and I are in the back of this SUV with her. "You guys ready?"

How exactly could we be ready for something like this?

"I guess so." I unhook my seat belt.

Judas looks out the window. "Should we be wearin' bullet-proof vests?"

"Omigosh stop." Cinny laughs. "Paparazzi is Italian for low-life, human roach, trying to avoid getting a real job. Ignore them."

We pile out of the car, and the voices shouting Cinny's name are instantly amplified to such a volume that my ears start to ring. It's chaos as the photographers clamor to make it to the front of the pack. Cinny grabs my hand as her security guard ushers all three of us into the restaurant.

We're sitting in a quiet corner. Through the floor-to-ceiling windows, I can see the human "roaches," as Cinny so eloquently referred to them, taking photos of us as we sip water.

"So like, y'all know they're taking pictures of you?" Judas is mesmerized with the whole spectacle.

"Of course we know," Cinny replies, a slight irritation to her voice.

"Isn't it awkward?" Judas continues with his questions, oblivious to the fact that Cinny isn't exactly receptive to them. I kick him under the table. "Ow." He glares at me.

"You get used to pretending you don't see them. And sometimes they're so damn sneaky you *don't* see them. I hate when that happens." She studies the menu. "You guys are gonna love their crab legs."

I note the price next to the crab leg lunch—115 dollars!

"Are these Sebastian's crab legs?" Judas asks.

Cinny looks up from her menu. "Who's Sebastian?"

"You know. From *The Little Mermaid*?" He grins. "Trying to rationalize the cost here."

Oh, God. Judas is so *embarrassing*. Except, Cinny cracks up laughing like he should be headlining at the Funny Bone.

"Judas." I turn to him. "Be normal."

"It's fine." Cinny smiles at Judas. "He's adorable."

"See, sis? I'm adorable."

Judas is many things. Adorable is not one of them.

"But on the real, Cinny." He crosses his legs and leans back to stare at the ceiling, and I brace myself. This is typically the position he assumes when he's about to go on an "information tangent," as I like to call them. "To make a profit…"

Yep. Here we go.

"…restaurants charge about a three hundred percent markup," he explains. "This Gush pricing is more like a three *thousand* percent markup. That sort of price gouging should be illegal. I'm gonna get the cheapest thing here. Just to spite them."

Cinny snatches the menu out of Judas's hand. "You're so silly. Besides, I already called ahead and ordered for all of us, since we don't have a ton of time. And lunch is on me. Also. I'm a millionaire. So like…don't sweat the small stuff."

"Thank you," Judas replies. "But Corporate America is depending on you millionaires to waste your money to feed unnecessarily into the American economy. It's why we're staring down the barrel of a recession."

"I'm sorry about him," I say. "He *wasn't* dropped on his head as a baby. I think that's the problem. The good news? He's going away to college soon."

"University of Pennsylvania, baby!" Judas pops the collar of his shirt.

"You both are too cute for words. I wish I had a sibling. Hang out with me tonight. There's a new Slate opening a few blocks from Times Square. It's all glass. There's a six-lane bowling alley. Pool tables. Game rooms. The place is pretty dope. I'm doing a set for the opening. Come be my guests of honor."

"An industry party?" Judas looks like a starving pup who spotted a meaty bone. I swear he's salivating. "I've never been to one of those."

"I'm going out with Damon and Angel. Remember, Cinny?"

"Oh yeah." Cinny frowns. "I forgot." She drums her long nails on the table. "They have a karaoke room at Slate. I'll put Damon and Angel on the list. You guys can sing boring old Lynyrd Skynyrd songs in a much cooler environment. Besides, there's gonna be soooo many celebs there tonight." Cinny sighs. "I wonder if the Smiths are still coming?"

"Willow and Jaden?" Judas repeats.

"I can introduce you," Cinny offers sweetly.

Judas turns to me. "Sis. Let your boys know. We're going to Slate. Discussion over."

"Yay." Cinny claps her hands. "It's official. I'll have my manager put everyone on the list. This'll be way more fun!"

Will it? I was actually looking forward to a more intimate night out, hanging with Damon and Angel and getting to know Lorin. "Wait. Lorin was coming, too."

Cinny rolls her eyes. "Fine. I'll get *Lorin* on the list, too. But nobody else. This isn't a charity event."

A waiter appears, pouring more water into our beautiful crystal glasses.

"Good afternoon, ladies and gentleman. Chef Adalene is pleased to have you dining with us for lunch and has prepared three lunch specials, which include Chef's original recipe for lobster bisque. Marinated in a crème fraîche and Dry Sack sherry with—"

"We don't need to hear the details. We trust it's good," Cinny interrupts. "But can we get three lemon drops with sugared rims? You guys have Carbonadi, right?"

"Yes, miss."

"Perf. Three lemon drops with Carbonadi. Stat."

"Excellent." The waiter retrieves our menus. "I'll return with your items shortly."

He moves off.

"What's a lemon drop?" I ask.

"It's so good. It's like syrup, lemon juice, and vodka," Cinny replies. "Perks of being a celebrity. Nobody *ever* cards you. Unless they're assholes."

"But we gotta go back to work," I remind her.

"Trust me. Working with Tag? Being drunk is ideal. I swear, kissing him is like having to kiss one of my pre-pubescent, middle school fans." She takes a big gulp from her goblet of water.

"Won't the paparazzi say we were drinking?" I whisper,

as if they can hear me from outside through a thick pane of glass. "Underage drinking?"

"I'll put a pic on the Gram and add hashtag Nonalcoholic." She holds up her phone and smiles. "Thank you, Instagram. Helping celebrities lie since 2010." She sets her phone beside her on the table. "So, Jerzie. Tell me something about you I don't know. I feel like you're the biggest mystery."

"Really?" I force out a weak smile. *Me? Mysterious?* "I can tell you something kinda bizarre."

She takes another sip of her water. "Hell yeah. Tell me, girl."

"How do you feel about 'I Defy'?" I ask.

She groans. "Not one of Robbie's greatest creations. The song has potential though. Something about it is weird to me."

"I fixed the melody line!"

Her eyes narrow. "You did what?"

"At rehearsal today. I came up with a new melody line. Robbie loved it. So I'm gonna get credit for helping him write the song."

"You lyin'." Judas turns to me. "That really happened, Jerzie?"

"I swear. It happened right before lunch. I was listening in on him and Alan, and it came to me. They loved it."

"Sing it. Right now," Cinny demands.

"In the restaurant?" I shake my head. "No way."

"Jerzie Jhames." Cinny smacks her lips. "You wanna sing on Broadway in front of thousands of people, but you can't sing to a nearly empty restaurant? Kinda sense does that make?"

I glance around the space. Quite a few tables surround us, but they're all empty. It really does feel like we have the place to ourselves. At least in this section.

"Come on, Jerzie," Judas urges. "I keep a box of earplugs next to my bed, you sing so much at home."

Fine. Why not? I can do this. I sit up nice and tall in the booth, clear my throat and begin singing the new melody line. I sing as softly as I can, but my voice still reverberates, and a few people on the other side of the restaurant stop eating to look over at me.

"Daaaamn," Cinny says when I finish. "That *is* way better. Robbie just got one-upped by a sixteen-year-old." She laughs.

"Seventeen," I correct her with a smile. "Today is my birthday. And I didn't one-up him. The arrangement is flawless. That's all him."

"I didn't know you wrote music." She meddles with her phone. "Listen to this, Jerzie." Music blares from her speakers. It's a really cool and catchy beat. Me and Judas bob our heads along.

"Sick." Judas nods. "This is dope."

"It sounds like Spade," I add.

Cinny claps her hands. "Dang, Jerzie. You're *good*. It is Spade. He produced the track. It's for a new song of mine. What would you sing over it?" Cinny asks. "We haven't found a songwriter we like yet, and the label wants the song like, yesterday."

Me and Judas exchange excited expressions. Is Cinny asking what I think she's asking?

"Sing me something. Consider this your job interview." Cinny slides the cell phone to the center of the table and starts the track over again.

Holy shit! She *is*.

"Uh, well." I rub my hands together. "I'm not super on

the spot. I've been listening to 'I Defy' for over a month. So for that, it was a little easier to come up with something."

"Girl, it doesn't have to be perfect. Make something up on the fly. Or don't." She drums her long nails on the screen of her cell phone. "I *am* trying to give you a shot here though."

I look at Judas, and he flashes a smile in support. "You got this, sis."

"Okay." I exhale. "Play it again."

Cinny starts the track again. I close my eyes, focusing on the baseline. Hearing the key changes. Memorizing the cadences. "It's in 6/8," I say more to myself than to Cinny. "I like the basic drum rhythm. But the guitar riff…" I nod. "Reminds me of Aerosmith. It's like Spade was channeling Steven Tyler."

"Who is Steven Tyler?" Cinny asks.

"Never mind." I close my eyes. "It's rock and roll." I listen so intently, my heartbeat feels in sync with the track. I slowly open my eyes. "I'd get grimy with it. Make it like an R & B rock *fusion*. Yeah." I start humming. "Okay. I don't have lyrics in my head. But what about a melody line like this." I sing the melody for Cinny. She's barely moving a muscle as she listens, her eyes more focused than I've ever seen them.

"That's what's *up*." Judas holds up his phone. "I could hear that comin' up on my playlist for sure."

I look at Cinny. "Well? I mean, I could do better if I had more time."

She taps her phone to stop the track. "I mean it was cute for *sure*. Like, you're crazy talented, Jerzie."

"Really, Cinny?" I place my hands over my cheeks. They feel blazing hot.

"Maybe not exactly what we're looking for though," she adds with a sad shrug.

I deflate.

"No, don't look like that." She leans back in the booth, studying me. "I'm gonna do you a favor. A real big favor."

"Yeah?" My ears perk up.

"I'm gonna set up a meeting for you with my manager. He has to meet you. You should bring a few of your original songs. You have music you can share, right?"

I can hardly breathe but manage a nod in reply.

"Good. Bring as much as you can. This industry needs more women songwriters. Especially women of color. Hell yeah. This has to happen."

"Cinny?" I say her name like she's got to be kidding me. "Are you being for real? Because this would be the most exciting thing to ever happen in my life." I'm smiling so hard my vision is blurring. "You would do this for me?"

"Jerzie. I'm happy to do it." She reaches across the table to squeeze my hand. "Who knows? Maybe you might even write a song for me one day. My manager has all the connects."

The waiter returns and sets three giant martini glasses in front of us, filled to the brim with a cloudy, yellow-tinted beverage. I stare at my nonalcoholic-alcoholic drink. I mean. It *is* my birthday.

"Will you tell on me if I drink this?" I turn to Judas. He's already got lips to martini glass.

"Uh. Yeah, you good, sis."

We both laugh.

He extends his glass in my direction. "Happy birthday, Jerzie."

"Happy birthday, Jerzie!" Cinny chimes in.

We all clink glasses. I take a sip. It's *delicious*, and within a few seconds I feel the cool drink turn warm in my stomach. I giggle.

Cinny's cell buzzes in her hand. She checks the screen. "Oh, God. I wish he'd stop *texting* me."

"Who's that?" I ask, feeling so puffed up, I'm in danger of full-on combustion.

She sighs. "Zeppelin."

It's like a swift kick to the gut. The warm feeling in my tummy turns cold and now there's an ache in my chest more powerful than all the good feels. My name somewhere beside Robert Christian Ruiz in the Playbill for *Roman and Jewel*, a meeting with one of the most sought-after managers in the music industry, and all I am is deflated. Like a shiny Mylar balloon days after the party, sagging in the corner of an empty room. Once the highlight of a grand celebration, now waiting for its next destination—the New York City landfill.

"He's scaring me." Cinny takes a photo of her drink. "Let me post this 'nonalcoholic drink' on Instagram quick before the roaches outside can sell their pictures and head to Starbucks to finish out their 'workday.'"

I watch as she posts the pic on Instagram, then sets her phone on the table. I know I shouldn't ask. But the curiosity in me cannot be tamed.

"What, uh, did he say? Zeppelin, I mean."

She grabs her phone and taps the screen. Then flips the cell around to show me. It's one message. From Zeppelin Reid:

Cinny. Please talk to me. Please.

Oh. My. God. I reach for my lemon drop but quickly decide against it. With the way my head is already spinning, I need water. I grab the water glass and take a sip, careful not to show Cinny how the message has battered my already bruised and broken heart. I'm struggling to keep my hands steady, my eyes from watering, my voice from cracking.

"That doesn't seem too scary," I say evenly.

She runs her fingers through her perfectly straightened hair, pulling it over her shoulder. "Yesterday he texted me like, thirteen times. Honestly, I'm afraid he's losing it at this point. He lost his job. He lost me for sure. And I guess he's lost you. Though I'm not sure what you and him were about anyway."

"I keep telling you," I say softly. "Nothing."

"And also, who's gonna hire him after getting fired from a Robert Christian Ruiz musical? He's done on Broadway. I hope he doesn't try to kill himself or something like that. His messages are starting to sound kinda desperate. Yesterday he did mention that living seemed like an exercise in futility."

Zeppelin, kill himself? No. No, Cinny is wrong. She's *wrong*. "He really said that?" My hands ball into tight fists under the table.

"He said it. And don't tell anybody I told you this." She leans forward. "But I heard from Lorin, the chorus girl."

"You mean the swing?" I correct her.

"Potato, pa-tah-toe." She flips her hair over her shoulder. "Background girl. Anyway. I was chatting with her one day, and I guess her and Zeppelin were kinda friends. She was hoping for more. Trust me. Anyway, she said Zeppelin's mom was a washed-up opera singer and couldn't get a job. So she literally hurled herself off a bridge or something and…" Cinny shakes her head. "Never mind. I'm sure Zeppelin wouldn't do something like *that*. At least I hope not. Anyway." She waves her hand as if swatting away a gnat. "New, nondepressing topic."

What sort of situation could Zeppelin be in right now? Is he really suicidal? And what kind of *asshole* is Cinny to ignore it with a wave of her hand? Zeppelin *was* right about her. From fake Instagram posts to lies on national TV, ignoring the plight of her friends—or ex-boyfriend. Which. I raise an eyebrow.

"You spent time at Zeppelin's apartment, right?" I say.

Cinny blinks. "Uh. Yeah. Of course."

I'm taking a huge gamble. But here goes. "What did you think of how messy it was? When I was there for the few minutes I was..." I pause to take another drink of my water. "I couldn't believe how...dirty...he is."

"Soo dirty." She nods. "I would always tell him to clean up. But you know how Zeppelin is."

My eyes narrow. Yeah. I think I finally *do* know how Zeppelin is. But more important...I know how Cinny is, too.

She turns her attention to Judas. "So what kind of girls do you like, so I know who to introduce you to tonight?"

I tune out their conversation. I've been so focused on how *I'm* feeling, I've forgotten about Zeppelin's feelings. The way the sadness can come over him so quickly. The way the light can dim so suddenly in his bright eyes. What he must be going through.

When I look up, the waiter has reappeared and is setting down perfectly plated fine dishes, bowls of soup decorated with basil and bright colorful spices, and baskets of steaming hot bread. I don't have much of an appetite, so I push my plates aside. Cinny and Judas don't notice I'm not eating—they're too busy laughing and planning for tonight's event.

I'm planning, too. I know my new road must include a quick detour. It really is all about perception. And from my viewpoint, this can't be the end of the road for Zeppelin.

I won't let it be.

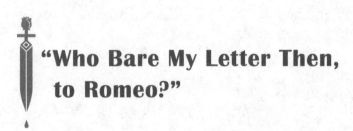

"Who Bare My Letter Then, to Romeo?"

"I know what I want for my birthday," I tell Judas as we stop in front of the doors of Forty-Second Street Studios. Cinny had to take a call (another one, that girl pretty much never gets off her phone) and is still sitting in her driver's car. "Let me borrow your phone till rehearsal is over."

"Nah, no way." Judas is texting on his phone as we speak. "Without my phone, I'd die here. Roaming about Times Square aimlessly waiting for you to get done. Plus, I need to research who is gonna be at this party tonight. See how good I need to look."

"Use your laptop. Connect to the wifi at Starbucks."

Judas shakes his head. "You can't have my phone, Jerzie. So stop askin'. You not gonna be invading my personal shit. Plus, Mom was very clear that you are not supposed to have unsupervised phone access. Sucks to be phoneless on your birthday, but I can't help you out."

Fine. I'm tired of being nice. I grab Judas by the wrist and pull him to the side of the busy sidewalk. "Give me your phone or I'll tell Mom you subscribe to a cam girl. A few actually."

Judas looks at me in disbelief.

A slow, devious smile spreads across my face. "I believe one of the websites is discomboobulate.com?" I scratch my head. "Not sure what's so sexy about watching a naked girl jump rope, but you're the freak. Not me."

"H-how do you know about that?" Judas breathes.

If I'm being honest, it was an accident. Trying to fix the Wi-Fi for Mom and Dad one day last year, and I stumbled upon the router logs. Judas's late-night internet activities seemed pretty tame, but I still remember thinking it might come in handy for blackmail purposes. And here we are.

"Judas." I cross my arms. "If you knew what I know about what you do on the internet, you'd be handing me that phone right about—"

"Take it." He hands it to me.

"Smart." I tap him on the shoulder. "Now what's the passcode?"

He tells it to me. "Don't invade my personal stuff, Jerzie."

"Judas Jhames, I'm so not interested in Nancy Drewing your boring life. I need your phone for a few hours. You'll get it back after rehearsal. I promise."

I rush into the building, pushing aside my guilt for blackmailing Judas into giving me his phone. The end justifies the means. At least, I hope so. I spot Nigel chatting with the stage manager and Rashmi near the elevator.

"Hey, you guys." I manage a fake cough, and the two men take a tiny step away from me. Rashmi steps forward, concerned.

"Are you okay, Jerzie?" she asks.

"Actually, is there any chance I could lie down in one of the break rooms for a bit? I feel a little sick."

"Don't throw up on me." Nigel studies the screen on his buzzing cell phone. "You know the musical rehearsing upstairs? They moved to tech a few days ago, so all those rooms are empty."

"I can take her up there," Rashmi offers.

"Perfect," Nigel replies. "I'll come check on you in about an hour."

About an hour? Excellent. I put on my best sick face and smile weakly. "Thank you so much."

There is something about an empty rehearsal room. The silence is so loud. It's like the energy of so many people and performances lives on in the temporary stillness. I sent Rashmi searching for banana-flavored LaCroix waters. I swore they're the only thing that can settle my tummy. They don't actually exist, so her pointless search for them will give me the alone time I need. I set down my backpack and lean against the wall. I use Judas's phone to Google Zeppelin's family's restaurant, Belle Torte. The number and address load onto the screen. I click the button to place the call. After a few rings, a girl answers.

"Thank you for calling Belle Torte. How can I help you?"

It's Marta!

"Marta? It's me. Jerzie."

"I'm sorry?" she replies.

"Uh, Patti LuPone? Zeppelin's friend."

"Oh!" She laughs. "Patti. Now I remember. How are you? Did you want to place an order?"

"No, no." I stand and pace around the empty space, talking softly even though no one is here to listen. "I'm wondering if Zeppelin might be there, by any chance."

"Zeppelin? We haven't seen him for days actually. Kinda weird."

"But doesn't he come to the restaurant to help out?"

"Normally. Yes. We've been short staffed lately, and he's always trying to help us. Maybe he's busy with the show."

The one he's fired from?

Marta goes on, "Because we can't get ahold of him. I'm glad he's busy though. It's a sad time of year for him. For all of us really. Busy is good. Patti…" she laughs "…I mean, Jerzie, we're pretty slammed today. I gotta jump off."

"Wait! Can I get his number? My, uh, phone…short… circuited and I lost all my contacts."

"Sure." She gives me his number. Yes! She gives me his number!

"Thank you so much, Marta!"

I hang up and quickly type in the number before I forget, nervously waiting while the phone rings and rings. Finally, Zeppelin's deep voice answers. My heart flutters in my chest.

"Sorry I missed you. Leave a message. Maybe I'll call you back."

The phone beeps and I take a deep breath. "Uh, Zeppelin?

Hi. It's Jerzie. Jerzie Jhames." *As if he knows another Jerzie?! Imbecile!* "This isn't my phone. It's my brother's. But I'll have it for the next hour or so. Call me or text me back, all right? I hope you're okay. Are you okay?"

I hang up. Gosh that was the *dumbest* message. I didn't even leave Judas's number. I tap the text icon and construct a message:

Hi. It's me again. Jerzie. The one who just left you the really dumb message. Here is my brother's number in case it didn't come up on the caller id. I'm worried about you. I care about you. I want you to know that I do. Care about you I mean. I always will.

I send the message and stare at the phone. Waiting. Hoping for that glorious ellipsis that shows up when people are texting right back. *Please, Zeppelin. Be okay. Text me back.* But there is no ellipsis. There is no reply. And thirty minutes later, there is still no message from Zeppelin.

I jump back online. I type the name Francesca Ricci into the search bar. Her Wikipedia page pops up, and I study the face that is so similar to Zeppelin's. It makes me want to cry. I click the link and scroll down to her death, noticing something I hadn't before. The *date*. The same as today. The anniversary of Zeppelin's mom's death is *today*? On my birthday?! This is why Marta said it was a tough time for their family.

I'm pacing again. Back and forth. Back and forth.

What do I do? Marta thinks he's busy at work. They must have no idea he was fired. I can hear the music from below now. In fact, I'm pacing in rhythm to it. I'm directly above one of the *Roman and Jewel* rehearsal rooms.

I start a new Google search:

how to check on someone who is far away if you think they're in trouble

That's quite the run-on sentence, but Google doth provide. It's called a welfare check. Okay. This sounds like what I need. Next, I search the Bay Ridge nonemergency police line and quickly dial the number.

"Bay Ridge Police. How can I help you?" a woman answers.

"Hi." I pause in my pacing, finally feeling like I'm connected to someone or something that can help. "I have a friend who I think is in trouble. And I Googled it, and it says I can ask for a welfare check." I'm breathing so hard I feel faint.

"Okay. Can you tell me a bit about what you think is happening?"

"My friend. His name is Zeppelin Reid. He's not answering his phone."

"How long have you not been able to get ahold of him?"

I look at the time. "A half hour."

The woman sighs. "Miss. How about you keep checking in with your friend and call us back when you're—"

"Miss." I can hardly breathe. "I know you don't know me, but I swear to you something is wrong. I can feel it in my gut. My friend. His mom killed herself seven years ago to date. Like literally, his mom died on this day. My birthday. Which, that's moot. But his family hasn't heard from him in days. And that's not like him. He checks in. And he wouldn't not text me back or call me back because I know he *just* had his phone because he texted Cinny."

"Cinny?" she replies.

"Yeah. Look, I know I sound crazy, but I'm not. Something is wrong!" I'm crying now. "And I can't drive because I'm only seventeen. Besides, I don't even know how to drive! Plus, I'm at work." I'm sobbing. "Please. I'm begging you. Check on my *friend*."

"Honey." The lady's voice has turned soothing. "You're gonna make yourself sick." There is a moment of silence before she says, "Tell me his name again."

"Zeppelin Reid." I wipe my eyes. Only a tiny bit of hope is restored, but I'll take it.

"And his address?"

Shit. I don't know his address. But wait. I know the name of his apartment building! "He lives at Belford Park Apartments in Bay Ridge. His apartment number is M-1202."

"M-1202. Belford Park Apartments. Okay. I'm getting it all down. What's your number?"

I give her Judas's cell number.

"It might take a while to get a unit over to the apartment. But when we do, I'll give you a call back. If I don't get back to you before my shift is over, I'll make sure to contact you first thing in the morning. Okay?"

"Thank you," I sob.

"Try to calm down, honey. Nine times outta ten, when we do these welfare checks, the person answers the door and all is well. I'm sure your friend is fine."

"Okay." I hope she's right. I hope we're not the one out of

ten scenario when no one answers and the police break down the door to find a nightmare waiting for them. "Thank you."

I end the call and slowly make my way to the piano pushed against the back wall. I plop down on the bench, logging out of Judas's Instagram account so that I can log into mine. It's the first time I've been on my account since the day I went viral.

I have so many messages. Hundreds and *hundreds* of messages. I want to take the time to read each and every one of them, but I'm on a mission here. I need to get a message to Zeppelin. Somehow. Someway. And I know he's not on social media. But maybe... I don't know. Maybe somehow this will get to him. I set the camera on the piano so I'm in full view, pausing to run my fingers lightly through my twisted curls. I hit the button to go live.

Within a few seconds, I have over a thousand people watching. So many messages are scrolling. My heart is pounding. People are listening. So what am I gonna say?

Not sure how Ram_Butt's lone message stands out among the masses, but I see it quite clearly as it scrolls by:

Ram_Butt_Booty16: Why you crying beautiful? And where the hell have you been?!

I laugh and wipe at my tears. "Today I'm gonna do something I've never done before on the Gram." I slide my fingers across the dusty white keys. "I gotta lot of new followers, so I guess I should start by introducing myself. Hi." I wave to the camera. "My name is Jerzie Jhames. Not like the state. That's J-E-R-S-E-Y. I'm J-E-R-Z-I-E. A much cooler way to spell it, if you ask me."

PacMac_123756: I love your name! It's so cool.

I smile. "Thanks, PacMac. It's growing on me."

Serendipity_DooDah: What are you gonna do Jerzie? That you've never done before on the Gram?

"I'm gonna sing," I reply.
A few hundred clapping hands fill the screen.
I lean forward and read another message.

UnicornQueen821: Are you gonna sing I Think I Remember You? That's my jam!

"I was thinking about singing a song that sorta expresses how I'm feeling right now. Or..." I pause. "What I'd like to say to someone. If he was listening anyway." I take a deep breath and play simple chords on the piano. Cinny said *he* said living was like an exercise in futility. What I wouldn't give to prove him wrong. I sing.

It's a song about friendship. A song about love. A song about someone knowing they can always count on you. Took me growing up, a little bit anyway, to understand the meaning of these simple lyrics. The song is one my dad used to play when I was a kid. I understand it now. There is nothing more powerful than the love shared between friends. Zeppelin is my friend. I wipe my tears and look back at the phone. Over five *thousand* people are watching me sit here and cry. So many messages are scrolling by.

Don't cry Jerzie.

Aww, I'll be your friend.

That's what friends are for! That's what's uuuup!

I love you Jerzie with a Z-I-E!

Right! Keep smiling girl.

Count on me! Count on me!

I smile at the messages. Nothing else matters. Not my parents. Not this musical. Not even the tears that are streaming down my cheeks. The only thing that matters is that I genuinely care about someone. I *feel*. That's all I've ever wanted. To make people feel. Who knew that started with me?

I wipe my eyes, blow a kiss to the camera…and end the live feed.

"Where Is My Romeo?"

"Yo." Judas extends his hand. "Gimme back my phone."

There's been no reply from Zeppelin, and it's been hours. No call from the Bay Ridge Police Department either. What do I do?

"Fine," I grumble. "Here." The subway is slowing to a stop in front of us. As I move to return the phone to Judas, it vibrates in my hand. An unknown number is calling! I snatch the cell back and click the button to accept the call. "Hello? Hello?"

"Hi, is this Jerzie Jhames?"

Judas is glaring at me.

I gesture dramatically and whisper, "What! It's for me."

"This is Genie Haddock with the Bay Ridge Police Department."

"Hi!" I follow Judas as we pile into the packed subway car and grab onto the nearest metal bar, positioning myself for a standing ride. "Is he okay? Did you talk to him?"

"Two officers dispatched were unable to do a welfare check with the information provided. No one resided at the unit M-1202."

The train lurches forward, and I stumble a bit, almost crashing into Judas. I wrap my arm around the bar to steady myself, the phone pressed so forcefully to my ear that it's causing me physical pain. "So he wasn't home?"

"I'm afraid no one lives at the address you provided. That particular unit was *empty*."

"That's impossible, miss. Unit M-1202. Twelfth floor? Are you sure? Belford Park Apartments in Bay Ridge?"

"The officers were adamant. The apartment was empty. No one lives there. In fact, they said it looks as if someone may have recently moved out. I'm sorry we weren't able to help you."

An empty apartment? "Is it possible to speak with the apartment manager maybe? Hello?" *Shit.* I look at the screen. Lost the call.

Judas snatches the phone from my hand.

"Finally." His head swiftly slumps and his thumbs move into position.

I tap him on the shoulder. "Judas. I might get a text. Or a call."

"Damn. Cut the cord." He twists around so that the phone is out of my eye line.

"Judas, please," I whisper. "I'm waiting on a message from someone."

"Stop buggin'," he whispers back. "Move on. It's over. No service down here anyway. Now back off."

Like I even have a choice. We ride the rest of the way in silence.

★ ★ ★

I stare at my reflection in the mirror. I'm wearing makeup. Something I don't normally attempt. My lips are tinted plum, my eyelids dusted with a glittery pink shadow, and I'm wearing my hair down, my twisted curls surrounding my face in perfect symmetry. And Aunt Karla dressed me before she headed off for work. A mini skirt, a Queen T-shirt that hangs off the shoulder and black leather ankle boots. I certainly look like a girl headed to an industry party, even if I don't necessarily feel like going to one.

Living is an exercise in futility? How could he say such a thing?

"Jerzie?" Judas taps lightly on the open door and steps inside the master bedroom. The scent of his cologne reaches me before he does.

I cover my nose. "Judas. Did you take a bath in body spray?"

"Smells good, huh?" He's fixing the knot on his metallic silver tie, which looks supersparkly against the dark blue of his dress shirt. "It's Tom Ford, Calvin Klein, Nautica, a few others I think. I got some of those cologne samples from a magazine of Aunt Karla's and rubbed them all over me."

"That's the dumbest and stinkiest idea you've ever had."

"Watch the ladies tonight. They gonna be all over me." He nods in my direction. "Nice look, sis. If I didn't know you, I'd never guess you were a drama nerd who listens to show tunes in her spare time."

"Very funny."

"Ride share should be here in a few minutes."

I slump down on the bed.

"So come on. Let's go wait outside."

"Judas." I cover my face with my shaking hands and mumble. "Would you hate me if I didn't go?"

He moves quickly to sit beside me on the bed. "Talk to me, sis."

"I'm not in the mood. Go without me. Have fun."

"And let you spend your birthday alone?"

"Judas." I burst into shoulder-shaking sobs. "I'm worried about Zeppelin."

"Who?"

"The guy Mom demanded I stay away from? The one who uploaded the videos of me and of Cinny?"

"Ooooh, the pale-face white boy you like."

"Yes." I roll my eyes, even as I'm sniffling and wiping away tears. "Him. Call me dramatic, but I think he's gonna try to kill himself today. If he hasn't already."

"That's deep, Jerzie. Why you think that?"

"Today is the day his mom did the same thing. Seven years ago she…killed herself. And today I couldn't get ahold of him. And the Bay Ridge police said his apartment is empty. Like, he moved out? What if he moved out and jumped off a bridge or something? Judas…" I look into my brother's eyes. "What if he's done something to hurt himself? Or what if he's planning to? I'll never forgive myself if I don't at least try to find a way to help him."

"Hold up," Judas says. "You had a welfare check done on your boy? Yo, that's intense. When?"

"Today. I used your phone to call the police." I sniff. "And they said the place was empty. Vacant. How can that be? I was just there."

Judas's phone chimes. He checks the screen. "Damn, Jerzie.

Ride share's almost here. Please come. Don't sit here crying all by yourself. I'm sure he's fine."

"But…" I stand, pacing in front of Judas. "Wh–what if he's not?" I cry. "Judas, I can't go anywhere. I'm too upset." I'm crying so hard now that my throat is aching, my vision blurry. "Go without me. Have fun. Don't miss out on an opportunity like this. I'll be all right."

"You really care about this dude, huh?"

I nod, tears spilling down my cheeks.

Judas stands. "I'll be right back, okay?"

He doesn't wait for an answer, just darts out of the room. I imagine he's checking to see if the ride share is outside, but a few seconds later he returns, out of breath, at the doorway.

"What are you doing?" I ask.

"I rebooted the Wi-Fi."

My brow furrows. "Why?"

"It takes about twenty minutes to reboot. Which means as of right now, the security cameras are deactivated."

I stare at Judas. "I don't get it."

"I don't want Aunt Karla to see me leave by myself. And then see *you* leave a few minutes later." He crosses to me. Hands me his phone. "Call yourself a ride share. After you check on your boy, come to Slate. With my phone, damnit. That's an *order*. You will not spend your birthday alone. A'ight?"

"Omigosh." I lurch forward and hug Judas. "Thank you so much. You *are* the best brother in the universe."

"*Man*. I been tryin' to tell you that!" He rests his head on my shoulder. "And I hope your boy is okay. I really do."

I hope so, too. "Judas?" I pull away and look into his eyes. "You *stiiiink*. Why did you mix all those cologne samples together?"

"What? You trippin', girl. I smell good."

I stand and fan away the pure stench of him.

"The girls will be like moths to a flame on me tonight. I swear they will."

"A moth flying into a fire is not a good thing."

We both laugh. It feels good to laugh. I hate to admit Dad was right, but he was *right*. Being alone this summer would've been a terrible idea. I'm with my big brother.

So thankful.

Aunt Karla's street is dark and eerily still when I rush toward the Chevy Impala that is my ride share, pull open the door, and slide into the car as swiftly and quietly as I can.

"Hey, how's it going?" the driver, a girl in her twenties, asks. I like her energy. She's playing Jay-Z's "The Story of O.J." I relax a bit and buckle in.

"It's going."

"What's in Bay Ridge?"

"Just...the love of my life."

"Aww. Man, I wish I had one of those," she says. "Anyway. Not so much traffic. We should be there in half an hour."

I type Zeppelin's address into the map app on Judas's phone so that I can follow the route and lean my head back. This is me throwing caution to the freaking wind. This time I don't need a substance to be unfiltered the way I was at Washington Square Park.

This is all me.

When the ride share pulls up to the curb of Zeppelin's brick apartment building, I tip the driver on the app, thank her profusely, and climb out of the car. As she's driving off into the dead of night, I peek through the gate of the parking area.

Zeppelin's motorcycle is parked in his spot! But wait, maybe that's a bad sign. How could his motorcycle be parked in his spot and his apartment be empty?

Because the police officers are wrong, that's why. They must've gotten the apartments mixed up somehow. I rush to the front door. Of course it's locked. But I see a lady inside, checking her mail at the boxes. I knock on the glass. She turns, eyes me suspiciously.

"Hi!" I wave. "I forgot my key card. Can you let me in?"

She moves toward me, pushes the door open. I step inside.

"Thank you. Sorry. I forgot my key card. I just moved in with my boyfriend. Twelfth floor. I think he's asleep, cuz he's not returning my texts."

"The elevator won't work without the card," she responds kindly. I must look trustworthy in spite of the blatant lies, cuz she adds, "Let me help you."

I follow her to the elevator. When the doors slide open, she steps in, waves her key card over the sensor and hits 12 for me.

"Thank you so much."

"I hate these new key cards. Makes everything so difficult. But no worries. What was your name?"

"Patti. Patti LuPone. Thanks again."

The doors slide shut, and the elevator lurches into movement. I have no real plan. The police said the apartment was empty. Maybe somehow they got it wrong. I'll find him. He'll be okay. If he's in a bad place, I'll talk him off the ledge. Help him see that living is not an exercise in futility. Then I'll take another ride share back to the party. All will be well. So now I have a plan. It's a good one.

I think.

The elevator slows to a stop, and the doors slide open on the twelfth floor. I step into the hallway and move cautiously toward apartment 1202. I pause when I make it to the door, take the deepest of breaths, and knock softly. No answer. I knock again. Nothing. I'm banging now. Still no answer. I'm banging and banging and banging and banging. No one is answering!

Finally, the door across the hallway is pulled open. An older guy peeks his head into the hallway.

"Hey, kid, you trying to wake the dead?"

I spin around. *Am I?* "God, I hope not."

"You lookin' for Zeppelin?"

"Yes." My heart is racing. "Do you know where he is? Have you seen him?" I step toward the man's apartment, hopeful he's the missing link that can lead me to Zepp.

"I haven't seen Zeppelin for a couple of days."

"Oh." My shoulders slump. "Oh. Okay."

"Not since he moved downstairs. Bastard got one of the apartments with a balcony."

I look up. *"What?"*

"Yeah, yeah. If you ask me, it's cuz the manager's got a sick and unhealthy crush on that kid. She's a cougar. Fifty-two and married. Zeppelin could be her son! Besides, it was my turn. I put in a request for a balcony unit, too."

"What's the unit number?" I almost scream. "Do you know?!"

"L-1101. It's the biggest studio in the building. Lucky bastard."

"Sir." I fold my hands in prayer. "Can you please let me in the elevator so I can go down to see him? It won't work without a card."

"Use the stairs." He shakes his head. "Today's youth. Pretty—but lacking in the intelligence department. Once you're on one of the floors, the stair doors are open. It's the law, you know. You can't lock stair doors. Fire hazard."

He slams his door shut and I look down the hallway. I spot the sign for the stairs and literally run toward it, my heels *click clack*ing on the laminate flooring. I pull open the door and race down to the next floor. When I find apartment 1101, I stop to try to catch my breath before I pound on the door with all my might.

No answer. I knock again. Nothing. I'm banging. Still no answer. He's not home. But he's okay. I mean, he took the time to move, so surely that's a good sign. Right? But my eyes are still welling with tears. I came all this way. I only want to know if he's really all right.

I slide down onto the floor in front of the door. I can sit and wait. For a little bit at least. But what if his neighbor got the numbers wrong? What if this isn't his apartment, after all?

I lean my head back just as the door is yanked open. I yelp as my head slams onto the wood floor of the apartment. I wince in pain and stare up into the face of…Zeppelin.

And yep. He's alive.

"I Will Lie with Thee Tonight"

"Jerzie?" I'd say Zeppelin looks a little dumbstruck. But more important, he looks *alive*.

I jump up. Rub the back of my head. "You're okay!"

"Why wouldn't I be okay?"

"I know it's the anniversary of your mom's death," I blurt. "I was doing a welfare check on you."

He doesn't move. His hand rests on his doorknob, and he's staring at me as if he's trying to figure out what to make of this. "Do your parents know you're here?"

"No. But..." I hold up Judas's phone "...I tried calling you, and you didn't answer. And then I called the police."

"You did *what*?"

"I called the police to come check on you, and they said your apartment was empty, and so I freaked. I was so worried. Your neighbor gave me your new apartment number.

Did you get my messages? And the one I sent to you on Insta-gram? I know you're not *on* Instagram. But. I was thinking maybe you might be. Like a random occurrence."

I survey the apartment. There are only a couple of stacked boxes to even indicate a move took place. It's in perfect order. Like he's been living here for months and months. "Why didn't you call me back, Zeppelin?" I cry.

"I didn't know you called. I accidentally stepped on my cell a couple days ago. Haven't had time to get a new one yet."

"But you texted Cinny today."

He frowns. "Impossible."

What? "Zeppelin. She showed me your text. It said some-thing like, please, talk to me. I read it. Stop lying to me! Be up front with me, okay? You owe me that!"

He finally lets his hand slide off the door handle, and the door slams shut, making me jump a little as he skirts around the remaining boxes and moves to his bed. He grabs his phone—his very shattered phone—and crosses back to where I stand near the door. "Here." He places it in my hands. "Turn it on and let's see if I sent a message to Cinny today."

I press the side button to power the phone on. It lights up, but after a minute, only a bunch of weird lines are displayed on the cracked screen. There's nothing really to see beyond that.

"See? My phone is completely inoperable. Texted Cinny? How?"

"But I saw a text from you."

"Trickery. She's fucking with you." He takes Judas's phone out of my hands. "Let me show you something. Unlock this for me."

I do and watch as he types Cinny's name and the date into the search engine.

"If you want the most recent pic of a celebrity, Google their name and the date," he explains. Pictures of Cinny load onto the screen. Zeppelin scrolls through them.

"That was today!" I stare at the pic of Judas and me entering Gush with Cinny among the bunch.

"I see she got the pics of her new BFF out into the wild. The girl works fast." Zeppelin points. "There."

It's a photo of Cinny sitting in some sort of club, lovingly embracing the spiky-haired white rapper known as Shivers.

"This picture was taken a few weeks ago. With her *boyfriend*. Shivers. Before you came around, he would come to rehearsals from time to time. See the date? This picture was taken when she and I were supposed to be secretly dating. My guess? The text you saw? She saved her actual boyfriend under my name to make it seem like I was texting her. I've had no contact with her. Not since I got fired from the show."

"No." I shake my head. "This is not what I'm talking about, Zepp. I don't need to see this to know you weren't dating Cinny. That much I've already figured out on my own."

"You have?"

"Of course I have. But the video uploads. The complicated story? Tell me now, Zeppelin."

He sighs.

"Zeppelin," I say softly. "You asked me to trust you. And here I am. Trusting you. You have to trust me, too. With the truth."

He pushes his hair off his face, and I note the dark circles under his eyes. It hasn't been that long since I last saw him, but he looks thinner than I remember. Paler, too. His eyes look swollen, his expression, pained.

"I didn't upload the video of you." He leans against the wall and stares up at the ceiling. "Or the video of Cinny. It's complicated, because it wasn't me."

"What?"

He looks at me now. "It wasn't me, Jerzie. I didn't do it."

"But… Zeppelin!"

"Please understand."

"Understand *what?*" I take a deep breath, struggling to be calm. "Zeppelin," I repeat, quieter this time. "You lost your job…your career, and you didn't even do it? *You're* not the one who uploaded the video?"

"I didn't lose my career. I can bounce back from this. I've bounced back from worse."

"So then who did it?"

"Three people were at my apartment the day those videos were uploaded. Damon. Angel. And Lorin."

Lorin. It had to be Lorin. She hates Cinny! "You have to tell Robbie."

"No. I don't."

"Zeppelin, this is your *life.*"

"I know, Jerzie. It's my life. But it's theirs, too." He heaves a sigh. "I guess I'm okay to take the fall for one of them. I'd do the same for you. You know I would."

"But, Zeppelin…" I want to beg and plead with him. He has to be rational. With a word, he'd be back in the show. He'd be Roman again. It's what everybody wants. Shouldn't it be what he wants, too? How can I make him see that getting his job back should be his top priority? The show needs him. *I* need him.

I stare down at my hands, doing that dumb thing where I'm trying to twist my fingers off. Somehow my gaze shifts to the door of his closet. From where I'm standing, I have a perfect view inside. It's practically empty except for a few items hanging and a tiny pile folded on one of the shelves. Now my gaze moves to the two remaining boxes stacked beside his bed. There is no way all of his clothes are in those two tiny boxes.

"I'm sorry. Where are your clothes?"

"I donated them."

"You *gave away all your clothes*?"

"I did keep the stuff I didn't steal."

I can only stand there, speechless, staring into the nearly empty closet.

"Most people can't afford to dress the way I do, and I came to realize I'm one of them."

I have no idea why imagining all of Zeppelin's clothes at some sort of Goodwill makes me feel like throwing up. "Did you do that because of me?"

"Yeah."

And now I'm crying. Damn my eyes and their never-ending tears. "Do you hate me now?"

"If by hate you mean love, then yes." He manages a weak smile. "I hate you. A lot. With all my heart."

I wipe my eyes. "Can I hug you, please?"

"God, I wish you would."

I rush into his arms.

"Zeppelin." I wrap my arms around his neck. He lifts me effortlessly off the floor, and my legs wrap around his waist.

"I've missed you so much." And here, in his arms, I could stay forever. I really could.

He stumbles deeper into his apartment, holding me tightly. He slowly lowers me onto his bed. He stares down at me, one hand holding his hair off his face, the other holding up his body weight as he leans over me. "Do you hate me, too, Jerzie?"

"If by hate *you* mean love? Then yes." I laugh and wipe tears off my face. "So much so, I question my sanity."

"Crazy in love. Right there with you." He crawls into his bed beside me, and we turn to face one another. Only tiny slivers of light peek through his closed blinds, but it's enough to see his eyes so clearly, his lips, his face. The sadness in his eyes. I trace my finger along his jaw.

"How are you here right now, Jerzie?" he whispers. "Is your family downstairs armed and ready to kill me?"

"My mom and dad are home in New Brunswick. My aunt is working. My brother is at a party at the new Slate near Times Square. With Cinny. He's waiting for me there and swears not to tell anyone where I've been. He knew I was worried about you. I thought you were dead."

"Impossible." Zeppelin wipes my tears. "If I were dead, you would know it, because my ghost would be driving you insane."

"Zeppelin." I shake my head. "Don't you want your job back?"

"I do. Yeah." He takes my hand into his. "After my final audition, when they told me I'd gotten the job, I was walking down Ninth Street in the East Village. Headed to Thomas's place to tell him the good news. And there was a street performer. She was standing there playing 'Casta Diva' on her violin. Do you know that song?"

I shake my head. It's not one I know.

"It's an aria. From Bellini's *Norma*. *Norma* was the production my mom was in before she had her accident. 'Casta Diva' was her favorite song. Tell me that was a coincidence. I wouldn't believe you."

Now it's me who reaches out to wipe away tears as they slide down his cheeks.

"It was surreal. That's not even a street where street performers usually are. It probably sounds weird, but it felt like my mom had come to congratulate me. To tell me she was with me and always will be. I stood there and listened to the whole song, crying on the freaking street corner."

I slide closer to him. "I don't think that sounds weird at all, Zeppelin."

"Broadway was never my dream. But music is my life. It keeps me eternally connected to her." He pauses to gently caress my cheek. "I know she's with me, Jerzie. I feel her around me. So many random miracles happen in my life. I know I'll always be okay. I know she's looking out for me." Now the sadness returns to his eyes. "But who's looking out for Lorin? Her sister is disabled and can't work, so she financially supports her *and* her sister's two kids. And Damon hadn't been able to find a job after *Sing Star*. Nobody would hire him. He was living with different friends. Couch surfing when he got the gig. And the production paid for Angel's work visa. He can't stay in the country if he's not working on *Roman and Jewel*."

Of course I understand now. "You're an amazing friend, Zeppelin. Don't ever change."

He pulls me close to him. "How long do we have? Before

you have to get back? I can give you a ride." He traces my lips with his finger.

"Before Cinny's party ends," I admit. "I'm a little like Cinderella, needing to get *to* the ball before midnight instead of away from it."

"If you don't mind riding on my bike, I can get you there before you turn back into a pumpkin."

"In a parallel scenario..." I frown. "Wouldn't your bike be the thing turning into the pumpkin?"

"Why are you such a nerd?" He smiles. "Promise *you'll* never change."

And suddenly we're kissing. And I'm not so sure if I'm doing it right, but I do remember that Zeppelin said there are one million nerve endings on our lips, so hopefully he's happy to have my lips touching one million parts of him. It's only when his hand slides under my shirt that I tense. He immediately stops and pulls his hand away to lovingly touch my cheek.

"You're in control, Jerzie," he whispers. "I'm happy to just lie next to you. Being with you is all I need."

"But you said you'd teach me things."

"I'll teach you everything I know. We can learn the rest together."

It's dawning on me that this touching thing goes both ways. I can finally run my fingers along all the muscles on his stomach. So I do that, reaching under his loose-fitting T-shirt. Which I guess prompts him to pull the entire thing off. And if I thought Zeppelin felt warm before, he's practically a furnace now that he's half-naked. I rest my hands on his chest, and for the first time, I feel his heart beating quite fast. As fast as mine.

We lie together for a while, kissing, holding one another tight. Touching in ways that sends energy pulsing through all parts of me. With every movement he makes, he pauses to whisper into my ear, to ask me if I'm okay.

I freak out only a little bit when he reaches into a drawer beside his bed and pulls out a box.

"Condoms?" I ask softly.

"I mean…" He laughs. "I know it's been a billion years. But I'm really in no rush. I'm gonna be your first everything. Including your first perfect gentleman." He hands me the box. "Happy birthday, Jerzie." He smiles. "Billion-year-old boyfriends know everything."

Of course he would know it's my birthday. But… "It's the same day as—"

"I know." He nods sadly. "Just another message from Mom. My darkest day turned bright from now on."

I sit up in his bed and with trembling hands, untie the simple red ribbon on the small box. Inside is an engraved silver bracelet. I study the inscription:

Maybe this time…

It's the song from *Cabaret*. The beautiful lyric. The one that makes me cry. Zeppelin's gentle hand wipes tears as they slide down my cheeks. He slips the bracelet onto my wrist. It feels cool, sending a shiver up my spine.

"Maybe this time." He wraps his arms around me.

"Definitely this time." I rest my head on his shoulder.

"I love you. I really do."

"I love you, too, Zeppelin."

"Oh Blessed, Blessed Night"

Riding on the back of Zeppelin's motorcycle, my arms wrapped around his waist, my head resting against his back, the wind rushing by so fast, the city so monstrous, so garish around us, it feels as if we are the only thing quiet; we are the eye of the great, raging hurricane known as New York City. I close my eyes and try to capture my feelings the way a camera can capture a moment in time. I want to remember this forever. Being here, with him.

Zeppelin slows to a stop at a red light and turns to me, shouting over the roar of his bike and the nighttime city traffic. "You up for a quick detour? It won't take long. Promise."

I nod. We're in Times Square, close to our final destination. A quick detour can't hurt. He turns into a parking garage, and within a moment, we're parked and walking arm in arm.

Times Square at night—it needs one of those signs for when

you arrive. Like the ones you see at theme parks, in line, before you get on a roller coaster. The WARNING in big bold letters, followed by a list of people who should turn back:

People with heart problems.

People sensitive to bright, flashing lights.

People who *don't* like to be scared shitless.

Zeppelin holds tightly to my hand as he steers through the crowd. I wouldn't call it bumper to bumper—more like arm to arm, because the people pileup is *real*. If I was walking with Aunt Karla in this kind of foot traffic, she would have veered off the main roads and found some sort of shortcut. Through a back alley. Around a building. *Through* a building.

I marvel at the woman's savvy traffic-avoidance navigation skills, but am also marveling at the way Zeppelin appears to revel in it all. He seems unaffected by the melee. Happy even. I give myself permission to be unaffected, too. And suddenly, I'm swept away by the magic of this strange section of midtown, where anything goes and everything incites the senses. My neck tilts back, my mouth watering as I inhale the aroma of street food and gaze up at the flashing neon billboards as big as our house back in New Brunswick, my ears buzzing from the roar of the crowd, heart racing from the warmth of Zeppelin's hand holding mine.

A man on skates, dressed in gold spandex from head to toe, spins in fast circles. Even his head and face are covered in gold spandex, and I wonder how he's breathing. He's attracting a ton of attention, spinning and spinning in front of the iconic red stairs, where people can sit and gaze peacefully.

"Never trust a man dressed like an Academy Award." Zeppelin holds on to my hand a little bit tighter, and I smile.

We turn down Broadway, and a show must be letting out, because hundreds of people flood through the doors of a theater we're passing, looking relaxed after a night of what I'm sure were phenomenal performances. Couples walk together, kids chat excitedly. Zeppelin steps around a cluster of older women who hold their Playbills tight as they load onto a tour bus. He moves to a stage door, where a line is forming.

"Marcel!" He shouts over a crowd-control gate to a beefy security guard, who waves at him.

"Zepp! *Yo.* Where you been, man?"

"Hibernation," Zeppelin says. "Hey, help me out? Can you let us in across the street?"

Marcel nods. "No doubt. Show just let out. Gimme like ten, and Imma get somebody to cover me here. I'll meet you over there."

"Cool." Zeppelin turns to me. "We're gonna cross."

He pulls my hand, and I follow him, weaving around cars stuck in crawling traffic. We quickly make it to the other side. Half a block later, we approach another theater, this one seeming all shut down like it's a Monday, the only day the theater takes off. But today isn't Monday.

I place my hands over my mouth, not sure why it took me so long to realize where we are. This is the Broadway Theatre. This is where *Roman and Jewel* will be running.

"This is us. Well, I mean, you." Zeppelin smiles weakly.

"What are we doing here?"

He steers me to the stage door. "Robbie and I have been emailing back and forth all week. He told me they'd be finished with the set, but they're having some pretty intense tech issues with the floor and flew in an expert from London who could only work during a certain time window. So I think they might be here now. Marcel's gonna let us in. Pretty sure no other cast member has set foot on this stage. You'll be the first. As it should be."

I clap my hands excitedly. "So cool, Zeppelin." Of course, then I realize this moment that is making me so giddy might cause him some pain. "Wait. Are you sure? We don't have to go in. I feel bad."

"Don't. It might be the only time I get to share the stage with you."

Those words sting. A lot. "What if I talked to them? To Angel and Damon and Lorin? I could get them—"

"No." Zeppelin shakes his head. "Whoever did it probably did it as a joke. I'm gonna guess they never intended for it to go viral, and I sure as hell don't think they ever thought they could lose their job over it. Robbie's looking out for me. He got me an audition for a show that's looking for a very special actor to play Kurt Cobain."

"Kurt Cobain?" How perfect would Zeppelin be as Kurt Cobain?

"It's called *The Death of Rock 'n' Roll*. It's the story of Nirvana. Off Broadway. Premiering at the Public Theater."

"That's where *Hamilton* started!"

"I know." He grins.

I lurch forward and hug him. Zeppelin *would* be great as Kurt Cobain. But he was born to play Roman. I'm about to speak these very words when the security guard Marcel makes his way to where we stand. He and Zeppelin do that overly masculine "hug" guys do where they bang shoulders and slap each other on the back.

"This is Jerzie." Zeppelin introduces me to the beefy guard. I wave. "Hi."

Marcel tips his head. "Nice to meet you, Queen."

I watch him unlock the door and motion us to go through. "Text me when you're leaving so I can make sure everything's all locked up."

Zeppelin holds up empty hands. "No phone."

I whip out Judas's phone. "I can text you."

Marcel gives me his number, and I save it in Judas's contacts.

"If anybody asks," Marcel says, "it wasn't me who let you in. I'm not playin' with you, man."

"No doubt." Zeppelin laughs.

After Zeppelin and I step through, the heavy door slams shut after us. Technically we're still outside. It's that space in between buildings. Night sky above us. Zeppelin leads me toward a door at the end of the walkway. We pull it open and step through.

It's pretty dark, so we use the light from Judas's cell phone to guide us around a few corners until, at last, we are literally backstage in a Broadway theater. It's not glamorous. It's the opposite, in fact. Stage lights on the floor, Fresnel lights lining the walls and hanging from the ceiling. Scaffolding. Setups of laptops and computers. Giant, dusty speakers. Multitiered carts stacked with equipment. Metal ladders, wires, cords—is that a *helium* tank?

Zeppelin and I crouch between some of the larger light fixtures on the floor. In front of us, the main stage is pretty much disemboweled, and crew members are working with a mass of wires and cables. A man who looks like he's in his

forties, with short, curly blond hair and a heavy British accent, laughs and chats with Alan Kaplan.

"That's the technician they flew in," Zeppelin whispers,
his breath tickling my ear.

"As long as it works, I don't actually care *how* it works."
Alan yawns. "*You* could be under there for all I care."

I can't believe he'll be at rehearsal bright and early tomorrow morning after having spent the night here. Broadway must never end for him. Behind them, I note the tiered
rows of empty theater chairs. Hundreds of them, all uphol-
stered with that classic, lush red fabric that looks like velvet.
To think, people will be sitting in these very chairs so soon.
Watching the cast of *Roman and Jewel*. One day, maybe even
watching me.

I glance up at the wood carved ceiling. I do this whenever I visit Broadway theaters. Staring at the ceiling with my
cell phone pointed up like your basic Times Square tourist
who crowds up the sidewalk by stopping midstep to stare at
buildings. But this ceiling...you'd swear Michelangelo rose
from the dead to supervise its intricate, detailed construction
with all the violet and indigo colors. Surrounding the pro-
scenium are gold archways lined with crimson and heavy, red
velvet curtains that look plucked straight from a theater in
the Southwark district of London, where Shakespeare's plays
were performed for the very first time. I imagine these curtains traveled through a time warp to get here.

Zeppelin and I crouch and watch. I've no idea why this
group of men, working hard to prep a stage against the backdrop of an empty theater, is so mesmerizing. Why did Zeppelin think I would enjoy this so much? How did he know?

I'm not sure how much time has passed when I get distracted by Judas's phone, lighting up in my hand. It's a text message from an unknown number:

Jerzie. It's Judas. You need to get here. Damon is letting me text from his phone. Hurry UP.

My stomach churns. The party's not over for another hour at least. I compose a message back:

Judas. Headed that way. Everything ok?

He texts back: Eh. I'll explain when you get here. You're not on the list though, so be creative about how to get in. But get in Jerzie. You gotta.

I place a hand on Zeppelin's shoulder. He turns to me. I show him the messages.

"What do you think happened?" he asks softly.

"No idea," I whisper. But that's a lie. Because whatever has happened, I'm certain it involves Cinny being her very terrible self.

"A Plague o' Both Your Houses!"

We opt to walk to Slate. It's only a few blocks away and saves us from having to find new parking for Zeppelin's motor- cycle. He squeezes my hand tightly as we near the building on Fiftieth. A red carpet has been rolled out in front of the new storefront. There are reporters, camera people, and se- curity guards lining the carpet. Screaming teenagers crowd the sidewalk, holding up cell phones, taking flashing photos, selfies, and videos. There's a monster traffic pileup as drivers slow to see what all the commotion is about. It's chaos. If I'm not on the list, how exactly are we supposed to get in? I look at Zeppelin, hoping maybe he might have some sort of solu- tion. He seems as dumbfounded by the scene as me.

An idea forms.

"I think I know what to do!" I shout over the roar, pull- ing an Aunt Karla and expertly weaving through the crowd until we've pushed to the front where the gates are set up. "Zepp!" I scream. "I'm gonna jump over!"

He widens his eyes. "Serious?"

"I'm so serious." The crowd-control gates reach to about my chest. We can easily jump over. I mean, I might need a boost. "You have to do it with me."

"So, breaking in is your idea?" He points. There are quite a few security guards stationed at different points, and two police officers, that I can see—there are probably more—stand near the front entrance. "You cool with being arrested?"

"We'll be fine. I think." *I hope.*

"That's the kind of confidence I like to hear." He places a hand on my back. "You sure about this, Jerzie?"

I kiss him on the cheek. He always feels so blazing hot. "I'm sure. Let's jump overboard."

Thankfully Zeppelin asks no more questions and moves fast. He gives me a boost, and then in a matter of seconds he's jumped over after me. I grab his hand and drag him along as I push around a few photographers to rush onto the red carpet.

I look over my shoulder. One of the police officers makes eye contact with me. *Shit.* Now two security guards are approaching from opposite ends. Zeppelin and I exchange worried expressions as we stand, dead center on the red carpet like two deer facing fast oncoming traffic. But then my glorious plan takes flight.

"Look! It's Jerzie Jhames! It's Cinny's best friend!" a voice screams.

Someone recognized me. Thank the internet, they *recognized* me.

The screams amplify, and reporters call out. I grip Zeppelin's hand tight, watching the security guards retreat to their assigned positions. We're safe.

I smile at the cameras, as if standing dead center on red carpets is something I do. I wave. I laugh. I pose.

"Jerzie Jhames!"

"Jerze! Over here."

"Jerzie, can I get a smile!"

"Right in this direction, Jerzie!"

"Jerzie, who are you wearing?"

"Jerzie Jhames, who's your date?"

This question, I take a moment to shout an answer to. "Zeppelin Reid."

"Zeppelin!" they yell.

"Zeppelin Reid, over here!"

Zeppelin leans down to whisper in my ear. "I have never been more impressed with you."

I laugh. If I'm being honest, I've never been more impressed with myself.

"Jerzie and Zeppelin! Can we get a kiss from *Roman and Jewel*?"

I turn to Zeppelin. I can hear the *click click click* of dozens of cameras as I step on my tiptoes, and Zeppelin leans in so that our lips connect. He wraps an arm around my waist, and I rest a hand on his cheek. Real-life Romeo and Juliet. Reunited at last.

We wave to the crowd and move toward the entrance. The two doormen simply step to the side. Neither bothers asking who we are, since people are still screaming our names. And suddenly we are through to the other side.

We're *in*.

Music blares. Lights are dim but the unique setup shines bright, since most of the furniture and accessories seem to be glowing neon. Feels like we've stepped through one of the billboards from Times Square and into an alternate dimension.

The best way to describe Slate: it's sorta like an adult, indoor playground. It spans three different floors. There are giant Connect Fours, human-size chess pieces on life-size boards where partygoers engage in laughter-infused competition. There's also the focal point of the entire place, a monstrous, spiral tube slide, like the kind you'd see at a children's park. It must start somewhere on the top floor and twist all the way down to the main level. How *fun*. Over the roar of the music, I can hear the sound of heavy pins falling onto hardwood from the bowling alley upstairs. People are crowded around all of the many bars Slate has positioned on each floor. Just as I'm about to compose a text to Damon's phone, I feel a tap on my shoulder and turn to face my brother, his silver tie glowing under the neon lighting.

"Judas!" I lurch forward and hug him.

He shouts, "Glad you made it back from your trip in one piece, sis!"

I turn to Zeppelin. "This is Zeppelin. He's okay!"

Judas extends his hand. "Happy to see you alive, man."

"Happy to be alive." Zeppelin and Judas shake hands.

"So what's going on?" I ask.

"Jerzie," he starts. "First of all, when I got to the door, I wasn't on the list. I thought maybe I could get in on your name. No dice. You weren't on the list either. I didn't have a phone or a way to contact Cinny, so I stood outside for like forever. Lookin' like a damn fool. Thank goodness I ran into your friends from the show. They sneaked me in through the back. Speaking of which, Damon's got the video on his phone, they're upstairs."

Video?

We follow Judas up a set of stairs lit and somehow glowing from underneath. When we reach the top, I see Angel, Damon, and Lorin playing a game of pool at one of the many tables. I can't help but glare at the three. One of them has added ruining Zeppelin's life to their plush résumé.

"Oh my God, he *lives*." Damon tosses his pool stick on the table, and suddenly all three descend upon Zeppelin in a mash-up of hugs and happy greetings.

"Why haven't you called me *back*?" Lorin is squeezing Zeppelin, her eyes tightly closed, her head resting on his shoulder. "I thought you were dead or something."

"You're not the only one," Zeppelin replies. "My phone got smashed. Couldn't contact anybody."

Lorin's eyes are welling up with tears. Was it her? Was she the one who did it? She *has* been moping around the studios.

"How'd you get in?" Angel asks us. "Don't tell me She-Who-Must-Not-Be-Named put you on the list? I won't believe it."

Zeppelin turns to me. "Jerzie used her internet stardom to get us past security. What about you guys?"

"Same," Damon admits. "That bitch didn't have *any* of us on the list like she said she would. Thankfully fans recognized me from *Sing Star* and I was able to get Lorin and Angel in by saying they're in the show with me. We sneaked your brother in after that."

"Cinny's performing in one of the upstairs rooms. Right

now," Angel says. "Select guests only. But Wesley recognized us earlier, and we got to watch her mic check."

"Wesley?" I repeat.

"Her security guard," Damon reminds me.

"And it's crazy dark in there," Angel adds. "So she didn't see us come in. She had no clue we were watching her."

"Show her the video." Judas motions to Damon.

Damon extends his phone. A video is playing on his screen. I watch as Cinny finishes one of her most popular songs. She brings the mic closer to her mouth. "So then I'll talk for a few seconds about the new song? Right?"

Not sure who she's talking to and can't hear their reply back to her. But Cinny replies, "I'll say something like, Spade produced this. We laid down the vocals tonight actually. Blah blah. It's gonna be my new single. Yada yada. Y'all are gettin' an exclusive listen. Then I'll start the song."

I recognize the song as it begins. It's the track Cinny played for me and Judas earlier today. But then she begins to sing. It's the melody I made up. The lyrics are not mine. But the melody *is*.

"She's singing my song." I look at Judas and smile. "She's using my melody?"

Judas shakes his head despondently. "Keep watching."

The song ends and someone steps to Cinny. She's still mic'd so I hear her when she says, "Omigosh thank you. Me and Spade wrote it. It's our very first collab." She laughs. "It's like our ode to Steven Tyler. An R & B rock fusion. We decided to get grimy with it. You know? I've been trying to get Spade to write a song with me for years, and he finally likes something of mine. Finally."

And then the mic turns off, and I can no longer hear her. Nothing else I wanna see anyway. An ode to Steven Tyler? Ha! She didn't even know who he was! I hand the phone back to Damon. The Earth is slowing to a screeching halt once again. Tsunamis are destroying the coastlines. Trees are being uprooted. But the world isn't ending. Just me being sensible is. Though, if I'm being honest, *sensible* went out the window quite a few hours ago.

"She's not gettin' away with this. *This* is where I draw the line."

I storm off.

"Jerzie, wait!" Zeppelin rushes to catch up with me, grabbing my arm and stopping me at the base of the stairs. "What are you gonna do?"

"Confront her!" I cry. "Zeppelin, I wrote what she's singing. I came up with it today. It was on the fly, but still. She told me it wouldn't work for what she wanted, and now she's trying to pass it off as her own? Zeppelin, it's not right. I'm not as good as you, okay? What's right is right. She's *wrong*."

"I know, but…" He takes my hand and pulls me away from the foot traffic flowing up and down the stairs. "Jerzie." Zeppelin's eyes look desperate under the glow of the lit staircase. "You can't *prove* it. She'll deny it."

"So what? She might deny it, but at least she'll know I know."

There's suddenly a lot of commotion coming from the third floor. Cheers, screams, people shouting Cinny's name. She's emerging. I dart away from Zeppelin and race up the stairs. I hear him calling after me, but I'm moving so fast, I'm not sure I could stop if I wanted to, racing up two steps at a time.

When I reach the top, I see a crowd has gathered at a door to one of the rooms near the back. Cinny's being guided by two security guards plus Wesley, and waving as she's being led toward an elevator. She's leaving? I can't miss this opportunity.

"Cinny!!" I scream so loud it gives her instant pause.

I push through the crowd and easily make it to the front. Cinny looks downright spooked to see me emerge. A few seconds later, an out-of-breath Zeppelin has made it to my side. He places a hand on my shoulder. Ha. As if that can stop me.

One of the security guards steps in front of her as I shake off Zeppelin's hand and approach.

"Nah, it's cool." Cinny extends her hand, gently pushing the guard to the side. "The fuck, Jerzie? What the entire fuck are you doing at *my* party with Zeppelin Reid?" She motions toward him. "You know what he did to me. Why would you think this would be cool? I should have him arrested for trespassing."

"Cinny, have a heart." Adrenaline is pumping, my heart is beating so fast, I feel faint. "He's your ex-*lover*. Don't be cruel."

"Seriously, what are you doing?" She crosses her arms. "You making yourself look mad stupid right now."

"Am I? Oh, by the way, how'd your set go, Cinny? How's your new *single*?"

She takes a step closer to me, whispering, "I was gonna tell you the good news. The label liked the melody, so we're gonna use it."

"Sweet," I whisper. "Do they know I wrote it?"

"Jerzie." She cocks her head. "Be sensible."

"I'm the very antithesis of anything close to sensible."

"What does that mean?" Her brow furrows. "Look, don't

be weird about it, but Spade isn't gonna put his name next to yours. You're like, nobody."

No, she did not. "So, you're really gonna pass off my work as your own?" I cry. "Cinny, I realize you're a hot-ass mess, but don't be *this* bad."

"Who are you, Jerzie?" She's speaking loud enough for people to hear now. Which makes her security guards take a protective step toward her. She waves them away. "Can't you motherfuckers see I'm not in any danger?" She turns back to me. "Jerzie, honey." She's smiling, talking softly again. She places a hand on my shoulder, as if we're having a peaceful chat. "You think you get to write a song with Spade?" She laughs. "You think you get to come out of nowhere? Out of the freakin' New Jersey sticks and one-up *me*?"

"Careful, Cinny," I reply. "I'm your *best friend*. You wouldn't talk to your best friend like this, would you?"

"Bitch, bye." She laughs again. "Literally. Bye. Get the fuck out of my party before I have you charged with trespassing, too." She looks over my shoulder at Zeppelin. "And take him with you. How's the unemployment line, Zepp?"

She tries to move away, but I grab her arm.

"Don't touch me!"

"Is your *boyfriend* here, Cinny? Your real one? The one you saved as Zeppelin in your phone because you're a maniac, a psychopath, and probably a sociopath, too?"

She snatches her arm away and steps back to me. "You think you're better than me, Jerzie? Little Miss Goody Two-shoes. 'Nothing's going on with me and Zeppelin, I swear to you, Cinny.'" She dramatically imitates me. "That's what you said. You're a liar, too! You're no better than me. Don't you dare judge me!"

"I *am* better than you," I cry. "I didn't tell you about Zeppelin because I didn't wanna cause trouble. To hurt you. Then I find out you were only *pretending* to like him, in some sick and twisted game meant to hurt me."

"I wasn't pretending!" she yells.

I notice the crowd that's gathered. Some of them have their phones out now and are recording this little interaction between Cinny and me. We're officially making a grand scene.

"I wasn't pretending. Okay?" She looks at Zeppelin now. "Please explain what it is about *her*? She came out of nowhere, and suddenly *she's* the one that gets your attention?" She looks back at me. "I'll never get what he could possibly see in somebody as basic as you. It's the new mystery of my life."

"Wow, Cinny." I shake my head. "At least I know what you really think of me."

"Trust me, I'm being nice."

My hands ball into fists.

"Oh, what?" She laughs. "You gonna hit me? Lay one hand on me! I dare *you*. Your ass will rot in jail."

Temporary insanity. I'm convinced now it's a thing. Because surely that's what comes over me as I take Cinny up on her dare, lurch forward, and grab ahold of all parts I can grab hold of. Her hair. Her clothes. Her arms, flailing about. In a moment of temporary insanity, you become mad. That's what's happening here. I am a madwoman.

We tumble onto the floor as more cell phones point and flash in our direction.

"Omigosh, they're fighting!"

"Somebody break it up!"

"Help her!"

"This is insane!"

"She's attacking Cinny!"

We are a tangle of limbs, hair, and screams for I don't know how long when, at last, my body is lifted off Cinny by one of her guards. Strong arms forcefully pin mine behind my back.

"Get a cop up here. Now!" Cinny cries as she's helped up by Wesley. "You saw it. She assaulted me! I want her arrested."

Her clothes are in disarray, her makeup smeared, her perfectly styled updo now lopsided and pointing in so many different directions she looks like she definitely lost this fight. I glare at her, tears streaming down my cheeks.

"Don't even think about coming to work tomorrow, Jerzie! My restraining order will ensure you can't even *see* a Broadway show, let alone be in *mine*!"

"I hate you, Cinny," I cry. And boy, do I ever mean it. "I'd rather have nothing and be a nobody than be anything like *you*."

"Good," she barks back. "Because having nothing and being a nobody is your destiny, Jerzie Jhames."

"Myself Condemned and Myself Excused"

Being arrested is not as bad as I thought it would be. Okay, full disclosure, I've never thought about being arrested. I *will* say that being read the Miranda warning, then stuffed into the hard and extremely uncomfortable plastic back seat of a squad car while hundreds of Cinny's fans stand on a New York City street corner laughing, pointing, and taking photos of me—*that* was probably not a life highlight. But the *ride* in the squad car is downright fun.

Okay, fine. *Fun* is an overstatement. Sure, I'm crying. And yeah, I'm a bit of a mess. Hair, pretty much disaster status. What was once a beautiful array of glitter, gloss, shadow, blush, and foundation on my face has turned into what I imagine a drowning clown would look like. My T-shirt is ripped, my skirt, too, and I can't even wipe my nose because my hands are in metal cuffs behind my back. So I may or may not have snot dripping down my face. But one thing I have intact.

My pride.

Okay, *fine*. My pride is not intact. But how many girls can say they fought Cinny, and then got *arrested*. On their birthday! That's nothing to be ashamed of.

Oh, God. What the hell am I thinking? That's *everything* to be ashamed of.

Voices blare through the officers' radios as we rush around busy nighttime traffic. I'm imagining what being in a jail cell will be like. I've binged every single episode of *Orange Is the New Black*, but that TV series sorta ends my prison studies.

"Do I get my one phone call?" I sob. "*Please* let me have my one phone call."

The officer who's driving laughs. "You been watching too many movies, kid. You can make as many calls as you need. Might wanna start with your parents."

Oh. My. God. My *parents*. I'm crying even harder now.

I have to take off my boots so that another corrections officer can frisk me. I guess the first frisk didn't count? It's a female, but that doesn't make it any less demoralizing as she runs her hands up and down my legs, butt, hair, and everything in between.

I'm walked to another section of the station, where I'm fingerprinted and positioned in front of a gray backdrop to be photographed. I've seen enough celebrity mug shots online to know this picture will be pretty much everywhere. For eternity. Now that my hands are free, I wipe my face as best I can and twist my hair until it's in a bun on top of my head.

Front. *Click click*.

Left side. *Click.*

Right. *Click click click.*

There. All done. Now everyone will have confirmation of my official arrest.

"Jewelry. Take it off." Another officer thrusts a plastic baggie into my hands. My trembling fingers remove Aunt Karla's rings, earrings, teardrop necklace and finally, I swallow, Zeppelin's bracelet. Taking it off leaves me feeling like a strong winter wind is blowing, chilling the air in the muggy hallway.

Now I'm led into a small, cluttered room where I'm seated on a chair in front of an older officer. He seems nice. Or maybe I think that because he's eating a cheeseburger.

"Are you wearing an underwire bra, miss?" the officer asks, his mouth full. "We typically have women take out the underwires before being transferred to a cell."

"A *cell*?" I'm crying again. "They said I wouldn't have to go to a cell."

He must be used to crying teenagers, because he takes another bite of his cheeseburger and nonchalantly continues with his paperwork. "So is that a yes or no on the underwire?"

I'm not even *wearing* a bra. "It's a no. Can I make a call yet?"

"Almost done here. Few additional questions." He takes another large bite. *Chomp chomp. Chew.* "Are you suicidal?"

"No," I reply. Though if I was, I'm pretty sure the stench of charred meat, cheese, and mystery sauce would not be the last thing I'd want to smell.

"Are you on drugs?"

"No," I reply again.

"Are you crazy?"

"Huh?" I look up.

He laughs. "Sorry. Couldn't resist. I heard you beat up *Cinny*? The singer?" He whistles. "Some nerve you got, kid."

"I didn't beat her up, sir," I wail in defense. "I just…" *Geez, what did I do?* I shake my head in agony and decide to exercise my right to remain silent on this one.

After the questions are complete, I'm finally led to a phone. Officer Cheeseburger dials the number I give him. It's not that I don't want to call Mom and Dad or Aunt Karla, it's just that this is the only number I know by heart. He answers on the first ring.

"Hello?" Judas's voice booms in the sterile space.

"Sir, this is Lieutenant Sandvig with NYPD."

"Uh. Okay," Judas replies.

"I have somebody here who needs to speak with you." The lieutenant motions to me.

"Judas?" I step up to the receiver.

"I'm here, sis. I'm waitin' on Aunt Karla. There's some sort of real bad accident, she's been stuck in dead-stopped traffic on the freeway for over an hour. As soon as she gets here, I'll hop in her ride share and we'll be there. Don't be mad. But I had to tell Mom and Dad, too."

"I'm not mad." I sniff. "Are they upset? On a scale of one to ten, how upset would you say they are?"

"Uh." Judas pauses. He must be standing on the street corner because I can hear the roar of city traffic. "Aunt Karla is holding steady at a 9.5."

I swallow.

"Mom and Dad?" he goes on. "I'd say they're hovering somewhere around one million."

I survey the space around me. There are three cops behind

the desk, and others moving through the hallway. So, privacy?
Not so much. It is what it is. I *have* to ask.

"Is he with you?" I ask. "Zeppelin, I mean?"

"Nah. Your boy just up and left."

He did not. "Are you serious?"

I'm sure Judas can hear the surprise in my voice because
he adds, "Sorry, Jerzie. He straight bounced. Didn't even say
bye or drop dead or nothin'. Am I on speakerphone? Like,
can cops hear me? Hello?"

"*Judas.* Can you please focus?" I'm crying again. I wipe my
tears. It's all right. I don't care if Zeppelin up and left.

But that's a lie, because it's not all right. And I do care. How
could he leave like that? How could he not make sure I was okay?!

"We got your back though, Jerzie," Judas adds. "Your family will be there soon, even if your boyfriend left you high
and dry. We got you. Hold tight."

As if I have anything else to do? "Thanks, Judas."

"Fa sho. Oh, and man, you beatin' Cinny's ass has about
22 million views on YouTube last time I checked."

"*Judas.*"

"Sorry. I am on speakerphone, huh?"

I groan. "Yes, Judas. You are."

"Well, whoever is listening… Cinny had it comin'. If it
wasn't Jerzie, somebody was gonna do it. That girl was due
an ass-whoopin'."

I look at the lieutenant. "Can you please hang up on him?"

"Wait. Jerzie!" Judas calls out. "I know you're like, a felon
now, but I woulda done the same thing. I mean, I didn't. Cuz
I'm on speakerphone and I don't wanna get charged with

nothin'. Black man without a record here. But I woulda. Hope that makes you feel better."

It does. A little.

"Sir?" The lieutenant is speaking to Judas now. "Would you happen to be able to connect us to Jerzie's legal guardian or parents? A telephone number where we can contact them would be nice. Jerzie claims she doesn't know her parents' number."

I listen as Judas gives the officer Dad's cell. So many things should be going through my head. But what am I thinking about? Zeppelin. It seems to always be Zeppelin. I can't believe he left me.

How could he?

The officers who brought me in said I wouldn't see the inside of a cell, but that's exactly where I'm taken next. Though it's not the sort of cell I imagined, with black bars and a bunch of angry gang members staring me down. It's a simple, tiny room; concrete walls, a door.

I sit on a concrete ledge cushioned with the sort of plastic mats you'd keep in a tent on a camping trip. Not exactly comfortable, plus I smell the distinct scents of blood and throwup. Uggh. Somebody probably died on this mat. But at least I'm alone and can officially suffer in silence. I assume the fetal position and close my eyes.

I realize I fell asleep because it takes me a second to remember I'm in a jail cell after the door pops open. *How long was I sleeping?*

A kind-sounding female officer says, "Jerzie Jhames?"

"Yes?" I stand, widen my eyes, and try to look alert.

"You're headed home. You can follow me."

I attempt to straighten out my wrinkled mess of clothes and begrudgingly follow the officer out of the cell, where I'm led back down the long corridor. Around a corner, we reach a desk, where my plastic bag of jewelry is slid across the counter and I sign some papers that I don't bother reading, though I do see COURT HEARING at the top of one. *Uggh.* I get copies of everything. I wonder if it would be frowned upon to toss it all in the garbage.

Next, I'm led through another door, down another long hallway, around another corner. Finally, I'm escorted into a vestibule where a series of doors will lead to my freedom. The officer gives me a nod, which I assume means, *Bye and have a nice life.* Through thick panes of glass in the set of double doors, I see Dad, his arm wrapped around Mom. They're talking to a man. I'd guess he's a lawyer. My lawyer. Mom and Dad had to hire a lawyer? I'm so superdead.

When the door is pushed open and I step outside, all three heads turn toward me. I'm literally cowering, hovering by the wall. Waiting on Mom to charge at me and scream, *What were you thinking, Jerzie?! We've all sacrificed so much for you!*

Knowing Dad will follow up with his own reprimand. *You have no regard, do you, Jerzie? For us. For your brother. For your aunt. It's all about you.*

Speaking of my aunt. Where is she? And Judas?

It's the man who approaches me first.

"Hello, Jerzie." His voice sounds familiar, and I watch as he runs a hand through his thick mane of hair. It reminds me of the way Zeppelin runs his hand through his hair. In fact...

Holy. Shit.

"My name is Daniel Ricci," he says kindly. "Zeppelin is my son."

And now I see him. Off in the distance. A very tired-looking

Zeppelin sits on a bench resting his head on one hand. He gives me a tiny wave with the other. He's close enough that I can see his eyes are red, his face flushed, hair in typical Zeppelin fashion—pretty much everywhere. But he's here. He's *here*.

"I got a frantic call from my son demanding I come and help you. I'd do anything for my kids. Zeppelin knows that. So here I am."

"And you should be damn grateful," Dad calls out.

"He was here before we were, Jerzie," Mom says. "You'd be spending the night in jail were it not for him."

"Thank you so much, sir." I speak softly, back to trying to twist my fingers off, staring at the dirty concrete. Not exactly the way I'd prefer to be introduced to Zeppelin's family— fresh outta jail and all. But like he said. Here we are. "Not sure how I can properly thank you."

"Don't thank me. Thank the dozens of videos Cinny's fans took and posted online. Videos that show provocation. This is not felony assault. I'd call it a…misdemeanor catfight, if anything. I'm pretty certain the judge is gonna toss it out altogether. But we'll cross that bridge when we get to it. For now. Go home. Get some sleep. Go to work tomorrow. You're gonna be fine."

Am I? "But the restraining order. Cinny told me she was gonna get one. I can't go to work."

"A restraining order?" Another hand through the hair. God, Daniel Ricci is *so* similar to Zeppelin. "That takes time, paperwork. If Cinny opts to take that route, she'll need to prove to a judge that you're a dangerous threat to her. That will be tough to pull off."

"I'm so embarrassed," I admit to him. "I hope this doesn't make you think badly of me."

"We all make mistakes, Jerzie." He looks at Zeppelin, and I note the sadness in his eyes. The same sadness I see with Zeppelin. "Heaven knows I've made quite a few in my life. Tomorrow is always a new day. To be better." He sighs. "Wiser."

I stare at him, wondering if he's real. There's a chance I could be imagining him. And of course now I understand Zeppelin's dilemma. It would be nearly impossible to hate this kind, gentle, and clearly remorseful man. And yet, Zeppelin's tried so hard to.

Mr. Ricci turns to Mom and Dad. "You have my info. Don't be afraid to reach out to me for anything. Anything at all. It won't be a bother."

Mom and Dad shake hands with him and say their goodbyes. I'd ask if I can say goodbye to Zeppelin, but I don't wanna press my luck or rock the boat any further. Cuz if I'm being honest, this boat almost sank to the bottom of the sea.

Zeppelin stands as his father approaches, and our eyes connect. He points to his eyes, places a hand over his heart, then points to me before turning and walking off with his dad.

I get the message.

I love you, too.

When we make it back to Mom and Dad's car, Judas is in the back seat, sound asleep. For some reason, seeing him stretched out stuffed into the back of Mom and Dad's car causes guilt to rise up my throat like bile. A very tired-looking Aunt Karla is leaning against the car, texting on her phone. She pockets it when she sees us approaching.

"Well, well, well." She flips her long braids over her shoulder. "Look what the cat dragged all the way to the local precinct."

"Can I say something, please?" I say. "Before you guys go in on me."

In the back seat, Judas is waking, stretching, and yawning. Good. He needs to hear this.

"To all of you. Mom, Dad. Aunt Karla. Judas, too. I know I messed up. I know I wasn't supposed to be with Zeppelin tonight and I...attacked...Cinny and got myself arrested and disobeyed you guys and dragged Judas into my mess. I've shamed my family." I point to my chest and *ow*, too hard. "I've shamed *myself*." I extend my arms. "On a national scale. I've been shamed. I'm so ashamed. Dear God, I am *so* ashamed."

"Jerzie, be *quiet*. You sound like a lunatic." Judas has lowered the back window and is peeking his head out of the car. "I already told everybody everything. Plus they saw the video. They know Cinny needed to get her ass beat."

"Judas." Mom places a hand on her hip.

"What?" He yawns. "She did."

Aunt Karla smacks her lips. "She stole your song and tried to pass it off as hers? That poor child needs more than an ass-whoopin', she needs some sort of intervention."

"A good psychiatrist is what she needs," Mom adds. "And to think, she got that poor boy fired, too."

Poor boy? Zeppelin is poor boy *now?*

"Maybe a religious conversion could help, too." Judas nods like his idea is the best one yet.

"And when she said having nothing and being a nobody was your destiny?" Dad whistles.

"The absolute *nerve* of that little girl." Mom shakes her head.

"Wait." I look around, studying the angry faces of my family members. "You guys are...defending me?"

"And then she got real brave." Aunt Karla yanks opens the back door as if she didn't hear a word I just said. "Talking about *I dare you to hit me.*"

"Bad gamble." Judas scoots over, making room for Aunt Karla. "Jerzie was like *ka-plow*. And Cinny hit the deck like *blam*."

Mom and Dad move around and pull open the front car doors.

"Bet she won't make any more dares like that." Dad slides into the driver's seat.

I watch them, going in on Cinny like she's the one with the problem. Not me. A smile creeps slowly onto my face.

"Jerzie, my dear." Mom reaches into her purse and pulls out my phone. I step slowly to her lowered window. Is she about to do what I think she's about to do? She extends the phone to me. "I think you've suffered enough. As promised. I never turned it on."

And suddenly it's in my hands. I'm holding my baby. I can't resist. I bring it to my lips, kiss it tenderly and say, in my best Sméagol imitation, *"My preciousss."*

"Jerzie Jhames!" Aunt Karla barks. "Girl, get in the car. Didn't I tell you cell phones are dirtier than landfills?"

I slide into the back seat beside Aunt Karla. "I thought you said they were dirtier than public urinals."

"That, too." She clicks on her seat belt. "And why am I in the middle? I'm the oldest. One of y'all needs to switch with me."

"You're the shortest." Judas slides his seat belt over his shoulder. "By default the shortest human always sits in the middle seat. Deal with it, Auntie. Or grow."

Dad starts the car, and I take a moment to absorb what is most likely, debatably, the greatest family of all time.

"Why the Devil You Come Between Us? I Was Hurt Under Your Arm"

I think I've used up all the hot water in Aunt Karla's house. Seriously, I've dried up all the water wells in Brooklyn. Wait. Are there water wells in Brooklyn? Anyway, I think I've sufficiently washed off the stench of jail. All I have to do is burn the clothes I was wearing and dump the ashes in the East River. Then the jail gods will see to it I'm never arrested again.

I crawl under the covers. Mom and Dad have Farrah's room for the night, so I've been reduced to couch surfing. After sleeping on a plastic mat in a jail cell, you won't hear me complaining. Besides, I've been waiting for the right moment to power up my phone, and it feels like the moment has come at last. I know there's gonna be an overwhelming amount of messages and texts. Friends from school, Riley wondering where the hell I've been, and messages from Zeppelin, too. Messages he sent before he knew I didn't have my precious.

Zeppelin. I twist the bracelet he gifted me around and around my wrist. It feels like a part of me now. Like I've had this thing my whole life. And of course the thought of him warms me up better than a hot shower ever could. He didn't leave me. He came to my rescue.

It's 3:00 a.m. Today begins the first tech rehearsal at Broadway Theatre. I will show up for work. Not sure if they'll let me stay. But like Mom and Dad said, *You show up with your head held high, Jerzie. You have nothing to be ashamed of.*

I know they're right.

I press the side button on my phone and wait for a moment as it lights up. I ignore the whopping 162 missed text messages. *Dang.* That's a lot. Instead, I tap the internet icon and type Cinny's name into the search bar. I wanna see the videos. I wanna read what people are saying about it. About us. About me. Only the link that pops up makes me tear off the covers, jump off the couch, and gasp. The top trending story isn't about our fight at all. I read:

Fans swarm the hospital as reports emerge that R & B superstar Cinny was involved in a head-on collision.

This cannot be real. I rush upstairs, knocking softly on Aunt Karla's door. A moment passes before it creaks open to present my very sleepy-looking Aunt. Her braids are wrapped in a silk scarf. She rubs her tired eyes. "What's wrong, Jerzie?"

I thrust my phone at her. She stretches out her eyes to read the headline. "Jesus."

"Aunt Karla," I whisper. "I feel terrible. I don't want anything bad to happen to her."

"Of course you don't, Jerzie. Neither do any of us."

"What if she's dead?" I cry.

"They'd send her back. She'd be way too much trouble in the afterlife."

"Aunt Karla."

"Jerzie." She sighs. "I don't know what to say except I'm positive she's fine. Call it intuition. People get into car accidents all the time. She's fine. Trust and believe, okay?"

I nod.

"Now try to get some sleep."

Maybe I sleep for a few minutes. Mostly I toss and turn on the couch, wondering if time has ever literally slowed down. Because I swear that's what's happening right now. The Earth has finally stopped spinning. Around 5:00 a.m, I get a text from Nigel. The first tech rehearsal is canceled as they wait on word about Cinny. This is so real.

After reading the text, I decide *sleep* is an exercise in futility. At least for now. All I can do is scroll through stories on the web, waiting on some sort of update to surface. On Twitter, #PrayersForCinny is top trending. There is an outpouring of support. It soothes my soul a bit. TMZ says Cinny's Range Rover was hit head-on. She and her driver are both reported to be in the ICU at Lenox Hill Hospital.

The intensive care unit? *This is bad. This is so bad.*

I wish I could text Zeppelin, but I know he doesn't have his phone yet. I can read his texts. I decide to do that. It somehow makes me feel close to him, scrolling through the old messages:

Why won't you talk to me?

Jerzie, please text me back ok?

I can explain if you'll let me.

If you answer your phone I can explain.

Jerzie, I really care about you. I swear to God I do. Please, please, please talk to me.

This was a bad idea. Now my chest aches, thinking of how Zeppelin must've felt when he was sending these messages. Wishing I could reach through time to let him know I'm here. That I believe him. That I care, too.

A new text message comes through. It's from Riley. I sit up. Riley!

Doooood. You beat up Cinny and now she's in the hospital? Confuse me?

I tiptoe to the front door, punching the code to disarm the alarm system and quietly step outside. The sky is still black, but you can see people running in the dark, walking their dogs. You can feel the city slowly waking. I sit on the top stair of the stoop and tap on Riley's name. She answers right away.

"Riley!"

"Jerzie? Where in the hell have you *been*?"

I laugh. "I knew you were gonna say that."

"I have been calling and calling and texting and texting."

"My mom took my phone away. I got it back a few hours ago."

"Oh! And I saw your song on Instagram. I was superproud of you. But it made me cry so hard."

I fill her in on everything—losing the phone, Zeppelin, the fight, the arrest, sleeping in a jail cell, Zeppelin's *dad* coming to my rescue.

"So wait. *Rewind*," Riley says. "Can we go back to Zeppelin's apartment? On his bed. Under his covers. Can we just go back to that?"

"Riley." I laugh. "Of all the things I said, that's the only thing you heard, huh?"

"Well, I mean. It's the highlight of the story. How was *that*?"

A black sedan catches my eye as it glides slowly down the street. Something about it feels strange to me. Almost like that car is here...for me. "Riley. Can I call you *right*, right back?"

"You better! I need to hear everything about this torrid love affair."

I laugh. "I promise to give you all the details."

I hang up and stand. The sedan slows to a stop right in front of Aunt Karla's stoop. The back door is pushed open to reveal...Cinny. My breath catches in my throat when I see her. Dressed in sweats, a hoodie, and sneakers. Face scrubbed clean of even a trace of makeup. Eyes tired. She waves and slides out of the SUV onto the sidewalk. I walk down to meet her. "I thought you were in the ICU?"

"The media always gettin' shit wrong. What else is new?"

"But you're okay," I say. "I'm glad you're okay. I was really worried."

"'Okay' is debatable. I have two cracked ribs, a spinal con-tusion, and some serious whiplash. Plus my head is pounding so hard I swear I could die right now."

"Cinny," I breathe. "That all sounds serious. You should be home. Why are you here?"

"Because I needed to talk to you. I *have* to talk to you." She points to Aunt Karla's front door. "Can we go inside?"

"My family is asleep," I explain. "And also…they don't… like you."

"Understandable. Would you be down for sitting in the car? I promise I'm not here to abduct you. I wanna talk is all."

I follow her into the SUV and we sit on opposite ends of the back seat.

"Steve?"

The driver turns. "Yes, Cinny?"

"Could you give us some privacy? A few minutes?"

"Absolutely, miss."

The driver pushes the door open and steps outside. When the door closes and Cinny and I have complete privacy, she starts doing that thing I do. Where I'm trying to twist my fingers off. *I thought I was the only one who did that.*

"I want you to know that I'm dropping the charges."

"Omigosh." I breathe a sigh of relief. "Thank you, Cinny."

"I bet that was kind of a nightmare. Going to jail?"

"I got out pretty quickly. Plus, I found out they can't post minors' mug shots online. So all in all, guess it wasn't too bad."

She leans back and stares up at the roof of the car. "On the way over here, I went to a website and took a Cosmo quiz. The 'are you a sociopath?' quiz. It said I wasn't."

"You sure it's accurate?"

"Look, Jerzie." She turns to me. "I know I seem like a terrible person. But from my perspective, I had been with Zeppelin for *weeks* before you showed up."

"Zeppelin?" My eyes narrow. "That's really what this is about? We're fighting over a boy?"

"We're not fighting. Not right now. I'm explaining. So you can understand. Zeppelin would be so amazing when we were in a scene together. And I'd think he *must* feel some kinda way about me. Then Alan would say hold for one reason or another, and Zepp would disengage and retreat. It was driving me fucking mental. The closeness. It felt *real* for me. I was lost in it."

My stomach turns sour. She wasn't lying. She did think there was something between her and Zeppelin.

"Why didn't you tell him that you liked him, Cinny? He had no idea."

She rests her head in her hands. "It's my regret. If I could rewind time, I would've said it. 'Zeppelin, I'm falling for you.'" She looks up at me. "How simple would that have been? Maybe things would've been different." She's quiet for a long moment before she continues. "But I didn't say that. I guess I was waiting on him to say it to me. Then I walked in on y'all in the bathroom that day, and I saw the way he was looking at you. And then he fuckin' chased after you when you left so quickly. I could tell right away. He liked you." She turns, staring at the window. I watch her pull her sleeve over her hand and wipe her eyes with the edge. She's trying to hide it. But it's pretty obvious she's crying.

"Cinny. We don't have to do this. You don't have to tell me any of this."

"Yes, we do. You need to understand." She takes a deep breath and continues. "After he ran off after you, I tried to rationalize it. Like, you're mad cute, right? So I was like, he saw a cute girl is all. But then I saw that damn video with you two." A tear slides down her cheek. She quickly wipes it away. "Jerzie, up until that day, Zeppelin had *never* kissed me in rehearsal. Whenever we'd get to a kiss, it was always on the cheek. I figured that was his thing and he was waiting for dress rehearsal or some shit like that before we kissed for real. But he kissed *you*." She shakes her head. "I confronted him. Like, the fuck? He swore it was the moment or whatever. I think he said, 'What's the big deal? Who cares?' And the next rehearsal he kissed me, trying to prove a point, I think. But I could tell he was mad uncomfortable, and again…he went running after you that day, too. That's when I found y'all in the stairwell."

I nod. It's all making sense now.

"I didn't mean to be all, stay away from Zeppelin like some crazy-ass baby-mama drama type shit. I just was like, I decided I'd earned the right to let him know how I felt."

"You had earned that right, Cinny. You could've told him."

"I was scared."

"Correct me if I'm wrong," I say. "But you have a boyfriend. Right? Zeppelin said he would come to rehearsals sometimes."

"I hang out with Shivers. Yeah. But he's a friend. And not a friend with benefits. Just a friend." She looks at me now. "Are you and Zeppelin friends with benefits?"

"Cinny," I say softly.

"It's whatever. I'm only trying to put together the missing pieces of the puzzle here."

"I don't think I feel comfortable answering that."

She wraps an arm around her waist, wincing in pain.

"Are you okay?"

"Hurts like hell is all," she says.

Is it her heart that hurts?

"Anyway. Me and Shivers. We mostly hang out for paparazzi pics and shit like that. We want people to think we're a real thing. Remember? I like for the media to exploit lies. It's when they exploit the truth that bothers me."

"Yeah. I get that."

We sit in silence for a while.

"I ripped your posters off my wall," I admit.

"Say what?"

"After I found out you got the part over me and I was hired to be your understudy, and after I cried for days. I ripped your posters off my wall. I had three. I took you off all my playlists, too. And then I unfollowed you on Instagram."

"Dang. Are you serious?"

"I hated showing up for work that first day. I hated... losing."

"I hate losing, too," Cinny says. "All my life, winning has been my top priority. Being number one. Being the best. It's what I do. I'm the happiest when I'm winning."

I give her a look.

"Don't judge me for it, okay? If Tom Brady said winning made him happy, everybody would slap him on the ass and congratulate him. But I say it, and I'm a bad person?"

"It's not that you're a bad person. It's just that there are greater experiences than winning."

"Like falling in love?"

Yeah. I sigh. *Like falling in love.* "Listen, Cinny. We both need to change our perceptions. We're not in competition with one another."

"Sorry, boo, but if two people are vying for the same thing, it's a fuckin' competition."

"Then you should be declared the winner, Cinny. You got the part over me."

"But you won Zeppelin's heart."

"Hold on." I sit up now. "I have a thought."

"I'm listening."

"A lot of people want the same things."

"True," Cinny agrees.

"If you ask me, it's not always a competition. Sometimes it's just life. *We're* not competing."

"How you figure that though?"

"Because." I smile. "A real competition has a clear beginning and end. Our careers have no end in sight."

She smiles now, too. "Maybe our existence has no end in sight either."

"Exactly! How can we be competing? We're just living another life."

"And maybe one after this one, huh?"

"Who knows?" I say. "Maybe."

"Fine." She nods in agreement. "I'm with that. I kinda like it, too. It's life then. It's *this* life. And we're just living." She exhales dramatically. "But can we agree I'm not a sociopath or a psychopath and what was the other thing you called me?"

"Uh. A maniac."

"Right. I didn't take the maniac quiz, but I think I'd pass that one, too."

"The 'are you a maniac' Cosmo quiz?" I laugh.

"Girl, now you know those quizzes are accurate." She laughs, too. "Look. Call me Tom Brady, but in this life, winning is my jam. It's all I know. And I took one look at you that day in the bathroom, showing up outta nowhere. I knew there was something special about you. And I was like, the fuck is wrong with this production. Why they hiring this understudy who's better than me?"

"Cinny, stop it. I'm not better than you."

"For Broadway you are, and you know it. You're so Broadway. I'm R & B. I'm MTV. I'm fucking fabulous, don't get me wrong. But *you're* Broadway."

I truly can't argue with her there. I am Broadway. It's all I've ever wanted to be.

"Still," I say. "It's life. It's this life. And in this life, you got the part I wanted. You're the lead. I gotta live with that."

"I'm a lead who has two cracked ribs," she admits. "So I'm a lead who will be out for the next six weeks to heal. Which means, Jerzie Jhames, that *you're* the lead. For now. You'll be opening the show."

Her eyes are welling with tears again. She looks pretty fragile in this moment. It reminds me of being in the conference room and watching her cry. Never thought my life would take me to such places. Watching an international superstar cry. Because of *me*.

"I'm opening the show?" I whisper.

"You are. I chatted with Robbie. And Alan. They're panicking a little, like the money-hungry *bitches* they are, but I told them you got this. They know you got this. You're a star, Jerzie. The show will be fine till I return. Plus, I heard previews sold out. Already. Everybody is dying to see this damn show."

"Serious?" I exhale. "But they're all coming to see you. Not me."

"They might be coming to see me. But they're gonna fall in love with you."

My new reality is ever so slowly sinking in. My all-time favorite composer, Robert Christian Ruiz, has a new musical. It's called *Roman and Jewel*, and in it...

I am Jewel.

"Don't trip though," Cinny adds. "Imma be there every day. Watching in the wings. You can't get rid of me. And when I heal, I'm taking my spot *back*. Best believe. I'm not going anywhere."

"Right." Of course she's not going anywhere.

"Gotta make sure I win my Tony to go with my Grammys," she says playfully. "And the future Academy Award."

I sigh.

"Aww, don't sigh like that, Jerzie. What's wrong with wantin' to win a Tony?"

"It's just that..." *Uggh.* I don't wanna be the one to tell her this. But. She'll find out soon enough anyway. "Well," I swallow. "Only the opening cast of a production can be nominated for a Tony."

"Wait, what? Is that really true?"

"Yeah. It's true."

"Damn." She shakes her head. "Karma is a bitch."

I raise an eyebrow. "What do you mean?"

"Wanna know where I was headed when we got into the accident? To the hospital to pretend you caused me serious injury. So I could make sure you got charged with a felony." She winces in pain again. "I should go. I only wanted you to know that I'm not a sociopath." She grabs my hand. "And I'm not gonna pass the song off as mine. Okay? I'm sorry about that, too."

My eyes widen. "You're gonna tell the world I wrote it with Spade?"

"Nah." She shakes her head. "Don't hate me, Jerzie. But Rome wasn't built in a day. I lost the guy. I lost the role. The future Tony—"

"Cinny, you haven't lost."

"Fine. Whatever. It's this life. But I need time to process my new reality—life can suck sometimes. I know that now."

"Cinny," I interrupt. "You'll be back and—"

She holds out a hand to silence me. "You're opening the show, boo. Not me. Shit hurts worse than my ribs." She pauses. "Look, I can't be singing a song you wrote. I'm not doin' that. We're going in a totally new direction. New track. Everything."

"But, Cinny. That's like cutting off your nose to spite your face."

"Say what?"

"It's this old expression. My mom and dad say it all the time. It's when you do something needlessly self-destructive. This song with *this* new melody? It could be the song that catapults you to a new level. To the next, next, *next* level. What if that happened? Who cares who wrote it?"

"I care," she says firmly. "I guess I'm biting off my face to destroy my nose then."

"Cutting off your nose. You know what. Never mind." Because if I'm being honest, I understand where she's coming from. I really do. Life is funny that way.

"Thank you for understanding, Jerzie."

I hug her very gently. "I'm sorry I called you a sociopath. You clearly are far from that."

"Thank you." She exhales. "And I'm sorry I got you arrested. And tried to ruin your life. And Zeppelin's, too. I wish he was still a part of the show. He was such a good Roman. You know, out of everything that's happened, him uploading that video of me hurts the worst. It just seemed so *unlike* him. I pegged him as one of the good guys. I swear I did."

"Cinny." I know I shouldn't. But it's like the words are pouring out of my mouth before I can even think it through. Zeppelin *is* one of the good guys. She deserves to know that. "He didn't upload those videos."

"What?" She sits up. "Who did it?"

Do I tell her I don't know?

"You know what?" Silent tears slide down her cheeks. She wipes them away. "I don't even care who did it. I'm just glad it wasn't him. You have no idea what that means to me."

I bet it means a whole lot. I move to push open the door.

"Hey, Jerzie?"

I turn back. "Yeah?"

"Jokes aside. Do you honestly believe in all this past life shit? Like, you think it could be real?"

I shrug. "Maybe."

"So then maybe in a past life, I took a guy *you* loved.

Maybe this life is for us to even things out. A new experience for us both."

"Maybe." I smile. "But if things are even. Next life? Can we like, meet up in Ibiza and dance and drink lemon drops and just have fun? That could be a new experience, too. Cuz all this is pretty tiring."

"Bitch, we can do that in this life." She laughs. "I'll make sure we do."

"I'll look forward to it. Bye, Cinny."

"Bye, Jerzie Jhames."

THREE WEEKS LATER

I'm staring at my phone in disbelief. "I cannot believe *BuzzFeed News* wrote an article about our show called 'Roman and Copycat'!"

Angel snorts. "That's funny."

"So what if our set is similar to *Dear Evan Hansen*?"

"Is it?" Angel asks. "Never seen *Dear Evan* before."

I slide my phone into my back pocket. "It's similar. Because our band isn't in the pit, it's onstage, and like them, we're using Ableton."

"Able-wha?" Angel scratches his head.

"It's this piece of software that plays loops and sounds to represent all the digital elements—text messages, social media chimes, etc."

"Oh." Angel yawns. He's given up on his violet contacts and has now switched to green. Like a lime, Halloween-cat sort of green. "You know a lot of stuff. Does it make your brain hurt?" He holds out his phone in front of us. "Say cheese. I need a new pic for the Gram, and this lighting makes my eyes glow. I look amazing."

I lean my head on his shoulder and smile. He quickly snaps the pic with his camera phone. We're sitting in the front row right now, watching the orchestra rehearse before the dress rehearsal officially begins in an hour or so. I swear the music is like a living, breathing organism.

"Listen to this music, Angel," I say. "Copycat? Ha! It's so hip-hop. It's so new age. It's so high-tech. We're badass. We copy no one."

"I don't care what *BuzzFeed News* says." Angel stretches out his legs. "I'm just glad tech is over. Twelve-hour rehearsals? I swear to God, if Alan adjusted one more light, I was gonna walk off and quit."

"Walk one step. Stop," I say. "Uh-oh. The light's too hot."

Angel imitates Alan. "Ooooh, now it's too *abrasive*. Could we warm that light on Jerzie so it's not too abrasive?"

I laugh. "Never mind. Now it's jarring. Mae? Mae? Is it jarring to you? It's jarring, isn't it?"

Angel places a hand under his chin. "Make it intimate. Not a cold light. Not a hot light. But a Christmas light. In fact…" he snaps his fingers "…make it a *night*-light."

We both crack up.

"We are a week from preview." Angel exhales. "I seriously can't believe it. You nervous?"

Nervous? That's an understatement. But I can't like, admit I'm nervous. Can I? Saying it out loud would make it too real.

Then the nerves would amplify. "Nah, I'm not nervous. We got this."

Mae taps her baton on her stand, and the music stops.

"From the third measure." She flips a page in her sheet music, adjusting her glasses as she studies the pages. "The oboe must be louder. Let me hear the B." The oboe makes the most beautiful sound as the note reverberates off the walls. "Violins with the A but *pianissimo*. The oboe is the star here." The violins play so soft and sweet, I place a hand over my heart. "Perfecto. Violins. Perfecto."

I turn to Angel. "How's Damon?"

Angel shrugs. "He's okay. He will be anyway. And we kinda like living together now. It suits us."

"Good to hear." I stand. "I should head up."

He studies his phone. "I'll be right behind you. Oooh, our pic already has six hundred likes. Told you I looked amazing. You look good, too."

I laugh and move toward the stage stairs, where Aunt Karla and Nigel are having a hushed conversation.

"Excuse me?" I step to Nigel. "Aren't you like, supposed to be working? Instead of breaking the rules, letting my aunt backstage where she's not allowed and openly flirting with her? You should be fired for this."

"First off." He holds up a finger. "*She's* the one openly flirting with me."

Aunt Karla laughs. "You wish."

"All my wishes come true." Nigel smiles. "But I probably should get back to work." He and Aunt Karla kiss on the lips. I cover my eyes.

"God. Get a *room*!" I exclaim.

Aunt Karla laughs. "Jerzie, stop acting like a teenager. You're the lead in a Broadway show. Grow up."

I stick out my tongue and move past them, up the small set of stairs where I almost slam into Lorin.

"Hey, Lorin," I say. "You ready for this?"

"*Jerzie,*" she whines. "I found more roaches in my dressing room sink. I'm so disgusted. I have an infestation."

"Aww, cute. A family."

"You think so? I'll have the exterminator drop 'em off with you."

"Cool. The mouse I saw last week in *my* dressing room can eat them for dinner."

"Uggh. Rats? These old theaters should be demolished. Have you seen Nigel?"

"Keep walking. You'll run into him."

Lorin rushes past me in a huff.

Onstage, Alan is pointing as he talks with the lighting crew. "I still feel like we're way too hot on Roman," he explains. "He looks as white as a ghost next to Jerzie. How do we fix it?"

I laugh. The man is never gonna move past the lights.

As I walk backstage and into the chaos of so many people coming and going, I see Robbie standing near the stairwell door, chatting with Elias and Nikolai.

"Jerzie." Robbie waves me over.

"Hey, Robbie." I will never be fully calm and composed talking to Robert Christian freakin' Ruiz! Never. But I can fake it till I make it. "Hey, Elias, Nikolai. How are you guys?"

"Nervous." Elias really does look nervous. "I had a dream last night that everyone forgot everything and you all stood onstage for two hours staring at the ceiling while the music played."

"Nothing to fear." Nikolai rolls his eyes. "He has that dream every time a show is about to go up."

"*Playbill* is here," Robbie says to me. "They wanna interview us about 'I Defy' and take some photos. Can we do it after you get through your hair and makeup and we get you all mic'd up?"

I'm sorry, *whaaaaa*? *Playbill* wants to interview me?! Oh, screw pretending like I'm calm. "Holy shit, Robbie! Are you serious? Yeah, man. We can do it anytime."

He laughs. "Perfect. Come to the stage when you're dressed."

"And try not to say 'holy shit' during your interview," Elias adds.

"Okay. I'll only say it in my head." I pull open the door and move into the stairwell.

"Jerzie. Hon?"

I see one of the dressers peeking out from the next level.

"Hey, Desi." I rush up the stairs to meet her.

"Are you free at all to come to like, a five-minute fitting?" she asks. "There is one dress where the hem needs to be adjusted."

"Sure. Let me run to the bathroom superquick. I'll come right back."

"Oh. You're a doll."

"That's what they tell me."

I rush up the stairs to the next floor, yank open the door, and move down the hallway. When I step into my dressing room, a very blond and tan Zeppelin sits at my vanity. "Aren't you in the wrong room?"

He stands. "I like yours better."

"Really? Why?"

"Cuz you're in it."

"Aww." I step into his arms. "I missed you."

"You saw me like, twenty minutes ago."

"Felt more like a long half hour." I look into his eyes and run my fingers through his newly blond tresses. "Will I ever get used to you with blond hair?"

"Does it look like I should be in a boy band?" he asks solemnly. "Like the kind of boy band where they wear matching clothes and do weird choreographed dances?"

"No, no." I bite my lip to keep myself from smiling. That's exactly what he looks like.

"You promise? Babe, don't lie to me."

"It's less pop, more rock 'n' roll. You've definitely got the rebel without a cause, Romeo meets Roman look going on right now. Roman being blond was a good call the producers made."

"And the fake tan. Does it look natural?"

"It's cute. You look like you just got back from the beach."

He exhales, relieved. I hear my toilet flush, and the bathroom door opens to reveal Ava.

"Oh. Ava is with me," Zeppelin says.

"You're gonna watch the dress rehearsal, Ava?"

"No." She pouts. "I'm not allowed to. Nigel's kicking me out. Dad's on his way to pick me up." Ava steps around Zeppelin, her bright blue eyes gazing at the lights on my vanity.

"Your room is way better than Zepp's." Her voice is soft and gentle. Kind. "And way bigger, too."

"They're the exact same size," Zeppelin says.

"No, they're not." Ava flips her long black hair over her shoulder. "Don't be jealous of your girlfriend. Your room doesn't even have its own bathroom."

"It has a sink. Same thing," Zeppelin replies.

Nigel sticks his head into the room. "Ava. Your dad is at the stage door."

"Aww," she whines. "I don't wanna go."

Nigel turns to Zeppelin. "And one of your dressers is looking for you."

"Got it. I'll head back to my room in a second."

"And, Jerzie." Now Nigel turns his attention to me. "Desi needs you. And Sound needs to test your mic."

"Got it. Headed to Desi in a second. Then to Sound. But Robbie needs me, too. We're doing an interview for *Playbill*."

"Oh." He winces. "That's the priority. Get dressed and do that first. I'll tell Desi they can use April to stand in for the fitting. You guys are the same height. I'm headed to the greenroom to find her."

"A greenroom? Can I see it before I go? Please?" Ava asks.

"Fine." Nigel motions for her to join him. "But full disclosure. It's not green."

We watch the two exit into the hallway, and I turn to Zeppelin. "Have you talked to Damon?"

"We talked. Yeah," he replies sadly. "He's doing another reality show. Seems like he's recovering. I hope so anyway."

"That was pretty good of him to come forward the way he did."

"Yeah." Zeppelin nods. "I always knew he would."

"You knew?"

"Of course I knew. He's a good guy. He's a real friend."

"And how are things with your dad?"

He shrugs. "Family therapy is a drag but we're all getting through it."

I study Zeppelin. The blond hair. The tan skin. The Roman wardrobe. "You're pretty sexy as Roman, you know."

"Yeah?" He runs a hand through his hair. "Well, you're *beautiful* as Jewel."

"I'm not even in costume yet."

"Oh. Well then, you're just beautiful." He grins.

I place my hands over my cheeks to cool them down a bit.

"Ahhh... 'See how she leans her cheek upon her hand. O that I were a glove upon that hand that I might touch that cheek.'"

"Don't tease me, Romeo."

He steps to me, wrapping an arm around my waist. I look up into his eyes.

"Ti amo, Jerzie." He kisses me so softly, so gently, on the lips. "Ti voglio bene. Or maybe I should say... Sei veramente importante per me. Or better yet. Le parole non bastano a descrivere il mio amore per te."

When Zeppelin speaks Italian, I swear I could melt into a puddle on the floor and dissolve into thin air. "English really needs more sexy ways to say I love you."

"Are you kidding, Jerzie? When Juliet says, 'Give me my Romeo, and when he shall die, take him and cut him out in little stars—'"

"'—and he will make the face of heaven so fine,'" I continue, "'that all the world will be in love with night and pay no worship to the garish sun.'"

"Now *that's* a sexy way to say I love you." He traces my lips with his fingertips. "So. Will I be able to lie next to you soon? Now that you've broken up with the real Zeppelin and are dating his blond, tan, boy-band cousin?"

"My room does have a balcony."

"With a security camera."

"That disengages for twenty minutes when the Wi-Fi is unplugged."

"Nice. I can sneak in to see you. We can call it 'rehearsal.'"

"Exactly. We'd be rehearsing."

"And we need to rehearse. This is Broadway. Gotta be good."

I lay my head against his chest. Our hearts seem to be in sync with one another. Both beating slow and steady. Speaking the language only hearts can speak. The one, true universal language where no words are needed to tell the story.

I think about what Aunt Karla asked me weeks ago. What do I know about love? What does anyone know, really? But with Zeppelin, I'm willing to try to figure it out. Even when the butterflies have all gone away, and all we have is our billion-year-old bond.

Because I believe it will still be us. And we will still be together.

And the world will keep on spinning.

And everything will be all right.

★ ★ ★ ★ ★

Acknowledgments

To complete a novel…it takes a village. So, of course, I'd like to thank mine.

First up. My brilliant agent and friend, Uwe Stender. You believe in me. You believe in my stories. I am eternally grateful for you. My phenomenal editor, Natashya Wilson, who has loved this story from its inception, back when it was only an email titled "Do You Think You Would Like This?!" Tashya—Zeppelin and Jerzie live so clearly in my heart and mind because of your guidance. And in some alternate dimension, Aunt Karla and Nigel are naming their baby after you. Thank you for EVERYTHING.

Big thanks to Inkyard Press for being the best publisher in all the land. Thank you Bess Braswell for all your hard work. I appreciate you! Thank you to my amazing cover team Erin

Craig and Elita Sidiropoulou—with extra special thanks to Illustrator Robert Ball. You three are my cover dream team!

To my Broadway experts: Michael Potts, Ali Funkhouser, Tory Kittles, and Virginia Louise Smith. Could not have done this without you guys. Extra special Broadway thanks to Ali Funkhouser. All mistakes are my own.

The research process for this book involved travel! Which was the first time I'd ever traveled to research a book. What fun seeing Broadway shows and venturing backstage. And thank you to New York City for welcoming me and not laughing when I would get lost day after *day* on the subway. And thanks to all the New Yorkers who were nice to me when I said, "Excuse me, do you know how to get to [enter destination]." On the right train headed in the wrong direction was the underlying theme of my travel time.

Thanks to everyone who read parts of *Roman and Jewel* back in its earlier forms: Natasha Deen, Kevyn Richmond, Christopher DeWan, Michael Willuweit, Ravyn Willuweit, Uwe Stender (thanking you again because you read this *so* many times), and Katya Lidsky.

Thanks to Linette Kim for always working so hard for me and a very special thanks to Laura Gianino. I was sitting with you in a dark corner of a restaurant when you encouraged me to write this story. It was your belief in me in *that* moment that began this journey. Thank you, friend.

Speaking of friends. So many friendships that kept me sane during the year and a half it took me to write this story: My mom. You are my best friend. I'm so grateful for you and can't wait to celebrate the book YOU will write someday. My sister, Shona. Thanks for always being just a phone call away. Mikey and Kiki, love you two so much. My daughter, Cameron, who puts up with me staring at my laptop for hours a day—love you, honey. My many lifetimes road dog, Greg Schwartz. Michael Willuweit and Kevyn Richmond—thank you for your friendship. Katya Lidsky, who is the kind of amazing friend I would dream up in a novel. My best good buddy, Bree Barton. My best good Cali cousins, Monique and Lisa. Love you two. And to all my family. Yes, including you, Dad. Love you! And welcome to the family, sweet little Ava. Great Auntie loves you and can't wait to meet you.

And to all my readers. Thank YOU for taking this journey with me.

Rise up!

Until next time,
Dana L. Davis